KAREN WOODS

First published in 2017

EMPIRE PUBLICATIONS
1 Newton Street, Manchester M1 1HW

ISBN: 978-1-909360-52-5

Printed in Great Britain.

In Memory of Darren Anthony Woods.

You are always in my thoughts and my heart.

Love you forever, our kid.

Acknowledgements

THANKS TO ALL MY READERS and my Facebook, Instagram and Twitter followers too. This book has been a long time coming and I hope you all enjoy the final chapter in Misty Sullivan's life. Thanks as always to my children Ashley, Blake, Declan and Darcy - love you always. Thanks to Craig for his support.

My writing continues and I hope you all carry on enjoying the stories I tell. Without all my readers I would have stopped writing a long time ago, so thank you all for your continued support. Big thanks to Rebecca Ryder for sprinkling her magic into my book and thanks also to John Ireland and Ashley Shaw from Empire.

My last thanks is to my son in heaven Dale. Goodnight Godbless I love you always.

Love Karen Woods
http://www.karenwoods.net

CHAPTER ONE

SHE HAD TO FACE IT, get her head back in the game and make sure everyone in the family knew her mother was about to take her final breath.

Panic.

This had gone on for far too long. She was in pain and there could be no other outcome but death. This woman was suffering, she was on painkillers galore and barely a day went by without her asking the Lord above to end her misery and let her body be free from it. Lisa was pleading with God to free her soul, to let her finally be at peace. She'd had enough, completely lost the will to live. Who could blame her? She couldn't enjoy life anymore. The things she'd taken for granted all her life were now a distant memory. Even combing her steel grey hair was a tough task. She was like a baby, totally dependent on her family.

Losing her mother was something Misty had known would happen eventually but nothing could truly prepare her for the moment. Looking over at the bed, she wondered if she should end her mother's life for her, stop her suffering once and for all. Maybe she could take a pillow and place it over her head until her lungs flooded with fluid and she was no longer breathing. Sometimes you had to be cruel to be kind and nobody would have blamed her. It would have been considered an act of kindness.

Lisa lay in the bed with her eyes firmly closed. She was barely awake these days. Could she see the pearly gates, was she already gone and just waiting for her final breath to end her time on earth? She was delirious. One minute she was talking gibberish and the next she was filled with regret for the choices she'd made in her life. It was such a sad time for all involved, heart-breaking to watch. There were stern words spoken in this room too, things that had been said that had left Misty petrified of what lay ahead in the future; heartbreak, tears, misery. Oh yes, there would be tears shed when all this came out, lives would be savaged from the secrets the family thought were safe. It was a past Misty would rather not have spoken about. She would rather the past stayed where it was - hidden away forever. But it was her mother who had opened her big daft trap and ruined years of keeping schtum. What a silly old cow she was, blabbing about business that didn't even concern her. How dare she meddle with somebody else's life? A fucking do-gooder she was, always thinking she knew the answers to somebody else's problems. She should have kept her nose out of it all and kept her trap shut.

Lisa should have forgotten the drunken words her daughter had confided in her when she was off her head and steaming drunk. It was the wine that did it, it always made her talk about private things she should have kept close to her chest. It was the same old story every time Misty drank. 'Loose-lips juice,' her husband Dominic called it but she'd fucked it all up herself if the truth was known. There was no one else to blame but herself. Misty crept over to her mother's bedside, tiptoeing, not wanted to disturb her. She stood watching her chest rising slowly, listening to every gasping breath she took as the machine filtered oxygen into her lungs. Lisa looked old and haggard, ready for the knacker's yard. If she had been a horse the medics wouldn't have thought twice about pulling the trigger and ending her miserable life. A single gunshot right into the side of her head would have done it. Why was her mother any different? Lisa's fingers were all skin and bones under scrawny, transparent grey skin. These were the hands that held Misty in her arms when she was a little girl. The same hands that lashed out at her when she couldn't cope with the way her life was heading and the same hands that had led Misty's life down the wrong path. Things that would have sent an average person to an early grave, pushed them over the edge. Nothing was ever plain sailing in her family and without her mother, Misty would have curled up into a small ball and died a long time ago.

She'd never have admitted this though. No. She always told everyone she was strong and could bounce back from anything. This was far from, the truth; she was weak and needed guidance more often than not. Lisa's lips were like dried prunes, nothing like they were when they were younger. No more bright coloured lipstick, no sexy pouting, there was nothing left but cracks and emptiness. These same lips had cursed and made some people hate her, even her nearest and dearest. No one was safe when her back was up. These same lips had finally let loose the secrets that would soon find their way to that arsehole… it wouldn't be long before he would be knocking at her front door, threatening her, demanding a payout. Asking for money to keep her secrets safe.

But what if she got to him first? She could do that for sure. How hard could it be to end that rat's life? Nobody would miss him. She'd have been doing the world a favour by ridding the streets of the wanker anyway! Yes, she could wait for him in the shadows of the night and nobody would ever know she'd done him in. She could, she really could get away with it if she wanted to. But his body, what would she do with that? Pigs, yes, that was the answer. She'd watched a TV programme about the big fat porkers who would eat every part of the human body bar the teeth. The cunt was only about seven stone wet through anyway, so it wouldn't have been a problem to get rid of him. The pigs would eat him up as a snack. His diseased flesh would make them have the shits though, he was rotten to the core, pure evil. Even one of God's creatures could never fully digest this vile creature. Maybe she could burn him, melt the bastard so nobody could ever recognise him. Yank his teeth out one by one and watch him suffer. Oh yes, given the chance Misty could be as sick as the next person.

Her eyes shot back to the doorway in the hospital room. Where were the rest of the family? They should have been here hours ago. The doctor told them Lisa wouldn't last the night. Surely that should have created some kind of urgency but everyone had their own life to lead. Max was probably styling his hair, backcombing it, staring at the mirror for hours. In his own words he was a faggot. He loved cock and never tried to hide the fact he was attracted to other men. He knocked her sick sometimes. He told Misty about every date he went on, every sexual encounter he'd ever had. He shared too much information really. He should have kept some of it to himself. Max never kept a man for long, he was hard work, a proper nightmare. In fairness, he'd had some right eye candy for partners in the past and even Misty had licked her lips when he'd brought them around to meet her; ripped bodies, sexy arses, everything that a woman would look for in a man. Wasted on him really. But then they would never look at a woman.

The confusing thing was, Max was anything but manly,

he was a big fucking fairy, as camp as they came. And vain wasn't the word for him. He'd had more pricks in his face than he'd had shoved up his arse if he was being honest. He lived for Botox, fillers, and anything else he could get to give him the youthful look he desired. He looked well though but kind of plastic, there was no movement in his forehead and he had big fat chunky cheeks. Sort of like a hamster storing nuts for the winter. Lisa had never really got her head around her son being gay. She always said he would grow out of it. She hoped he would start fancying girls, start reading fanny mags like normal lads his age and realise the beauty of the female body. He never did. Lisa was a straight talker and some of the questions she'd asked her son would have made your toes curl. She went straight in for the kill, shooting straight from the hip. No messing about. She asked him directly why he would ever stick his dick up someone else's shitter. She held nothing back, it wasn't right in her eyes. An arse was for shitting out of nothing more, nothing less. It was so wrong to her. He was a back-door bandit, end of.

Misty glanced at the clock behind her. It was all she'd heard for the last few hours. Tick-tock, tick-fucking-tock. It was doing her head in now. Well, that and her mother's heartbeat monitor. Beep, beep, it was enough to drive somebody insane. Why didn't the big man in the sky just come down and take her and stop pissing about? Was he teasing them, making them wait? Hadn't he seen her suffer enough? For fuck's sake, she'd been to hell and back in the last week or so and still he was there watching one of his so-called children suffering. Was he having a laugh or what? Perhaps she should talk to her mother, ease her passing to the other side, let her know she wasn't alone. But what was left to talk about now, she'd fucked everything up with her meddling. Her and her mouth had dropped her right in the shit. Dominic would shit a brick when she told him the cat was out of the bag. He'd dreaded this ever getting out, prayed every day nobody would ever find out the secret he held close to his chest. But she would never tell him it was her who spilled the beans. No, she'd cover up the truth and say anything except what really happened.

Dominic hated Misty drinking and always told her she had a drink problem. What the fuck did he know about how much she was allowed to drink anyway? Who was he, the bleeding alcohol police? Misty had told him time and time again that if he didn't like it, he could fuck off out of her life, she didn't need him, she didn't need anyone in her eyes. But was that the truth? Not really, because when the drink got a grip of her she only ever wanted her husband near her to fight off the demons in her head. They played with her too, tormented her, refused to let her rest. Her past was on constant repeat in her mind as she replayed her mistakes over and over again...

Dominic told her she had mental health issues and he was probably right. Nobody acted like she did when she was drunk. She'd go from one extreme to another; love and hate, light and dark, laughing and crying. She was up the wall. But it was all that bastard's fault, not hers. He'd fucked with her head, made her lose all faith in humanity. Misty could still see his face when she closed her eyes, feel his warm stale breath all over her skin. She could still hear every hurtful word he had whispered in her ear but she'd never tell anyone that, it made her weak, fragile and vulnerable. Misty kept that to herself.

She was glad that Gordon was six foot under, unable

to hurt her anymore. Every now and then she would go to his resting place and make sure the cunt was still boxed up. She'd spit on his grave too. Not very ladylike but she hated him with a passion. This man had killed the feminine side of her many years ago, she was a fighter now, ready for whatever came her way. Some nights she wanted to go and dig Gordon up, just to make sure he was still there. To make sure he was rotting away beneath her feet, maggots eating his evil flesh away so nothing was ever left of him. They should have burnt the wanker and made sure he never had any chance of coming back. Misty had attended Gordon's funeral. She had hidden away from public view, stood behind a large oak tree as she watched his parents grieving in the distance. Misty needed to watch him being lowered to the ground, needed to make sure he was dead and out of her life forever. She could feel him around her sometimes, his presence. The air changed, it wasn't sweet anymore, it was dirty and unclean when his spirit was lurking. Did Gordon ever come back to watch over her, to ask for forgiveness, or just to torment her? He was still with her alright and she knew it. Every time she was feeling low or upset he was always there, laughing, sneering at her, loving the fact that her life was just as fucked up as his had been. Maybe she should have asked a priest to come to her house and exorcise him. Yes, she should have got rid of him once and for all then wouldn't she?

Misty reached over and touched her mother's cheek gently. It was empty, cold and rough to the touch. Perhaps now was the time to say her final goodbyes. The rest of the family would be here soon and she may not get out what she wanted to say. She might regret not speaking her mind without being judged. This was her time now, private words that no one else could hear. There wasn't a soul about, nobody to report back what she was about to say. This was the time to clear her head, to get things off her chest without the family meddling in her affairs and making her hold her tongue. A mother and daughter's relationship should have been strong, a bond that nobody could ever break. This wasn't the case with these two. This relationship had been smashed, ruined, fucked up years ago. There was no love lost.

Misty inhaled deeply, lungs filled with enough air to let her speak her mind. Her eyes lifted slowly as she licked the corners of her dry lips. Her voice was low. "I know you can hear me mother, so, I'll just say what I have to say without you butting in. Funny really isn't it, that for the first time in my life I can speak to you without you sticking your oar in. You'll listen to every word I have to say now won't you." Lisa's eyelids flicked rapidly, she was listening, her mouth glued together with the morphine flowing through her body. Her daughter was taking a liberty here, this wasn't fair. Lisa would have ripped her neck open and shit down her throat if she wasn't on her death bed. Nobody ever won an argument with this motor mouth, she had an answer for everything and she dug deep too. There was no line she wouldn't cross to get her point heard. Evil her mouth was, words were said that she never be taken back. Not that she gave a flying fuck if she hurt anyone's feelings anyway, she had no shame. If you upset her then you should have been prepared for what she would come back with. She was a battle-axe, old school. An old fishwife who would air her dirty laundry in public if she had to.

Misty edged closer to her mother's bedside. Her fingers stroked the crisp white hospital sheets. She kept her voice low and began to speak. "You just couldn't let sleeping dogs lie, could you? Why the hell you thought you could work this out on your own is beyond me. She'll find out now and then what? You're just an interfering old bastard who should have left this well alone. Didn't you think I'd been through enough without this hanging over me too?" She held her head back and gritted her teeth tightly together before she continued. "What, did you think I should have gone through more pain? Yes mam, you always said I didn't know what real heartache was didn't you. Were you that jealous that I'd found happiness in my life and you never did, that you wanted to ruin me?" Lisa stirred in her bed, her fingers rolling into tight balls at the side of her legs, she could most definitely hear her. Misty smirked and twisted her head back over her shoulder, checking one last time that they were still alone. Her mouth was close to her mother's ear. "I'll sort this mess out once and for all. You mark my words. I'll deal with whatever I have to, to protect my daughter. That's what a proper mother does. Not that you ever give a flying fuck about protecting me did you?" There was a few second's silence, Misty swallowed hard and her eyes clouded over, emotions rising high. "Make sure you tell God that too because he will know the truth. Oh yes, he'll know all about you and your wicked ways. Tell him mam, cleanse your soul and admit to all the fuck-ups you've made. Tell him about every last person you've hurt." Misty chuckled and raised her eyebrows. The corners of her mouth began to rise. She was loving this, sick really but she was enjoying every second of her mother's pain. "Don't bank on any angel wings either mother. We both know you're no saint."

Misty gripped the edges of the white pillow on the

bed; her fingers digging deep into it, her knuckles turning white, she was thinking, her eyes flicking one way, then the other. Surely not, was she going to finish her off, stop her breathing? Misty bit hard on her lips and inhaled deeply. "No mother, you'll suffer to the end. Why should I make this any easier for you when all my life you've made me feel pain? You can suffer like I did." She smirked and sat back down on the brown leather chair at the side of the bed as she continued talking. "It's kind of funny isn't it, mam. You no longer have any control over me. How does it feel to be defenceless? It's not nice is it? Welcome to my world for once. Let's see how long you last." Misty played with the cuff from her pink jumper, her eyes focused on one spot on the floor. Swallowing hard, she continued. "If anything ever happens to Charlotte I'll never forgive you. She's my world and I'll do time for anyone who ever tries to hurt my baby. Did you hear that mother? I'll go to jail for any cunt that comes within an inch of her. I will, I will." There was an eerie silence and the clock seemed to be ticking louder than it was before. Misty waved her hand in front of her mother's eyes, there was no response, she never flinched. "I know you can hear me, you know what you've done and I'll never forgive you, not now, not ever."

It was nearing midnight and Misty stood with her arms cradled around her daughter Charlotte as her mother took her final breaths. Dominic held them both in his arms and shook his head slowly, he was helpless. Lisa's death was long overdue and at last, this ordeal was nearly over. Nobody liked watching anyone pass to the other side and if he would have had his own way he would have stayed well away from the hospital. There was no love lost between Dominic and his mother-in-law and over the years she'd said some hurtful things to him, words she could never take back. Daggers in his back. The bitch said he wasn't a real man otherwise he would have put his wife in her place a long time ago. Slapped her, ragged her about. Yes, that's right, she wanted her son-in-law to beat up his wife; probably just like her husband had beaten her when she'd got above her station. What kind of woman would ever wish pain and misery on their own flesh and blood? The woman must have been tapped in the head.

Charlotte stood snivelling. She was seventeen years old now and looked like her mother did when she was younger. But she wasn't innocent by any means. This girl had attitude and lots of it. She feared nobody, not even her parents. Lisa opened her eyes and struggled to move about in the bed, exhausted. This was never going to be a peaceful passing. Her eyes held fear, they were wide open. Misty used a firm hand to secure her in the bed before she rolled out of it. "Mam, come on, keep still." Dominic helped as she continued to move about and between them both they made sure she was secure. Charlotte looked over at her grandmother and choked up. It was time, the end was near for sure. Lisa needed to speak, to get her final words out. She reached over and gripped her granddaughter's hand in hers, squeezing at it, pinching her young pink flesh. "I love you sweetheart. Be careful, very careful, he knows about you now. Never be alone with him ever. He's evil, evil."

Misty moved closer, and started to talk above her. What the hell was the daft old cow trying to do? For crying out loud, why didn't she just die and leave them in peace? Charlotte pulled a sour face and was none the wiser. Misty shot a look over at her daughter and tried to play it down. "She's delirious love, mixed up, ignore her. She's been talking a load of bollocks all day long. It's the medication, she's high as a kite." Misty turned her head and studied her mother. Surely she only had a few last breaths left in those diseased lungs of hers. How long did it take for her to be out of their lives forever? Lisa's eyes met Misty's and she stared deep into her soul. Her eyes said it all. There was no love lost here today and no final words that would ever right the wrong she'd done. As if someone had turned the power off inside Lisa's body stopped moving, her eyes still fixed on Misty. Everybody in the room froze. There was a moment of complete silence.

Was she gone? Was it all over?

Dominic ran outside and called the doctor into the room. He was panicking and had to make sure she was gone. Was the wicked witch finally dead? Misty stood back and covered her mouth with both hands, not a word. Was she shell-shocked, or was she waiting like everyone else to see if the torment was finally over? Charlotte looked at her grandmother and raised her eyes over at her mother. "I think she's snuffed it, mam." Bleeding hell, that was a bit harsh, she could have chosen her words a bit more carefully. How dare she speak like this at such a sad time. No bleeding respect whatsoever. But, it seemed mother and daughter were as bad as each other. None of them had an ounce of respect for this woman.

Misty rubbed at her arms and stepped forward. She was putting on a performance that any leading lady would have been proud of, the bullshit was rolling from her tongue. "Is she dead Doctor, she just wriggled about and then nothing? Please tell me she's not gone." Charlotte screwed her face up and slowly shot a look at her mother. She knew more than anyone how she felt about her, so why was she acting like she gave a shit? Dominic stood back while the medic did his job. His eyes danced with excitement knowing this meddling bitch was out of his life forever. Charlotte had seen enough near the bedside and moved to the back of the room. This was knocking her sick and it was nothing she wanted any part of. If her nana was gone, then she was gone. What was the point in hanging around this place anymore, being morbid and talking about Lisa as if she was a woman that was going to be missed? Nobody would pine for this old trout, not even her ginger tom cat. In fact, since Lisa had been taken into hospital, nobody had seen sight or sound of it. It had got off on its toes for sure, scarpered. Probably run away from the doom and gloom its owner created.

The doctor stood back and nodded. It was now confirmed, Lisa was dead. "I'll give you all a bit of time with her. I'm so sorry for your loss. She's at peace now. There was nothing more we could have done for her. She suffered right until the end, poor lady."

Misty stepped forward and shook the doctor's hand. "Thank you doctor from the bottom of our hearts. We know you've done all you can for her. We'll stay for a short while and then we'll go. I think we could all do with a stiff drink. It's been a long day."

"Take as much time as you want. I know how hard this must be for you all." Charlotte flicked her eyes down to her wristwatch and licked the corners of her mouth. She didn't need any more time here. As far as she was concerned, she'd said all she had to say. She was ready to leave. She reached into her pocket for her mobile and started to text her best friend Mandy. The doctor left the room and they all stood looking at each other. What now, should they hug each other, talk about Lisa's life and all the good times they had with her? Misty inhaled deeply and walked to her mother's side. Should she kiss her, cry on her chest, tell her how much she loved her, how much she would miss her? Dominic watched his wife eagerly. He knew more than anyone that she would never do that, she was an ice maiden, she had a stone heart. "Come on then," Misty said at last, "no point in hanging around here being miserable. Let's go home and get a drink or something. If she's gone then she's gone. There is nothing more we can do." Dominic swallowed hard. She was drinking again. His wife was always finding an excuse to crack open another bottle of wine. But dare he mention it to her? She might need a drink tonight, after all her mother had passed away. He kept his mouth shut for now. It wasn't the time or place to confront his wife about her drinking. Charlotte headed to the door, followed closely by her father. Misty was fixed to the spot, her eyes just looking at the woman lying in the bed. After a few seconds she followed them out too. Not a single tear fell, there was no emotion whatsoever. Max and Denise were on their way but it was too late, Lisa was gone.

CHAPTER TWO

"MAM, STOP PECKING MY HEAD. I'll get up when I'm ready. I'm not a kid anymore, for God's sake ease up on the pressure and leave me the hell alone. It's up to me if I go to college or not. Get out of my room, you're doing my head in. All I can smell is your hanging beer breath." Misty stood over her daughter, wobbling about as Charlotte snapped. "Move out of my face, you're a disgrace. It's not even nine o'clock and look at the state of you, move away from me."

Misty punched her clenched fist into the duvet. She was going sick, trying to make her daughter be quiet, stop her whining. "I'll bleeding drag you out of the bastard bed if you don't move your arse out of it. Stop winding me up every chance you get. I'm sick of it, bleeding sick of it. I've not even had a drink, so you're making it up in your own head." Misty booted the bottom of the bed and stood dragging her fingers through her hair. She needed a drink now for sure, she was stressed out. Charlotte dragged the covers over her head and turned back on her side. Her mother didn't scare her, she was used to her violent outbursts. There were banging noises as drawers were slammed shut. Misty was still in the bedroom, same shit different day. Here it was, the usual spiel she gave when she had a hangover. "I'm treated like a slave in this bastard house. All I do each bleeding day is clean up after you lot. Well, it stops here, do you hear me, you can all start picking your own shit up for a change. I've had enough. Let's see how you all cope then when I'm doing fuck all. I'm not a servant."

Charlotte kept calm, there was no way she was biting, getting involved in anymore drama. "Blah de blah mother, change the record and give me a bit of peace. Go and get yourself a drink, you're a much nicer person when you're pissed." Her mother froze, it was true, she was much calmer when she'd had a skin full. She'd cuddle everyone, see no harm in any living person. Misty stormed out of the bedroom with a face like a smacked arse. She was hungover, headache from the night before. It was only a few drinks she'd had so what was the big fuss about, she was grieving, dealing with her mother not being here anymore. Surely she deserved a little tipple to numb the pain she was feeling in her heart? But her daughter had said she was much nicer when she was drunk. Was that the truth? Was the drink getting a grip of her and she wasn't aware of it? Addictions are like that aren't they, they take hold when you least expect it and take over your life.

Dominic hated that she was a lush. All night long he'd been moaning at her, counting her drinks, rolling his eyes every time she poured another glass of wine. Why the hell didn't he just leave her alone and get on with his own life? Their marriage was on the rocks and she was pushing him to his limits, calling him, refusing to listen to a single word he said. He was nagging her every day and night, lecturing her about how she should be the wife he married not the washed-up wreck he kept seeing every night when he came home from work. He'd told her she was letting herself go, not looking after herself anymore. How dare he say that to her! His wife, the woman he loved. So what if she'd not had a wash for a few days or applied any make-up, it wasn't a against the law was it? It seemed like history was repeating itself here. Her mother's life was now hers. Was she depressed? Messed up in her head? She didn't know anymore. Misty headed down the stairs and into the front room. Her eyes shot about the floor, what a shit-tip. Empty bottles of wine were scattered all about the place, ashtrays filled to the top with cigarette butts. Dragging her fingers through her hair she plonked down on the sofa, exhausted with the day that lay ahead. What had happened to this woman? She had everything she ever wanted in life; a loving husband, a nice home, a top of the range car, everything she ever needed to be happy. What had gone wrong?

Misty reached over and sparked up a cigarette. The cleaning could fuck right off, she was in no mood today for anyone or anything. She wanted to be alone with her thoughts, calm down, have a few glasses and chill out. Maybe she was depressed. She had no energy anymore, no get-up-and-go. Misty's hands trembled, shaking rapidly. They were always like this now if she was being honest. Well, until she had a drink to steady her nerves. Maybe she did have a problem, maybe she didn't. A thick cloud of grey smoke filled her face as she sucked hard on her fag. With her feet tucked neatly under her bum-cheeks, she reached over and grabbed the remote control for the television. The living room door opened slowly and Misty looked over at her daughter with disgust. Here it was, round two. "I don't know why I bother anymore. Fuck your education. You can go and get back to bed for all I care. Go on, ruin your life and see if I give a flying fuck how you turn out. Don't say I didn't warn you."

Charlotte flicked her long dark hair over her shoulder

and started to apply her pink lip gloss in the mirror. "Stop talking to me like that. You're turning into your mother. Just look at yourself, when was the last time you even combed your hair you scruffy cow?"

Misty stubbed her cigarette out in the ashtray and bolted up from her chair. She was getting it now, no one spoke to her like that and got away with it. She ran at her with all guns blazing. How dare anyone say she was like her mother, nobody was that bad? Lisa was a crank, an evil cow. This was an insult. Misty's warm breath sprayed into her daughter's face. "Don't you ever say I'm like her. I'm nothing like my mother. Do you hear me, nothing like that woman!"

Charlotte backed away and stood with her hands on her hips. She had no fear. If her mother wanted a fight then she would scratch her eyeballs out. It wouldn't have been the first time these two had comes to blows either. There was no respect, no boundaries. They just said what they wanted to each other without any regard for the other person's feelings. Charlotte raised her voice high, "Yes, you are. Look at yourself mam, you're slowly turning into her. You drink every night and when was the last time you even cleaned this place up? I was proud to call this my home a few years ago but not any more, it's a shit-tip, a scruffy dirty dump. No wonder my dad is thinking of leaving you."

Misty went nose to nose with her, her hot stale breath spraying into her face. "So, you clean it up then Mrs fucking know it all. It's none of my shit anyway. It's all yours. Day in, day out I clean this shit-tip up and for what?" She held a sour expression before she continued. "So you two can mess it up again. And as for your dad leaving me, does this face looks like it gives a fuck? I don't need a man to make me happy, I'm much better off on my own!"

Charlotte grabbed her bag from the side of the chair and hooked it over her shoulder. "I'm off, you just sit there feeling sorry for yourself all day as per usual. Whatever it is tormenting you, you need to get help with it and sort your napper out. It's ruining you. You're making everyone miserable."

Misty snapped, her fists curling into tight balls at her side. "Go on, fuck off out before I punch your lights out. And don't come back for all I care! I'm sick of hearing your bullshit." Charlotte banged the door shut behind her as she left. She'd hit a nerve. Oh yes, she'd delivered a knockout blow alright. The truth hurt sometimes didn't it? Misty sank to her knees and dragged her fingers through her hair. She needed a drink, something to calm her down, to take away the tremors. With haste, she ran to the kitchen cupboard and sank her head low looking for the wine, the vodka, anything that would take the edge off how she was feeling. There it was, hidden away at the back of the cupboard, bingo. With both her hands, she gripped the bottle tightly and screwed the top from it. This was all she needed to stop the way she was feeling. The bottle pressed firmly against her lips, liquid dribbling down the side of her mouth. A warmth riding down the back of her throat. The vodka calming her from the inside. Misty tucked the vodka under her arm and headed back to the living room. "Fuck them, fuck them all," she mumbled under her breath. A few more gulps and she was starting to feel normal again.

Nothing was ever right in her head until she was drinking. It took her to a place she felt safe. A place where there were no problems. Nobody knew what she was facing. How could she tell anyone where her head was at? It was all fucked up and when the truth came out, she would be the one in the firing line for sure. Her lies, her dark past, her secret she had kept hidden away all this time had now come back to bite her on the arse. Maybe she should go and see Tom today, look him in the eye and tell him he wasn't getting another penny from her family. But what if he was willing to go all the way with this and tell everyone what she'd done? She would be a laughing stock. People would judge her, slate her for lying to her daughter. Staring at the four walls, Misty kept necking mouthfuls of vodka. She had to sort this mess out and fast. She was living on borrowed time.

Charlotte sat on the bus listening to her music, her head nodding to the baseline, lost in the moment. She was in no mood for anyone today, she was on a right downer. Fuck her mother and her problems, the sooner she got away from her the better. Every day it was the same, misery on top of misery. She needed her own place, somewhere she could chill away from all the drama in her family. The music she listened to took her away from all her problems, the stress of everyday life. Maybe one day she would write some lyrics of her own, open her heart and put pen to paper with her own heartfelt words. She was sick to death of the way she was feeling inside, frustrated. No one ever listened to her anymore. It was just drama after drama every bastard day. Life was a big crock of shit and she didn't care what happened to anybody around her. She had her own shit to deal with. Fuck education, fuck trying to please everyone in her life, she'd given up trying. Oh hello, hold on a minute who was this coming to sit near her? He smelled lovely, sweet aromas filling her nose. Charlotte sat up and took her feet down from the chair in front of her. She pulled her hoodie down slightly and got a better look at this piece of eye candy. Her jaw dropped and she was more than interested in him. She had to say hello, introduce herself before it was too late. She'd not seen this guy before, he was drop dead gorgeous. He was nothing like the lads in her circle, this one had good looks.

Charlotte pulled her earphones out of her ears and smiled over at him. She fluttered her eyelashes, flirting. What the hell was he doing, he didn't even smile back at her. She had to up her game, get him talking. Nobody ever ignored her, she always got what she wanted. Taking a deep breath, she finally caught his eye and opened the conversation. "Do you know what time it is please? My watch has gone mental and I don't have a clue if I'm running late or not?"

The lad casually pulled his sleeve up slowly and shot a look at his wristwatch. "Half nine it is." Charlotte kept looking at him in hope that the conversation would continue but nothing. Not a bleeding word. The cheek of him, did he think he was above her or what?

Charlotte flicked her hair back over her shoulder. She upped her game. "I've not seen you on this bus before, are you from around here or what?" This was like getting blood out of a stone. Usually it was her who was the one who was difficult to talk to, not the other way around. Hard work her friends called her. Charlotte was checking every inch of him out, he was nothing like she'd seen before, something about him was attracting her. His colourful aura dazzled her eyes, mesmerising her. She swallowed hard and had a crack at him again. No one got the better of her ever.

"What's your name anyway, you don't speak much do you?" He blushed and sat fidgeting nervously. His cheeks burned more with every second that passed. What was wrong with him, he should have been jumping at the chance to talk to a girl like this. Didn't he know who she was? Every guy in the area wanted to talk to her, hang about near her, she was gorgeous.

You could tell this guy was intimidated by this beauty. Of course, he'd had girlfriends in the past but nothing like this one, she was tip top. He had to play it cool, act casual. He swallowed hard and spoke. "Call me Reek, that's what my mates call me. What's your name?"

That was better, at least now he wanted to talk to her, she thought she was losing her touch, she started to relax. Charlotte twiddled a strand of hair dangling at the side of her cheek and fluttered her eyelashes. She was working this for sure. "You can call me Charlie. My proper name is Charlotte but I hate it, it sounds like a librarian's name don't you think? Charlie is much better."

Reek sniggered and nodded his head. "Yeah, it does sound a bit naff, doesn't it?" She snarled over at him. She didn't want him to agree with her for crying out loud, she wanted him to say it was a beautiful name. She nudged him gently in his waist and chuckled. "So, where you from then?" There were no flies on her whatsoever, she was straight in for the kill, no playing hard to get.

Reek licked his lips slowly and coughed to clear his throat. You could see he was trying his best not to look like a prize prick. "I've just moved back to Manchester. I've been away for years and my daft mother decided that she wanted to come back here of all places to start over again; a new college, new friends the lot. Barmy she is, we were settled where we were."

Charlotte smiled over at him. "Awe, poor baby has no friends anymore. Do you want me to look after you?" She sat smirking at him, watching him, digesting him. Reek sat back in his seat and smirked over at her. She was different than the girls he'd met before, she was upfront, cocky and full of herself. His mother had warned him about girls like this and told him they were nothing but trouble. But there was something about this one that intrigued him. Maybe she was trouble but he was in it now and he wasn't letting this chance pass him by. "I'll be sorted when I find my feet. Manchester is wild, everything just seems to move so fast around here. Even the way you lot speak is fast. I can't understand your accent."

Charlotte screwed her face up. Was he having a pop at her, thinking she was some kind of scruff who didn't know how to talk properly? She digested what he'd just said and sniggered. "So you're a posh boy then! Good luck with that around here. The lads will eat you alive," she edged closer to him and kept her voice low. "Do yourself a favour and don't be saying stuff about this place because trust me you'll end up being knocked on your arse. No one likes a silver-spooned prick."

Reek backtracked, he didn't mean anything by his comment. He blushed and stuttered. For fuck's sake he'd messed it up now, lost his chance to talk to her for longer. "Deer, I'm not posh, far from it. I'm just a bit different that's all. Reserved, shall we say."

Charlotte looked out of the window and saw that her stop was nearing. There was no way she was letting this one get away, she liked him, she wanted to see more of him. "Why don't you come down to the pub tonight. There's a few of us going there. It's good music, it should be a laugh. The Black Bull, come down if you want. What kind of tunes do you like?"

Reek held his head to the side and stroked the end of his chiselled chin. "I like most stuff, chart music and all that." Charlotte stared at him in disbelief. Was he being serious or what? Surely he was trying to have her over. He should have been listening to some house music, bassline stuff not corny boy bands. Quickly, she grabbed a pen from her bag and gripped his hand in hers. She scribbled her phone number down on his slightly tanned skin and flung it away from her body with a quick flick of her wrist. "If you get brave and fancy something different give me a ring." Charlotte stood up and knocked his knee with hers. "Move it then, this is my stop." Reek was frozen, staring at her, lost for words. She nudged him again. "Derr, I'm going to miss my stop if you don't move it. Come on gawp, move out of my way."

Rico stood up and quickly glanced out of the window checking the area. He was in a panic now. "I'm getting off here too. It looks like we're at the same college. Fancy that, fate maybe." Charlotte let him walk from the seat first and checked out his sexy peach-like bum cheeks. She had him hooked now, there was no way she was brown-nosing anymore. If he wanted her then he would have to put in a decent graft to get her talking to him again. There was no way she was making it easy for him. They both left the bus together. Charlotte stood still for a split second. Should she wait for him or walk inside the college together? No, she never even said goodbye to him, she got on her toes and completely blanked him. Reek was shell-shocked, had that really just happened? He shot his eyes down to his hands and stroked a single finger over the number written there. He lifted his head up slowly with his mouth still wide open. As he watched her in the distance he punched his clenched fist in the air. What a result this was, get in there. This girl was mint, much nicer than any girl he'd been out with in the past, she was gorgeous. Today had just gone down in history as one of the best days in his life. Nothing ever happened like this, he was back in the game. Manchester wasn't such a bad place after all.

Charlotte marched into the college like she owned the place. She was always a popular girl amongst her group and never struggled to make new friends. Everyone wanted to be her and most of the lads there would have given their left arm to have a date with her. Just one kiss, a hug, anything to improve their street cred. Mandy Dolan stood blasting a cigarette at the corner of the building. Blowing a thick cloud of grey smoke from the corner of her mouth, she clocked her friend approaching, shot her eyes down to her wristwatch and shouted towards her. "Late again. What's up with you lately, why can't you get out of bed in the morning? Move your arse or we'll be late again. They've already warned us about disrupting lectures and all that. We'll be carted if you don't sort yourself out!"

Charlotte let out a laboured breath. "Don't ask what kind of morning I've had, nothing goes to plan in my life. You know that more than anyone. That silly cow is pecking my head constantly. I swear Mandy, if you only knew the shit she's giving me lately you would cry with me. I'll punch her lights out if she carries on talking to me the way she is doing." The girls stood huddled together as the wind picked up.

Mandy sighed and placed her hand on top of her best

friend's shoulder. "Charlotte, your mam has just lost her mother, she's probably heartbroken that's all. Just be a little bit more sympathetic. Times are hard for her, just give her some space."

What was going on here, this was her best mate, where was the support? A bleeding sell-out she was. A double agent. Charlotte looked at her and gasped. "Oh just be quiet Mandy, if you're chatting shit too. I hate it when you get on your high horse. You know fuck all about my life, so just leave it there. I'm going to the canteen to get a drink. Stay here and sort your head out. I don't want to be around you when you're being a dickhead. Why are you sticking up for her when you know what she's like?"

Mandy flicked her cigarette butt into the side of the building. She smiled over at her bestie and held her open arms towards her. "Aww, you've seen your arse this morning haven't you? Come here and let's hug it out. I'm just trying to help that's all."

She moved towards her in the hope that she would lighten up. Charlotte growled. "Piss off now, don't wind me up. You know what you're doing. I'm not in the mood, trust me." Charlotte stood snarling over at Mandy, she was ready for snapping, flipping out. Her temper was something she had issues controlling. It was like a monster that strangled her and once it started, there was no going back. Sometimes when it happened it scared her, she wasn't in control of her actions. The red mist just took over and anything could happen when she lost it. Perhaps she should have had anger management therapy, anything to help control her rage. Mandy gave up trying to make her smile again, she was a lost cause. When she was like this she was better left alone, she'd calm down sooner or later, she always did. The two of them started to walk to the canteen together in silence. Charlotte slammed her body onto the chair and kicked her legs up across an empty space facing her. She wasn't sitting like a lady. No, she was sprawled across the furniture without a care in the world. Her mother had always said she was a tomboy and she was right. This girl acted like one of the lads, even the way she spoke.

Reek walked past slowly with a couple of other boys. The Geek Brigade they were, nobodies. It was time to earn his street cred. He spotted Charlotte and made sure everyone in his group heard what he had to say when he spoke to her. "I'll ring you later. I've decided I'll come down the pub tonight and see what it's all about." The other lads with him looked at each other, who the hell was he talking to? They knew more than anyone that Charlotte didn't speak to dickheads like him. She smiled over at Rico and nodded her head slowly, not a word was said. His feet seemed glued to the floor as he waited on a reply. Come on girl, speak, say something, don't leave him stood there like a twat. But no, she never replied she played it cool. She could see him scratching his head as he left her side. His mates were whispering to him as they walked away. There was no way they wanted anyone to hear them. Charlotte would have knocked ten tons of shit out of them if they were using her name without her permission.

Mandy looked over at her friend and pulled a sour face. "Who was that Clampett talking to?"

Charlotte chuckled and raised her eyebrows. "To me, cute isn't he?"

Mandy's face dropped and it was too late to tell Charlotte to be quiet. Paul Jones was behind her, listening to every word she was saying. Built like a shit-house door he was, he had a toned, ripped body. She could see him now. What the fuck did he want? She'd told him months ago they were over so why was he still hounding her, begging for it. Charlotte kept her cool and nodded at him. "What's up, did you want something?" She was dicing with death and she knew it. She was game as fuck though, he didn't scare her. He was a tosser in her eyes. Paul clenched his teeth together tightly and his chest expanded as his ears pinned back. Who the fuck did this cheeky bitch think she was talking to? Paul was a main head, a warrior who could end her life at the drop of a hat. He bent down slightly so she could see the whites of his eyes.

"Listen cocky arse, carry on talking to me like a prick and I'll show everyone here just how easy it is to end your worthless life." They locked eyes and Mandy was on standby to whack something over this big bastard's head if he so much as touched a hair on her friend's head. She was a nutter and a charge sheet from the dibble was the last of her worries when it was kicking off. Mandy was ready, alert and ready to attack, she gripped the corner of the plastic chair near her. Paul Jones was a crank, a bully who preyed on weak, vulnerable people. Charlotte had had a fling with him ages ago. A few kisses that's all and this tosser thought he owned her, control freak. Ever since she'd carted him he was out to prove a point. Nobody dumped him, not even Miss Fancy pants here. Paul circled the table and stood looking at Charlotte as she walked away. The corners of his mouth started to rise, she thought she was clever didn't she, who the hell did she think she was taking the piss out of him, the bitch. She made his blood boil and something in his eye told you this wasn't the end of this matter. He'd break her fucking neck, make her suffer. No one had him over, not even Charlotte.

CHAPTER THREE

MISTY WAS SPRAWLED on the sofa when her husband came home from work. She was in a world of her own. She couldn't be arsed with anything by the looks of her. She was just staring about the room in some kind of deep trance, unaware her other half had come into the room.

As soon as Dominic walked inside the living room he knew she'd been on the bottle again. Fuck, fuck, fuck, not this again. He could smell it, see it in her eyes. A bleeding disgrace she was, out of it. Where was his tea, the loving arms greeting him after a hard day's graft, nothing, she just lay where she was. He shook his head and let out a laboured breath. When was this nightmare going to end, when was she going to see what she was doing to herself. This was a problem now, something he knew needing sorting, probably sooner rather than later. For years he'd watched the woman he loved self-destruct. Day by day she was falling deeper and deeper into a sad miserable life she'd created. It was always somebody else's fault though, never hers. So what, she'd had shit in her life but hadn't everybody? Bleeding deal with it like the rest of us have to. Every day it was the same old story of how people had shit on her and how people she'd trusted had let her down. Blah de fucking blah love, join the club. That's life, sort it out like the rest of us have to. Never once had she asked him how he was feeling, it was always about her, selfish bitch. That may have helped the situation, showed him she cared about him. But, no, it was always about her and her fucking doom and gloom world she lived in. Misty had a short memory and she'd forgotten he was the one who was there when nobody else was. He was her backbone really. For years he'd brought up another man's child as his own and never breathed a word about it to anyone. Surely that counted for something. And where was his praise, his thanks for keeping his mouth shut about her dirty secret? It was hard for him too, so bleeding hard and she needed to see just how much he'd given up to be with her. Every time he looked at his daughter he could see that bastard's eyes looking back at him, her facial expressions, her bad attitude, it was all Gordon. Nobody ever gave Dominic a second thought, it all revolved around his selfish wife. He'd even suggested counselling for her, maybe going to see a professional regarding her mental problems. Anything to try and help her. But there was no way she'd ever admit that Gordon had affected her life in any way, shape or form. That would have meant she was a failure in her eyes and that he'd won. No, she would never admit that, she was in denial.

But it was there for everyone to see; Gordon had raped her, abused her for years. He'd turned her into a bitter, twisted, depressed, wine-swigging bitch. There were no other words for her. Maybe Dominic should have left her when he had the chance, done one, when she told him she was carrying another man's child all those years ago. He'd asked himself why he'd stayed with her time and time again. He must have been tapped in the head. The woman had brought him nothing but trouble. Maybe, if he had the chance again, he would have run as far away as possible from Misty and never looked back. The whole family was fucked in the head, crazy. They all needed help, even he did now because he was part of it, part of the drama, part of this hostile, toxic home life. Misty had lashed out at him more than once too, she was violent, just as her own mother had been. The beer made her worse, played with her head and made her sink into a dark hole of depression from which she could never escape. He'd tried everything. God only knew this man had tried his best to help his wife and you could tell by his expression that he was nearing the end of what had been a long winding. Sometimes his wife said she would never drink again after a binging weekend. But it was all a load of bollocks, it never lasted. She always made excuses as to why she needed another drink. Is that what alcoholics do, deny they have a problem? Was she really a pisshead? Misty was a stresshead and with each day that went by, he was falling out of love with her. How sad was that? Yes, he often questioned why he came home every night to the same old shit. To see his wife lying there like the messed-up slob she was.

Maybe he should have started to look for someone who cared about him. A woman who wanted to do all the things he wanted to do. That would show her wouldn't it? She'd be fucked if he carted her and made a new life with someone else. Yeah, a good-looking leggy blonde with big tits, that would show her what he was about. Dominic was a good-looking man and his body was still toned from all the hours he spent at the gym. His wife even moaned about him going there but it didn't deter him, he needed to exercise to keep his sanity. He needed to lift weights, push himself to his limits to keep his head clear. Dominic sighed and shook his head, was this really his life? Lisa had gone now and it had been months since Misty's mother's death.

He did have a heart. He did care that she was grieving but come on, she had to help herself first didn't she. Probably start with getting a wash and combing her hair, she stank like a buffalo's arse if the truth was known.

He looked over at her lying on the sofa. Slowly he moved forward with caution. Was she even awake? Her eyes were barely open. His voice soon made her alert. "I don't suppose you've made any tea again have you? Misty, are you awake?"

She stirred and rolled on her side to look at him closer. Licking her lips slowly, she reached down and gripped the bottle by the neck from the floor. It took her a while to focus. Her head wobbled about from side to side. She chuckled, slurred her words as she replied. "Here, get a few swigs of this vodka. It's all you need to keep you going all day. Not all that healthy crap you keep eating. Get a mouthful of this and chill out."

What a bitch she was, there no stopping her, she was rubbing salt in his wounds. Dominic gritted his teeth tightly together and snarled at her. "Turn it in Misty, do you think I need this when I've just walked in through the fucking front door."

He should have kept his mouth shut and completely ignored her. She wriggled about on the sofa to get up. Her eyes were wide open, ready to attack, mental look in her eyes. "Listen, you smarmy bastard. I've just lost my mother and you're only arsed about something to eat. You know where the fridge is so go and make something yourself, you're not disabled are you? I can't believe you could be so bleeding heartless?"

Dominic placed a flat palm in front of her eyes, blanking her face out. "Just sit yourself back down. I'll make my own fucking tea. I don't want fuck all from you if this is the way you're going to act about it. A bit of tea on the table when I come in from a hard day's graft is all I want. Is that too much to fucking ask?"

Here it was, the usual abuse that she flung at him when he'd asked a simple question. "Go and find some other idiot who will put up with your shit. See how long you last then. Go on, see if they will put up with you?"

Was this woman having a laugh or what, the cheek of her. He should have walked away, packed his stuff and spit in her eye. But she'd hit a nerve, stabbed at his jugular. Walk away man, don't let her get to you. Stop, before you say something you might regret. It was too late. Dominic stormed back to where she was stood, he was going to punch her lights out, smack the fuck out of her, you could see it in his eyes. He'd had enough. Nobody made his blood boil like she did. Probably the months of torment had now come to a head, he was raging. He could smell her stale breath as he went nose to nose with her. "Move out of my face before I do or say something that I might regret. Honestly, don't push me." Misty was never one to back down and today was no different. Her mother was a fighter and so was she. It was in her blood, never back down. It was like she wanted him to hit her, to punish her, to wipe the smile right from her face. She sneered at him. "Oh, can you hear yourself cocky balls. If you want to hit me then feel free. I've shit bigger than you so be prepared to get a good belt back. You're forgetting I can give as good as I get."

She held a menacing look in her eyes and raised her eyebrows high. Was this really happening, did he really want him to punch her, give her a crack? His chest was rising frantically, on the verge of rolling his fists into tight balls and pummelling them into her face. He needed to shut her up, stop her abusive mouth. Just a few seconds more and she would have seen another side of her husband. Been put on her arse. The back door swung open and Max stormed inside. He froze, eyes dancing to one side of the room then the other. He could see something wasn't right. Dominic backed off and stood dragging his fingers through his hair. What was he thinking, was he really going to hurt his wife? He was white, traumatised.

"Have a word with your sister Max and see if you can sort her out. I'm sick to bastard death of her. Take her somewhere, but just get her out of my sight before I strangle the crazy bitch." Max edged into the room and made his way towards Misty. He could see the look in her eye and knew she was ready to pounce. She would have killed him stone dead if she'd got her hands on him, scratched his eyes out. Max knew this more than anyone. She was lethal when she was fuelled with alcohol. He hurried to her side and held her back by the waist as she screamed after her husband.

"Why don't you just fuck off! I might be happier without you mithering me every bleeding day. Yeah, come to think of it, it's you who makes me feel like this. Go and ruin somebody else's life and leave me the fuck alone. You've always been the same thinking you can save me. I've had enough. Fuck off and save some other fucker who needs it because I don't." Dominic clenched his teeth tightly together. Had she really just said that to him? He was frozen, his lips were moving but no sound was coming out. His nostrils flared as he rested his flat palm on the door frame. There was no way he was taking this lying down, enough was enough. She'd pushed him too far.

"Is that right, then tell me to leave. Go on, say it and I'm gone." Game set and match, he'd called her bluff. The ball was in her court now. She wasn't expecting this, her jaw wobbled. Misty swallowed hard, aware that everyone was waiting on her response. Of course, she didn't want him to leave but he'd backed her into a corner now and was demanding an answer.

Max sighed and shook his head. He whispered under his breath. "Don't do it Misty, just walk away and calm down. You know you don't mean it." No way, she would be weak if she did that. If she admitted she was wrong he would laugh at her and think she was a push-over. There was no point thinking about this anymore, it was a no-brainer. Slowly, she sat back down, her eyes still looking at him, cocky stare. Popping a cigarette into the side of her mouth, she flicked the lighter and dropped her fag into the bright yellow flame. "Do what you are doing. You know I'll never beg you to stay. Piss off, I don't need you."

Dominic hovered where he was, he just couldn't do it anymore. He turned quickly and all they could hear were his feet pounding up the stairs. Max held his ear to the door and plonked down next to his sister. "You're tapped in the head you are. Are you really going to just sit there and just let him go? You should be up those stairs now begging him to stay. You're well out of order, not him. For fuck's sake, stop him before it's too late! You'll be fucked without him and you know it."

Her head twisted slowly towards Max. He was getting it now. How dare he comment on something he knew nothing about. He was her blood, her brother. How could he sell her out in seconds, fucking Judas. He was getting a mouthful now. "You sort your own bleeding life out. You don't see me sticking my nose into your business, do you? And, let's face it, you have more problems than me if we're putting our cards on the table here!"

Max sat back in the chair and folded his arms tightly across his chest. She was right, but he wasn't the one on trial here today it was her. Come on then big boy, get it out, tell her straight just how much she was messing her life up, here's your chance to be truthful. Max bit hard on his bottom lip before he spoke again. He was going for gold. "Have you seen what you're doing to yourself! That man up there," he raised his eyes up towards the ceiling before he continued, "he worships the ground you walk on and you just treat him like a piece of shit on the bottom of your shoe. You'll be sorry if he goes. You just watch, the minute you hear that front door slam you'll be gutted. Stop him leaving before it's too late."

Misty sucked hard on her cigarette. He was right and she knew it. But it was too late for that now, she had to bite the bullet. She could never apologise. She screwed her face up and replied. "Does this face look like it gives a fuck? I may as well be on my own anyway. I sleep down here most nights on my tod. So there's no love lost here I can assure you. The man is a hindrance, always moaning. I'm better off without him."

"He's your world, you dickhead. Remember Misty how much he loves you. Everything he's done, he's done for you. The man lives and breathes for you. He worships the ground you walk on." His words fell on deaf ears, she was just sat smoking her head off, oblivious that her marriage was falling apart right in front of her eyes.

Dominic sat on the edge of the bed looking at his

belongings. There it was right before his eyes, his life in four black bin liners. A load of shite really, there was nothing of any value. He used to look so smart in his day. Snazzy clothes, designer labels but lately he'd just got himself into a rut and let himself go where the fashion department was concerned. It was her fault, that lazy crank downstairs. How could he even think about buying clothes when the lazy cow wouldn't look after them? She didn't iron at the best of times and usually he was the one putting a wash in to make sure he had clean clothes for work, not her. His mother was right, she was always right where his wife was concerned. Why didn't he just listen to her? She'd pleaded with him not to marry Misty Sullivan but he totally ignored her and did his own thing anyway. He was young, in love, smitten. He supposed he'd have to go back to his mother's house now with his tail between his legs and admit he'd dropped a bollock. He could see her face now, all smug knowing she was right about his wife all along. Mothers are always right though aren't they, where their kids are concerned? The rain hammered against the bedroom window. It was dark already outside and he knew if he didn't leave now he would be back to square one. Could he do it this time, would he have the nerve to see this through? He sat staring at the four walls, looking for the answer.

Misty swigged a large mouthful of vodka and passed it over to Max. "Here, get a gob full of that and straighten your boat race." Was this apologising in her own way? Maybe it was, maybe it wasn't. She always kept her cards close to her chest. Nobody was allowed to get inside her head. Charlotte came in through the back door and shook her hair. "It's pissing down out there. Look, I'm soaked.

Brrrrr." Max smiled over at her and raised his eyes. It didn't take long for her to get the drift of what was happening. The silence, the atmosphere could have been cut with a knife. Kicking her shoes off, she sat on the chair bringing her legs up towards her chest. "What's been going on, why has she got a face like a smacked arse?"

Misty flicked the invisible dust from her shoulder and twiddled her hair. Her eyes were closed slightly. "It's that dickhead again. You know he's always having a pop at me for nothing. I was just resting when he came home from work and the verbal abuse he fired at me was well out of order. I've told him to leave. I can't put with that kind of behaviour. It's mental cruelty." What a barefaced liar she was, she wouldn't know the truth if it hit her in the face. Charlotte shot her eyes over to Max and she could tell by his reaction that all was not as it seemed. There were footsteps upstairs, banging noises.

Charlotte raised her eyes to the ceiling. "Who's upstairs?"

Max answered her without any hesitation in the hope that she could have a word with her mother to sort this mess out before it was too late. "Your dad, he's packing his stuff and leaving. They've been at it again, terrible it is, such a crying shame to watch."

Charlotte opened her eyes wide and let out a laboured breath as she hissed over at her mother. "What, and you're just sat there getting pissed when my dad's upset? Go upstairs and sort it out, for God's sake. I knew I should have stayed at Mandy's tonight. I hate coming home to this house when you two are at war. It's not normal, why don't you give it a rest and chill out?"

Misty snapped, why did she always get the blame for

anything that went wrong in this house? So what, she'd had a few drinks to calm her nerves, it wasn't like she was staggering about the place causing any trouble was it? Max tried to stop this from going any further. They would have been dragging each other about by the hair if they'd have carried on. He looked directly at Charlotte and raised his eyes. "Go and make sure your dad is alright, love. He's been up there for ages on his own, just check he's okay."

Charlotte bounced out of her chair and hurried from the room, stomping her feet. Max studied his sister and his eyes began to well up. Where was his old sibling, the lovable, fun, kind and caring person she used to be? Was she gone forever? Would he ever see her again? Fuck knows, it was such a big mess. He had to try, talk some sense into her. Make her see what was at stake here. He sighed and shook his head slowly. "I miss my mam, I know she was hard work but she was ours Misty, our hard work. You can't just blank her out of your mind. You need to talk about it. Please open up and tell me what's going on. I can help if you just let me."

Misty closed her eyes and bit hard onto her bottom lip. Had he hit a nerve, was she ready to break down and discuss what was really bothering her? Misty gripped the edge of the cushion, her knuckles turning white. That old cow had wronged her and she would never forgive her for it, ever. She sat up straight and folded her arms tightly in front of her, defensive. She was so cold-hearted, there was no emotion whatsoever. "I miss nothing about that woman. I can't help the way I feel either, so don't look at me with them big daft eyes because you don't know the half of it where she's concerned. She's evil. I'll never forgive her for what she's done to me. So don't even go there." Max rolled his eyes and carried on listening to his sister. "If I had a pound for every bit of pain that bitch has caused me then I would be a rich woman, minted I can tell you. You can blow her trumpet all day long for me but you can't polish a turd. She was a cunt, a heartless self-centred woman who cared about nobody but herself. It's the truth. I can't help how I feel."

Max sniggered, his mother had always said and he found it endearing that even though his sister declared she hated her, there was still part of her still alive in his sister.

You can't polish a turd…

Max changed the subject. He wasn't wasting any more time talking about his mother, pointless. "Denise said she's coming around soon to see you later. She knows you've been drinking more than you should be and she's worried about you. Well, we all are if I'm being honest." The living room door flung open and Charlotte marched inside, with Dominic following closely behind her. Misty clocked his black bags on the floor near his legs. He was really doing this, he was deserting her. Fuck, fuck, fuck, this wasn't supposed to happen. Usually he went upstairs and calmed down, forgave her. She gulped and itched the end of her nose.

Charlotte was the peacemaker here today and she was hoping this could be put to bed and everyone could kiss and make up. "Mam, I've told my dad you don't mean what you've said, so stop pissing about and put the man out of his misery. Go on, tell him you're sorry. Tell him to go and put all his stuff back in the drawers."

This woman was her own worst enemy, nothing, not a word, stubborn cow she was. She'd live to regret this for sure, her and her daft bleeding pride. She eyeballed her husband for a split second and dropped her eyes low to the floor. "If he's going then let him fucking go. I'm done anyway. I've had enough of all the drama".

Max shook his head slowly and raised his eyes over to Dominic. There was nothing left to say. Dominic picked his belongings up and hooked them over his shoulder. He snatched his car keys from the side of the table. Not a word. He never even looked at her once. The back door slammed shut and he was gone. Misty swallowed hard and turned her head slightly to watch him leave through the living room window. Misty just sat gawping out of the window. She said nothing, not a word. She sat back in her chair and played with her fingers nervously. Her stomach churned, he was gone. For fuck's sake, he'd really left her this time. What was she going to do now? They say pride comes before a fall and on this occasion they were more than right, she'd fallen flat on her face.

Charlotte pulled her mobile from her pocket and lay flat on the bed. Bored she was, fed up with her home life. Drama after bleeding drama every bastard day. No day was ever the same, there was always something going on. She had a pissed-up mother who didn't know what day it was. And now a father who'd given up on her too. What was the point anymore, she was beyond caring.

Charlotte had been to the pub tonight and Reek had come in to see her, just as he'd promised. She didn't speak to him much though. No, she played it cool and kept him on his toes. Maybe she should just flick him a quick text message. A few words to tell him she was glad he turned up. Reek looked like a fish out of water though; shy and bashful, a geek even. Even the way he was dressed tonight was a complete letdown. Black pants and a shirt he wore. He had no dress sense whatsoever. He looked like a nerd. But maybe she could change that, take him shopping, get him some decent swagger. Maybe show him the shops to buy his clothes from, the brands, the designer stuff. Lying back with her mobile in her hand, she flicked through the emojis. Just a smiley face was all she sent to him, enough to let him know she was happy he'd made the effort to turn up. Perhaps she should have made more of an effort with him, introduced him to the cooler kids in her circle of friends, put him on the map so to speak. Mandy knew Charlotte had a thing for him without her having to say a word. All night long she kept catching her gawping at him. He wasn't even her usual type, he was a muppet in her eyes. Reek was punching above his weight for sure. He was nowhere near Charlotte's league and if he thought he had a shot at the title, he had another thing coming. He was getting warned off, told straight to go and mix with his own sort. The geeks, the good kids.

Mandy had told one of her other friends this and as soon as she got the chance, she was putting this dickhead in his place. It would be child's play, just a warning to make sure he kept well out of her way. A text alert on her phone. Charlotte turned her screen to face her and smiled. He'd replied already, what an eager beaver he was. Why didn't he play it cool? Didn't he understand that no girl liked a pushover. They needed a challenge. He should have been more of a bad lad and given her a run for her money. A player. She supposed Reek was innocent to the ways of the world. The way it was in Harpurhey anyway. He needed to learn some life skills and fast. It was right to say he was a full-time dickhead. He had no street credit and no understanding of how things worked here. Maybe he could start by selling a bit of weed, just to get him on her level, a bit of sniff even. That's what most of the other lads her age did to earn a bit of cash, so why couldn't he do a bit of shifty work too? She could help him set up a graft phone, get him some drugs on tick until he managed to pay for it. Oh, this girl knew her shit when it came to making a few quid. Her ex- boyfriend Paul was a well- known drug dealer in the area and maybe that was why she was attracted to him at first. He had cash, he was minted for his age. But what girl would want a guy who was all over her like a rash, Paul was needy. A fucking headache really that she didn't need in her life anymore.

Paul had served his purpose anyway. He'd got her Jimmy Choo shoes. He could go and fuck a duck now if he ever thought he was getting another go at her again. Paul was a raging lunatic, tapped in the head. He needed to be kept at arm's length, watched very carefully. Shady he was, underhand. Charlotte snuggled deep into her bed. Lifting her mobile phone up closer, she studied the text that had just appeared on her phone. "Do you fancy coming to my house tomorrow? I will cook for you." She covered her mouth with her hand and sniggered. Was this geezer having a laugh or what? Who did he think he was, bleeding Jamie Oliver? Nobody had ever asked to cook for her before, he must have been soft, a big fairy. Men didn't cook did they? Once the laughter subsided she decided to reply to his message. A diner date was not what made her tick. She started to type a message back to him. "Nah, I'm not into that cooking lark. You can take me to Nando's if you want though. We can get a proper scran instead of that posh stuff you're gonna make me." She sent the text then read over it. She was stressed now, how did she even know what he was going to make her? Her dialogue was cringeworthy too, common as muck. But she'd sent it now it was too late. She sat staring at her phone waiting on a reply, nothing. Perhaps she'd hurt his feelings, ruined her chance of getting to know him better. She rolled on her side and began to flip through her photographs on her phone. There were some great snaps of the gang tonight. She used her fingers to zoom in on one photograph in particular. Her eyes were wide open. She could see Reek in the background. She just sat staring at the image of him. The corners of her mouth began to rise, she was smitten for sure. Okay, he wasn't her usual cup of tea but with a bit of work this geek could be perfect. There was another text alert…

Stop being a nobhead. I'm a good cook. Just come and give it a try. Stop being a weirdo.

She smiled and twisted her silver Pandora ring around her finger. Take your time, think about this before you answer this time. Don't send something you didn't mean to send, think about it first. Maybe she could go to his house but nobody could ever know. Yeah, she'd keep this on the low and tell nobody for now. She replied but this time she made every effort to be nice and polite to him.

Thanks for the offer and okay I'd love to taste your cooking. But, I don't like fish, or prawns, or seafood or anything that has crept about in the sea. So, good luck with your menu. Can I be cheeky and ask for a dessert too. I've got a sweet tooth and I love chocolate.

There it was, all ready to be sent. One last final read of the message and she pressed the send button. Reaching over to her TV, she flicked it on. It was time to relax, time to stop her mind from racing and time to stop stressing about family life.

Misty lay in bed, restless. Stretching her hands over to the other side of the bed, she felt the coldness of the sheets. It felt like her heart; cold and empty. A single tear trickled down the side of her cheek landing on her lip. Why the hell did she let him go, she'd fucked up big time. This could have been sorted out, put to bed and made better with a few words, 'sorry' being one of them. He'd had enough of her problems now, she could see it in his eyes. She'd ground this man down to the ground. Sucked every bit of happiness from him. She knew this more than anyone. Perhaps he was better off away from her. He might have started to enjoy his life then, without her screaming at him all day long. And she'd nagged this man too, made his life a misery. She couldn't even remember the last time they'd had sex, when she'd kissed him, told him she loved him. It was a distant memory to her. There was no passion anymore, no kissing, no cuddling, she'd just switched herself off from her marriage months ago, maybe years ago if she was being honest with herself. But why? What was the real reason she let one of the best things in her life just slip through her fingers without a care in the world? Marriages go stale, everyone knows that, but this was something more meaningful, deep rooted, there were big problems that no one would ever resolve. They were her demons and she had to face them before she could ever move on. Misty punched her clenched fist into the pillow and pulled the cover over her head. Sleep was never going to happen tonight for this woman and although she lay there for over an hour staring into space, her mind was racing, itching for something. There was no way she was getting any shut-eye. But how could she when things were lying so heavily on her mind, her husband and that bastard who'd threatened to ruin her life, her family? It needed sorting out fast. She knew he'd be knocking on her door within days, threatening to blab her secret, threatening to spill the beans. Misty flung the duvet from her body and dove out of bed. She was talking to herself as she wobbled over to the wall, trying to find the light switch. "I'll show him, I'll show them all. Since when have I ever needed any cunt in my life to sort my problems out? I need no one, I never have." Grabbing her house coat, she slipped it over her shoulders and made her way out of the bedroom.

Misty sat in the front room and plonked down on the sofa. The night was a lonely place when you were feeling this low. Every second that passed felt like an hour. Her head looked like it was going to burst with all her problems. She was smoking like a trooper, one after the other. It was a wonder her lungs hadn't collapsed. She needed a plan, something to be set in stone. If she confronted Tom she needed to have a backup plan, something to scare the living daylights out of him, shit his pants with fear and make sure he never darkened her door again. Misty knew people who could do this for her. It was all about the money. If needed she could always pull a few quid together to rid this bastard from her life forever. The refuge centre she'd left years ago always had a few quid in its budget. Nobody would ever suspect her of having it away, no way in this world. Now, that was an idea. Maybe she should call there and see how the girls were doing after all this time. She sat cracking her knuckles, tense, ready for snapping, small beads of sweat forming on her forehead. The bottle of vodka was staring at her, temping her yet again. She knew that no matter what, her answers were not in the bottom of any bottle, but this stuff made her calm and sorted her head out... The drink had a grip of her for sure and each day she was fighting her own personal battle to deal with it. It just gradually got out of control.

Misty drank socially at first and then to help her sleep but nowadays it was to live, to feel normal, to function, to hold a conversation. This woman needed help before it was too late. But with her husband off the scene now, who cared enough about her to get this addiction in line? Misty had to tell someone what was going on and fast. The denial was over, she had gremlins to face and the sooner she did it the better. She bent down and reached for the bottle of vodka, there was enough inside it to calm her down. With haste, she held the bottle to her mouth as if her life depended on it. What a crying shame to watch this woman self-destructing like this. She was desperate with every mouthful she took, liquid dribbling down the side of her mouth, on to her chin. Misty plonked back in her chair and held the bottle tightly to her chest, like a baby, nursing it, stroking her fingers up and down the cold glass. She was humming now, whispering a song she used to sing when she was younger.

CHAPTER FOUR

DOMINIC WOKE and rubbed his knuckles into the corners of his eyes. He looked to the left of him and for the first time in years, his wife wasn't there. His eyes clouded over and he gripped the pillow next to him tightly. Had he done the right thing, maybe he'd overreacted? It was only words she'd fired at him, that was all. But words stuck, once they were fired there was no taking them back, they dug deep in his heart and crippled him. Dominic inhaled and his chest expanded as he looped his arms over his head. He'd actually had a good night's sleep given the circumstances. No moaning wife by his side, no cars skidding about in the car park near his home. Peace and tranquillity at last. It was Saturday morning and there was no need for him to get up early, he could have a lie in, a decent wank without anyone interrupting him. Legs akimbo, he was ready to give his cock a real good shake. His mother would be in the bedroom soon, he just knew it. He had to be quick. His eyes shot around the bedroom. Maybe masturbation would have to go on the back burner for now. Was he really in the mood anyway, his heart was low.

Dominic shot his eyes over to the door. For the last twenty minutes he had heard Helen pottering about outside the bedroom door. He just knew she was there lurking outside, waiting to know the ins and outs of a cat's arsehole. She loved a bit of gossip and there was no doubt about it, she would hold nothing back where his wife was concerned. And why should she, she ruined her son's life in her eyes. Misty was never good enough for her boy, not now, not ever. Every mother wants the best for her son but Helen was so over the top with her boy. He was her only child and perhaps if she'd had a few more kids, she wouldn't have been so over-protective of him. Dominic was her world, her reason to get up out of bed each morning. Ever since her husband had pissed off and left her, she'd suffocated her son with love and affection. He could do nothing wrong in her eyes. This woman would die for her son.

Raising his hands above his head, Dominic scratched hard at his scalp. What the fuck had gone on in his life for him to deserve this? He'd been nothing but nice, caring, supportive and hardworking. He should have been over the moon that he was away from all the drama but his heart was heavy, he was missing his family already. But how could he be missing someone who abused him mentally and physically, was he off his nut or what? Was he just stuck in a rut and knew no better? No, surely he'd had enough of the crank. This wasn't normal, it was fucked up. As predicted, the bedroom door creaked open slowly and there she was, ready to start the interrogation. Helen crept inside slowly. He watched her closely. "Good morning sweetheart, did you sleep well?" This woman was so false. There was no love lost between her and Misty and she'd stopped pretending there was any kind of bond between them a long time ago. Misty was scum in her eyes. A council estate skank who would never be accepted into her family. She'd ruined her son's life. He could have had so much more. The family had always been well-known where they lived and although her son had moved to a nice area, it was still full of people like his wife. Benefit cheats, lazy bastards who didn't have a day's work in them; thieving bastards. His mother had told him to buy a property near her but that wife of his had the final say in the matter and she wanted to be as far away from her as possible. There was no secret about this. Misty was a bitch and every day her son was still married to her, it made her stomach churn inside. But her son was back home now. What a result! She could cook for him, clean his room. It would just be like old times. Her and her boy back together again. This could be the end of her nightmare.

Stepping toward the window, she gently tugged open the cream silk curtains. The sunlight burst inside the bedroom and made the room fresh and light again. She smiled over at Dominic and her heart melted, you could see the happiness in her eyes. "I'll make you some bacon and fresh tiger bread if you want love. Best butter on it too. I bet you've not had Lurpak on your bread in years, have you son?" Oh, she was rubbing salt in the wounds now. She might have given him a break seeing as he was so upset.

Dominic folded the pillow under his head and shot a look over at his mother. "Leave it out hey. I don't need to hear it, especially not today."

Helen was never one to let sleeping dogs lie, she continued, hoping to get her words out. "I don't know how you've managed to stay as long as you have. She's a dirty cow. When was the last time she gave that house a good scrub anyway? I didn't want to mention it but the last time I was round at yours, I felt like telling her myself. Honest, I felt dirty when I came home. I was itching, I think something bit me, a flea or something."

"Mam, fuck off out of here and just let me wake up.

I've come here to sort my head out not to listen to you going on about shit. My marriage is falling apart and all you're bothered about is a fucking clean house. Give it a rest will you, please, just piss off and let me wake up."

Helen's jaw dropped. His language was terrible, just like that foul-mouthed wife of his. She slowly stepped towards the bedroom door and in her own true style, she had to have the last word. "Don't you bite my bleeding head off because of her. I've told you a hundred times before how I feel about that woman and nothing on this earth will ever make me change my mind. Anyway, do you want something to eat or not?"

"If I do, I'll make it myself. Mam, just close the door on the way out."

Helen made her way out of the bedroom, humming she was, overjoyed that her golden balls son was home. Dominic closed his eyes and you could see he was in two minds if he could even stay under the same roof as his mother. She was hard work, full of shit about how money made the world go round. So what, he'd had to work for all he'd had in his life and in fairness, he was never one for material things. He had a wife and a family and that was all he ever needed to make him smile each day. Well, until now. It was such a shame. This man never even had his own child, Misty always said in time they could have a child together but that time never came. There was always something going on in her life and a baby was a hundred miles away from her thoughts. It hurt that he'd brought up someone else's child and never once had his wife see that he was craving one of his own too, his own blood, a proper bloodline to keep his name alive after he was gone. The arguments he'd had about this were endless but things never changed, she was spiteful. Dominic had endless women trying to grab his attention every single day but he was loyal, never once was he unfaithful to his wife, or so he told her. Really he should have slept with them all, banged their brains out, had children to them for the way his wife had treated him. Letting out a laboured breath, he closed his eyes and tucked the duvet under his chin. Maybe his wife would be missing him too. She might have realised by now just how much he meant to her, he wasn't holding his breath though, she was stubborn, hard work. He was pissed off now and even the wank he was planning had turned sour, he was in no mood, none whatsoever.

Denise banged her knuckles hard on the living room window. She could see Misty sat in the chair and it was clear she was ignoring her. Her fat face squeezed up against the glass pane and she peered inside. Misty could see her now, caught her bang to rights. "Open the door, I'm freezing my tits off out here."

Misty sighed and got up from the chair with effort. This was the last thing she needed. She just wanted to be left alone to sort her head out. Denise was loud and the way she was feeling, she would have ended up telling her to fuck off home. The door opened and in came her auntie. "Morning campers, stick the kettle on love. I'm spitting feathers here. I've just come from the shops. I've got us both a cream cake each," she clicked her fingers at the side of her. "Go on then, move that bony arse of yours and make us a brew." Misty trudged into the kitchen and took the small white box from her auntie. Denise plonked down in the chair and started to speak in a loud voice, so Misty could hear her in the kitchen. "I can see you got your act together and cleaned this house up."

Of course, she was being sarcastic, the gaff was a shit-tip. There was no reply, not that she expected one. She straightened the cushion behind her back and shot her eyes around the room. There were empty bottles of vodka, clothes all over the place, plates still with food on them lying about, the place was a dump. Misty leaned forward over the kitchen and waited for the kettle to boil. Even this was an effort for her, she had no energy, no passion for life anymore. All she wanted was to sleep, no bother, no nagging, just to be left alone. Denise sat up straight as Misty walked into the front room with two mugs hugged tightly around her fingers. Her expression was stressed. "Get a grip of one then, instead of bloody just staring at me, it's burning me. My fingers are gonna fall off if I hold them any longer."

Denise sat forward and hooked one of the mugs from her finger. Misty hurried to place her own drink on the floor next to where she was sat. Denise blew onto the top of her cup and slurped a small mouthful. "Bleeding hell, it's hot, did you melt the kettle or what?" Misty sat down and folded her legs underneath her, making no reply. Denise studied her and before long, she started the conversation Misty had been dreading. "I believe you've been drinking all the time. It stops now do you hear me, you need to turn it in before you get ill?"

Before she could finish her sentence, Misty was on the defensive and stopped her dead in her tracks. "Listen, don't listen to a word Max is saying. I've just been having a shit time that's all. You drink don't you when you're fed up, so before you start I don't need a bleeding lecture. Just let me sort my own shit out in my own way."

Denise growled over at her, where was the respect talking to her like this? She'd fucked it now, she was getting told and it was her own fault. Denise clenched her teeth tightly together. "Whoa, cut the fucking attitude lady. I'm here because I love and care about you, not to judge you. I don't care who's told me to be honest. I have eyes you know and I can see for myself you're struggling. You're a pisshead, so stop lying to yourself." Misty bit hard on her bottom lip, there was no running away from this one. No back-chat, she had to listen. Her auntie took a breath and swallowed hard before she spoke. "I've seen your mam in the same boat as you are. Our Lisa liked a drink as you know and we both know it was the root of all evil with her. Are you forgetting all the times we found her half dead because of the drink? What about the nights she went missing and we had to search every boozer in Manchester to find her?"

Misty's eyes clouded over. Of course she remembered it, how could she ever forget. She was the one looking after the family at the time. The one feeding them, cooking and cleaning and making sure they all got fed. It was a big ask, too. At the time she was only young herself, a child. Lisa would never have admitted it but she'd struggled with drink all her life. It was gin that took her fancy, mother's ruin they nicknamed it and in this case, it lived up to its name. Denise let out a laboured breath and looked her niece straight in the eye. "You're an alcoholic. There you go, that's me being open and honest with you. I've watched you for months and although it kills me inside to say it, you have a problem just like your mother did."

Misty's eyes were wide open, her heart beating

frantically in her chest. Small beads of sweat appeared on her forehead. She was having a panic attack for sure. All the colour drained from her cheeks and she was as white as a ghost. No! This wasn't right, she wasn't like her mother, she'd never be like her. Misty clenched her teeth tightly together and she didn't care who she speaking to, this was an insult, a fucking cheeky remark that hit her hard. She was never going to take it lying down. It was such a low blow.

"Denise, I'm nothing like my mam was. Don't you dare come around to my house and start chatting shit about something you know nothing about. Look at your own life before you start sticking your beak into mine."

There it was, the best form of offence was attack. Denise nodded her head slowly; like mother like daughter. They were both feisty and would never in a million years admit they were wrong or in trouble. She had to up her game, break her down and make her see what she was doing to herself. "Oi, stop it now before I put you flat on your arse. Since when have you ever spoken to me like this? I swear Misty, carry on and you'll be on the floor with a white chalk mark around you before you know it. Wind your neck in and fucking listen to what I have to say to you. I'm not here as your bleeding therapist. I'm here to make you see what is happening right in front of your eyes. Are you blind or what, can't you see what the hell is going on right under your nose?" Her eyebrows raised high as she continued. "Go on, when was the last time you cooked Charlotte her tea, or your husband for that matter? You just sit there all day, every day with your head in the clouds. Wake up and smell the coffee love, you have a problem."

Misty snarled over at her, no way was this true! "I do

cook all the time. It's not my fault if no one eats it."

Denise let out a sarcastic laugh. "Are you having a laugh or what, give your head a wobble woman. I've been sat here on plenty of occasions when Dominic has had to come in here after a hard day's graft and cook his own tea. That man is going through hell living with you and you know it. This is serious shit. You're going to lose everything you care about if you carry on, including your husband."

Misty squeezed her fists together at the side of her legs. She could punch her lights out, throw her out of the house, kick her right up the arse on the way there too. Count Misty, calm down before you do or say something you'll regret. She closed her eyes slowly, her mouth was moving but no words were coming out. Her cheeks were bright red and she looked like she was going to burst with anger any second soon. Denise stood up, she was ready. If Misty wanted a beef, she would give it to her alright. The two of them locked eyes and just stared at each other a little longer than they needed to. It was Misty who backed down first, she'd had enough, she was deflated. She needed a shoulder to cry on. She broke down. "I've had a lot of shit to put up with Denise. There is stuff you don't know about. Please, don't ask me about it because I'll start crying and once I do I won't be able to stop."

There she was, the woman Denise remembered, the kind caring girl she had helped out and stood up for through all the years that had passed. She was the apple of her eye and no matter what, Denise would always support her niece. "Come here love and give me a hug. Nothing is ever that bad that you can't talk about it. Misty, we go way back and you know whatever you tell me will never leave my lips. I cross my heart and hope to die." Misty shrugged her shoulders. Yeah right, as if she was going to spill her secret to Denise. This woman couldn't hold her own piss. She was a blabbermouth, a gossip. Denise squeezed her niece in her arms tightly. "Sit down and drink your coffee. I'll get us them cakes out of the kitchen."

Misty watched her going into the kitchen and sighed. Her head was bursting and if she didn't deal with her problems soon, she was going explode, have a heart attack. And this fucking cake muncher wasn't helping her either. She knew now she would have to sit down for hours and talk about other problems in her life. Denise knew her like the back of her hand and would never let up until things were sorted. Here she was now coming back from the kitchen. Honest, the woman was sucking the cream out of the side of the cake as if her life depended on it. Okay, she'd lost a bit of weight recently but it wasn't normal to be that bleeding hungry twenty-four hours a day.

"There you go my princess. It's bloody lovely, it's got jam and cream and vanilla in it. Get it down your neck before I eat it too. I'm bleeding starving."

Misty hadn't eaten anything proper for days. It was just the vodka that was feeding her. She was underweight and her skin was blemished with spots all around her mouth. Placing the cake towards her mouth, she gagged. Her palate wasn't used to food anymore, it was only the vodka she could stomach and this cake was making her stomach churn. Denise was watching from the corner of her eye. "Misty, just try it. I'll eat what you leave but just try and get something down you." She opened her mouth and sucked the tiniest bit of cream into her mouth. That was it, no more, she was going to spew.

"So," Denise said, "You may as well come clean and

tell me what's been going on because Max will tell me if you don't."

Misty sat back and folded her arms. "Okay, Dominic has left me, he went last night after a heated argument. We just seem to be at loggerheads all the time. It's like he doesn't understand that I'm grieving. He's pecking my head all the time."

"Come on love, Dominic has always been there supporting you. The man hasn't got a bad bone in his body."

"See, I knew you would say that. Nobody sees what goes on behind closed doors and he's hard work. He comes over as nice as pie to everyone else but when it's just us two, he's horrible."

Denise shoved the last bit of cake in her mouth and carried on speaking with her mouth full. "You need to tell him to come home, you need him now more than ever. Charlotte needs him too. He keeps her in check and makes sure she's alright. You know what she's like when she's on one. You're forgetting he's the one who goes walking the streets for her at night when she doesn't come home."

"What, so you're saying I don't look after her now. For fuck's sake I'm not that bad?"

"I'm saying stop being a stubborn arse and sort your marriage out."

Misty sulked, why did no one ever have a bad word to say about her husband? Surely he'd played his part in the downfall of their marriage. Denise softened her tone, she wasn't here to blame anyone, she just wanted to sort some stuff out. "Ring him, tell him how much you love him and that you're sorry."

Misty swallowed and sucked hard on her lips. "Not a fucking earthly. Do you think he can talk to me how he wants and I'm just going to take it? Day in, day out he's constantly on my case over this and that. He does my head in and perhaps I'm better off on my own. Only time will tell."

Denise was right and by the looks of Misty, she needed him back quicker than she thought. Alright, he was moody and high maintenance in her eyes but he kept her niece safe, he knew her inside and out. Denise digested what she'd just said and tickled the end of her chin. "Well, that's the wrong attitude isn't it? Stop being a smacked arse and go and get your husband back. Worse things happen at sea." There was a few second's silence and Denise sat forward, ready to tackle the main issue here today. She sat playing with her fingers, aware it could kick off at any second now. "Anyway, let's address you drinking all the time. Don't just dismiss it as if it's not a problem, because it is. It's going to be the ruin of you if you carry on."

"Oh, here we go again. I have a few drinks at night to help me sleep and now I'm a raving pisshead. I don't believe this, insulting it is."

"It's not just at night, you're drinking through the day too. Shahid in the corner shop has told me just how much you drink, so cut the crap."

Misty's eyes were wide open, what a grassing cunt that shopkeeper of hers was and when she saw him next, he was getting told. In fact, she would start shopping somewhere else. His prices were sky-high anyway and he'd been ripping her off for years. What a grassing fucker he was but now the truth was there for her to see, there was no running away from this or covering it up. She chewed on her fingernails and dropped her head. "Maybe I have had a few too many lately but I'll sort it out in my own time. I don't have a drinking problem, Denise. Do you really think I'm a lush?"

"If I'm being honest, then yes. Look at the state of you. When was the last time you had a decent wash or combed your hair? Look around you Misty, it's all falling apart and you're oblivious to it. You need to step up and get your shit together fast before it's too late."

Misty let out a laboured breath and admitted defeat. "Alright, alright. I get it and I'll sort it out but for now, can we just talk about something else. All anyone ever goes on about lately is me and my life. You all need to chill out and leave me the fuck alone."

Denise's job was done here for now and she'd set the ball rolling. Of course, she would keep an eye on her in the future but for now, all she wanted was for her to get Dominic back home where he belonged. "Please, will you ring him and try and sort this out?"

The back door opened and Charlotte walked inside, she was smiling and dancing about as she listened to the tunes she had playing on her mobile phone. Denise chuckled and stood up and opened her arms out fully. "Come here and give me a big cuddle you cutie." Charlotte danced over to where she was and started to dance with her. Misty was in a world of her own and never said a word, the miserable cow. "Will you help your mam get this place in shape lovey. She just needs a bit of help until she gets herself back on her feet. Just help by doing bits, like hoovering up, washing the pots, anything as long as you're helping in some way."

Charlotte nodded, she could have said no and caused mayhem but for once she agreed. What was up with her, this was unusual even for her. Had she really agreed to do some housework? This girl never did a tap! Denise watched her leave the room and rubbed her hands together with excitement. "See, that's a start. All we need now is for you to get sorted. Do you want me to book you in for your hair done? That will cheer you up. Go on, you go upstairs and get a wash and I'll see if the hairdressers can fit you in and sort that mop out." Misty didn't answer her, she just drifted upstairs like a ghost. She needed a drink, just a few swigs to help her calm down. But she'd drained the lot earlier, there wasn't a drop left. Today was going to be tough for sure. If Denise was with her there would be no way she could nip anywhere to get the alcohol she craved, she was trembling inside, sweating.

Charlotte rummaged inside her wardrobe, she needed to look mint tonight, something to really impress him. Should she wash her hair, curl it, plait it, or just shove it on top of her head in a scruffy bun? If she made a big effort he would be able to tell though. But if she was going to make him fall madly in love with her, he had to see her in her full glory. Yes, she'd wash her hair and blow it so it looked all bouncy and sexy. Maybe she could ring Mandy to call round to do her make-up too? She'd seen Reek earlier in the day and he quickly spoke to her as she walked past him. Mandy was curious and in the end she had to tell her friend about the date. The two of them had words about it too. Honest, Mandy had spat her dummy out and hated the fact that this muppet had clinched a date with her best mate. Why didn't Mandy just give Reek a chance and see how it all panned out? No doubt, Charlotte would have carted him after a few dates anyway, she was like that, she got fed up easily.

Misty looked like death warmed up as she slid her coat on. In fairness, she'd only really been out to the corner shop over the last few months and she was getting anxious about heading out onto the streets again. She needed to ditch Denise, get rid of her and fast. The two of them left the house together and Denise was proud of herself. She liked to think of herself as a bit of a fixer, a listener and a problem solver. God, she'd seen enough problems in this family to last her a lifetime too. Looking over at her niece, she smirked to herself. Today had been a good day and with any luck, Misty would pull herself together and get her life back on track. Sometimes that was all somebody needed, a good kick up the arse, a few home truths. Yes, today had been a good day.

Misty was edgy and fidgeting about as she sat in the reception area, waiting for her appointment. Denise sat next to her shovelling a packet of cheese and onion crisps down her neck, crunching them, licking her fingers. Honest, she never stopped eating. Every time you saw her she was munching something or other, food junkie. It was a shame really because all the weight she'd lost lately she was just piling back on. She may as well have admitted to herself that she was never going to be thin. She wouldn't have suited it anyway. When she lost over five stone a few years ago she looked ill, her cheeks collapsed and her eyes were sunken. No, she looked miles better with some weight on her. Misty checked her wristwatch with cunning eyes. "Denise, you shoot off. I'll be alright here on my own. I'm going to be hours here anyway because I'll have my colour done too, so you get off and go and do what you have to. No point in staying here being bored. I'm fine, honest."

Denise looked out of the window and nodded her

head. Yes, she could have done with going now as she had lots of jobs to do herself. With a quick peck on Misty's cheek, she stood to her feet. "Right, as long as you are going to be okay. I'll call around tomorrow to see you. And just for the record, I don't mean to moan at you. I just care about you. I love you to bits, that's all." Okay, okay, she'd heard it all bastard day now. Just go will you woman. Misty sat on the edge of her seat as Denise left the shop. Slowly, she peeped out of the window and made sure she was gone. She licked her lips slowly and made her way to the reception desk. "I'm just nipping to the shop to get some fags. I'll be back soon. Is that alright?" The dippy blonde behind the counter quickly checked the diary.

"Yes, that's fine, you have fifteen minutes yet before your appointment anyway."

"Brilliant, see you soon. I won't be long." Misty stormed out of the salon and headed down the main road. There was a corner shop not far from where she was and she headed there with speed.

Misty twisted the red lid from the bottle of vodka with trembling hands. She was stood in a deserted alleyway at the back of the shops. Bringing the cold bottle to her mouth, she hesitated. "Just one last time, I swear, just one last time," she whispered under her breath. Misty sucked hard at the bottle, desperate to get the liquid inside her.

CHAPTER FIVE

RICO STIRRED THE PAN with a wooden spoon. His mother stood behind him supervising; proud as punch she was, knowing she had taught him well. She was a great cook herself and her culinary skills had improved over the years. Francesca had been to night school to learn how to cook. She'd gone there out of boredom really, when she was living in Leeds. She saw it as a chance to make new friends. That was where she met Frank, such a lovely kind man who she had a relationship with for over a year. It just wasn't meant to be though. As time went on, the guy bored the life out of her. Francesca was used to the hard men, the ones who could give her a thrill, smash her head in. Frank was too clean cut, there was nothing exciting about him whatsoever. He was the first man she'd slept with in a long time.

She had never really got over Gordon if the truth was known. He damaged her, messed with her head. Francesca fell to bits when Gordon was laid to rest. Even though he was a total bastard with her, his death hit her hard for all sorts of reasons. Rico would never really know his dad, never have that father and son bond. It was so sad really. She'd spoken lots to Rico about his dad and she held nothing back either. He had to know how bad he was, the threat he'd been to her and anyone who was involved with him. Even though it killed her to say it, she told Rico his father was better off dead. Tom, Gordon's brother, was the danger now. He was a sick twisted fucker and thought the world owed him a living. He'd turned up at her house a few times in the past threatening to take her son from her. He still loved Francesca and he never forgave her for selling him out. She'd told him they had a life together but as soon as Tigger come on the scene she dumped his sorry arse and never gave him a second look. Every time he turned up at her house he always reminded her of that. The time they'd shared together, the promises they made to each other. It was all bullshit in her eyes, words she'd said when her head was all over the place.

Francesca stood behind her son and smiled. "Rico, you're so romantic. I don't know where you get it from. This caring nature is so nice. I hope this Charlotte appreciates all the effort you've gone to for her?"

He never flinched and carried on cooking. "Mam, stop being so on top. Charlotte is a lovely girl and she's not like you think. She's alright you know."

Francesca stood looking at him with her hand on her hip. "She's a street girl Rico. A wise head, just like I was back in the day. These girls are only after a good time, a free ride - just don't be sucked in by all her banter. She will run rings around you if you let her. That's why I'm keeping a close eye on her. You know if she thinks she can take the piss out of you, I will punch her lights out?"

Rico smirked. He loved winding her up. "Mam, you're nearly a pensioner, you can't be fighting at your age."

"Oi, don't underestimate me. I can still do a bit. You don't know about me when my cage is rattled."

Rico started to snigger and turned around to face her. "Mam, I hope you're going to go out and give us a bit of space. I don't need you sat here all night ruining my chance of getting a decent snog."

She rolled her eyes. "I hope that's all you're getting son. Don't be doing anything you'll regret. Put a sock on the end of it if you're thinking about having sex. You don't want any kids spoiling your career do you?"

Rico shook his head. He had a great relationship with his mother and they always talked openly about sex and any other issues he may have encountered. Francesca was as straight as they came, held nothing back, she told it as it was. Rico continued, "so, does that mean you are going out tonight then or what?"

"I thought I might just join you both for something to eat before I go out."

Rico screwed his face up and was ready to start moaning. She punched him in the arm and chuckled. "I'm joking, chill out. I'm going to nip round to Sally's to have a few glasses of wine. She's a bit of a glass eye but I'm hoping after a few she might loosen up."

Rico turned the gas on the stove off, his sauce was made. His expression was serious now. "I know I've only known her for a short time mam but she makes my heart skip a beat. Honest, she makes me weak."

Francesca let out a laboured breath. This was the first time ever she'd seen her boy falling in love with a girl. She could sense it, see it in his eyes when he spoke her name. "Just be careful. Like I said, take it slowly at first. Don't ever be anyone's fool son."

Charlotte had upped her game. She didn't look as boyish as she usually did. Her make-up was subtle, her hair all curly and bouncy and fresh-looking. There was no hoodie on tonight. She was dressed in faded jeans with a white blouse tucked inside them. As she knocked at the front door she stood fidgeting about, anxious, afraid he would be able to see right through her and realise she liked him a lot more than she was admitting. She rapped on the letterbox and stood back. Charlotte could see the shadow of someone approaching the front door. The door opened slowly. Francesca stood smirking, her cheeks slightly flushed.

"Oh, look at you, don't you look lovely," Rico's mother said in an animated voice. Charlotte dipped her head and flicked her hair over her shoulder.

"Is Reeks in?" Francesca pulled a sour face.

She hated that nobody ever used her son's proper name. 'Reeks' sounded common and her son was far from that. She held the door open and invited the girl inside. "Come in, he's just getting ready." Charlotte plodded into the front room and Francesca was hot on her trail. She could get a few minutes with her without her son listening to their conversation. She needed to let this girl know she was watching her, ready to pounce on her if she put a foot out of place. The front room was lovely, fresh and nicely decorated. Everything seemed to have its place and there was no clutter anywhere. Charlotte sat down and her nostrils flared slightly. "Something smells nice."

Francesca smiled and shot her eyes behind her. "He's been cooking for hours for you. He's a big softy really. Most lads his age would never think twice about cooking for a friend. They all eat shit; KFC, Nando's and all that crap."

Did this woman say she was his friend? Charlotte looked on edge, she needed her onside. "He is lovely. At first, I thought it was a bit strange that he wanted to cook for me but when I thought about it I realised that a man who likes cooking isn't such a bad thing after all. I mean, my dad does most of all the cooking in our house anyway. He loves new recipes, trying stuff out. So, it's all cool."

Francesca raised her eyes. "Does your mother not cook then?"

"Yes, but at the moment she's in a bad place. My nana died not too long ago and she's really struggling with it all. Her head is all over the place if I'm being honest. She's not cooked anything decent in months."

Francesca held her hand over her heart. "Oh, I'm sorry to hear that. Losing someone close is always hard. Trust me, I know. She will get better, it's just time isn't it? And at least she has your father to support her so it's not too bad."

Charlotte shrugged her shoulder and continued talking freely about her home life. "My dad's left. He's had enough of her drinking all the time. He's put up with her for ages now and she's still insisting she doesn't have a problem beer but she does."

Francesca looked concerned. "And you, do you think she has a problem with alcohol?"

Charlotte had to think for a few seconds, she wasn't sure. Was her mother a pisshead or did she just like a few drinks? She closed her eyes for a few seconds and thought about it. "Yeah, now I've thought about it she is. She even drinks when she gets up in the morning. I've seen her, she thinks I haven't, but I have."

"Can you not tell her she needs help?"

"Are you having a laugh or what, she would go sick. I swear my mam is not the kind of person you could have a chat with about something like this. Honest, you don't know her."

The talk Francesca had planned had gone right out

of the window now. For crying out loud, what kind of family was her son getting into? She didn't like it. Rico walked into the room and his cheeks blushed as he saw her for the first time. Charlotte looked over at him and her jaw dropped. He was mint; tall, dark and handsome, she couldn't take her eyes from him. Francesca spotted the way she looked at her son straight away. She wriggled about in her chair and stood up. "Right, I'm going to get a quick wash and I'm going to see Sally. I'll grab something to eat on the way there, probably a pizza or something. You two behave while I'm out. No funny business." Rico smiled over at Charlotte and didn't even hear a word his mother spoke, he was in love, oblivious to anything else around him. Francesca edged out of the room and never took her eyes from the love birds. She could see trouble ahead. Yes, this girl was nothing but trouble.

They were alone, their precious time together. "You look lovely," Rico whispered as he came and sat down next to her. Charlotte crumbled and her cheeks went bright red. Nobody had ever said anything to her like that before and she didn't know how to react to his comment, she just blushed. Should she say he looked nice too? No, that would have been corny, brown-nosing. She licked her lips slowly and just smiled over at him, lost for words. Silence. "I've made us Spaghetti Bolognese. It's my signature dish and everyone who has had some said I should be a chef instead of studying law. My mam thought I was gay when I found an interest in cooking, honest, she said it wasn't normal."

Charlotte chuckled as she checked him out, she could hear his words but she seemed lost in the moment. She wanted to kiss him, touch his face, run her fingers through his thick dark locks. She was hungry for his touch. "Are you hungry?"

Charlotte shook her head and she was back in the moment. "Yeah, but wait until your mam goes out before you dish it up. I feel a bit embarrassed sat here eating in front of her. I'm funny like that. I will go under if she's watching me."

Rico flicked the TV on and shot a look over at her. "Can you play Call of Duty?"

Charlotte began to relax and took her jacket off. "Yeah, of course I can, I'm mint. Put it on and we'll have a few games." Rico hurried to get the PlayStation rigged up. This was top, a bird who could play his favourite game. "Do you have an internet name you play with?" Charlotte asked curiously.

Rico began to smile and as he pressed the button to start the game up he turned to face her. "Yeah, Fast Ferret, what's yours?"

Charlotte began to giggle, she held the bottom of her stomach. "Fast Ferret, what the hell is that all about. That's not a warrior name, it's crap."

Rico held his head down, he thought it was a great name. He twisted his head back towards her. "Ok, what's your screen name?"

She was on the spot now, she had to pull it out of the bag. "Red Sonia," she whispered under her breath. Surely, he could not take the mickey out of her over her choice of names. She explained the name further. "Red Sonia was a decent female warrior. Have you seen the film? The woman is an icon".

Rico was oblivious to who she was, he was confused. "Who the hell is she? I've never heard of her before."

Charlotte sat on the edge of her seat now. Was he born on another planet or what? "No, stop it, Everyone's watched the film. You've seen Conan the Barbarian right?" This lad was like a fish out of water. And it was only now that she could tell how different they really were. Chalk and cheese. She knew he was different, that he didn't fit in, she had to act fast. "Right, I need to download these films so you can at least know who I am talking about." Rico agreed, and in his own head he hated that his mother had shielded him from all the top films when he was growing up. The action films, the violence, gun crime, drugs. Francesca was like that, she would always vet any films he was watching. The moment she heard a gun being fired or saw any blood, she would turn the TV off. There was too much hate in the world and she wanted her son as far from it as possible.

Francesca stood at the living room door and watched the two of them playing on the game. Charlotte was just as bad as him. Her legs were moving about as she held the control pad in her hands. Her hands were all over her boy, she was pulling at him, shoving at him and squeezing at him as the game intensified. Her heart was low and she knew deep down that she was losing her son to this girl. Her voice was low. "I'm going now." There were guns being fired, men shouting, bombs exploding in the background, she stepped nearer and repeated herself. Refusing to be ignored. "I said, I'm going out now." Rico twisted his head rapidly. "Alright, see you later then." That was it, no goodbye, kiss my arse or anything. Was this the start of things to come? Her stomach churned and you could see by the look in her eye that she wasn't comfortable with what was going on here. Should she pretend to be sick, stay with them to make sure there was no hanky-panky?

Charlotte smiled at Francesca as her game finished, she'd been shot and was out of the game for now. "Have a great night. Do you want us to save you some food?"

This was so nice, fancy her even thinking about Francesca. Perhaps she could share her son after all. "Yeah, if there is any left. You can put me a bit out. I'm going to grab a pizza but by the time I get in I'll probably be starving. I'm a bit of a midnight muncher if the truth is known. I can't help myself."

The game was about to start again and Charlotte got herself ready to begin another game. "See you later Mam," Rico shouted behind her.

Charlotte walked into the kitchen. Rico had really gone to town trying to impress her. There were candles all over, small yellow flames on every ledge. This was breathtaking for her. It was romance for sure. Rico guided her to her seat like a real gentlemen. She'd seen this behaviour before on TV and always wondered if men actually did this in real life. "There you go princess, welcome to Reek's restaurant. Tonight's menu is well thought through and you will find no prawns or fish will touch your delicate palate. See, I listen to you don't I?" He pulled the chair out while she sat down. The chair legs scraped along the floor as she took her seat at the table. She'd never been treated like this before, she didn't know how to act. Her eyes danced around the table. There were so many forks, knives and spoons in front of her she was beginning to panic. What the hell was each one used for? Her heart was beating faster than normal as he placed her food in front of her. Should she use a spoon? A fork? For fuck's sake, she didn't know. Charlotte watched Rico plating up his food and sat with her hands placed neatly on her lap. She was waiting for him, watching what he did. Yes, that was a good idea, she'd follow his lead. Rico placed a basket of crusty bread in the middle of the table with a small dish of olive oil at the side of it. She watched him carefully as he came to sit opposite her. "Tuck in then. What are you waiting for?"

"Derr, I was waiting for you so we could eat together," she chuckled. Rico picked up a spoon and a fork and she copied him. Finger food would have been so much better. This was a nightmare to eat. How on earth could she get the stringy spaghetti into her mouth without sucking it in? Charlotte started with the sauce. She dipped the edge of her spoon into it and slowly guided it into her mouth. "This is good. A lot better than I thought it would have been. You're not a bad cook are you?"

"Cheeky, why, did you think I was a crap cook or something? I told you I was a master chef." The two of them sat eating and chatting across the table. This was the start of something special for sure. They just hit it off from the start. He made her laugh, he made her heart melt inside.

★

Misty looked at Tom's house in the distance, eyes squeezed tightly together trying to focus. Today she'd already necked a quarter bottle of vodka and she was more than ready to approach this junkie. The wind was howling today and it was pissing down. Dark grey clouds hung overhead, depressing weather yet again in Manchester. Swerving the traffic on the main road, she headed towards Tom's gaff. He should be in by this time. It was late and he'd probably be settling down for the night. As she approached his abode, she squirmed. His windows looked manky, bits of grey net curtains stretched across the window, rain-splattered panes of glass. Misty sucked in a mouthful of air and headed down the garden path, dodging bits of wood, old wheels, dollops of dog shit. As she crept inside the dark dingy doorway, she started to gag. This place stank of cat piss, a strong aroma that hit the back of her throat. Misty pulled her coat up slightly to cover her nose. Shaking the rain from her hair, she composed herself, deep breaths, cracking her knuckles. Right, she was ready for this bastard, she stepped forward and flicked the letterbox rapidly. Misty danced about on the spot, teeth chattering together. Her nerves kicked in and she knew the moment the front door opened, she was ready to go to war. She had to make him see what he was doing, make him back down and say he would never tell Charlotte who her real dad was. She patted her coat pocket and gripped something inside it.

Where the hell was he? Could he not hear someone knocking at the door? Misty knocked again and this time she booted the bottom of the door. She'd wake him up, make him aware she meant business. The loud banging would put the fear of God up the little rat. He would think it was the dibble for sure. He was probably running about the house now getting rid of all the knocked-off stuff he had scattered about. Probably people's belongings, stuff he'd robbed from houses. His arse would have fallen out for sure. Hold on, a yellow light came on inside, somebody was in. Misty chewed hard on her fingernails, a shadow approaching the doorway. Should she just run at him as soon as she saw him and give it her best shot, windmill him, kick the fuck out of the scrote? Why hadn't she brought an iron bar with her, a hammer, she could have done some damage with that? She patted her pocket again softly.

The door opened slowly and a pair of eyes appeared

in the gap. A low shaky voice. "Who do you want?" Misty squeezed her eyes together, she didn't know this person or recognise the voice.

"Tom, I want to see Tom. Go and get him."

The door opened fully and a woman was stood in front of her. A gummy fucker she was, hardly any teeth inside her mouth, just a few brown stumps here and there. "He's out, he'll be back soon. Who are you, what do you want him for?"

Misty rammed her foot inside the door and prised it open with her fingers. She wanted to see who she was dealing with. She'd bang her out if she gave her any backchat, scratch her eyeballs out. "I'll come in and wait for him if that's okay." Misty gave the door a good shove and barged inside, she wasn't waiting for an invitation.

The woman was hysterical. "Oi, you can't just walk in here like that. Get the fuck out of here before I fling you out myself."

Misty froze in the hallway and her head swivelled around slowly. She weighed the woman up and down and stepped forward. She could deal with this junkie, snap her jaw with one decent punch. She went nose to nose with the woman. "Listen you, whoever you are! I'm staying here until Tom gets home, so like it or lump it."

The woman was up in arms. She stormed into the front room waving her arms around. "Proper cheeky you are. Who are you anyway, don't tell me he owes you money too because trust me he's skint, he's got fuck all!"

Misty began to relax, there was no threat here anymore. She sat on the edge of the black ragged leather sofa and shot her eyes around the gaff. It was a shit-tip, clutter everywhere. A crack-pipe situated in the middle of the table, burnt silver foil scattered about the floor. There was drug paraphernalia all over the place. Misty growled over at the woman, still aware she could be attacked at any time. "He owes me nothing. I just want to speak to him about stuff."

The crack-head started to itch at her skin, pinching at it, rubbing at it vigorously. "I'm his girlfriend and he hides nothing from me. So, you can tell me what you want him for, go on, I'm listening?"

Misty bit hard on the bottom of her lip. Who on earth did this scruff think she was talking to? Her patience was wearing thin and she was in no mood for this. She eyeballed her and pointed her finger over at her, swaying it about. "Park your arse down there love and relax. This is nothing that concerns you. Me and Tom go back a long way and when he sees me, he'll know why I'm here."

"So, who are you, at least tell me your name?"

Misty stroked the end of her chin and nodded her head slowly before she introduced herself. "I used to know his brother Gordon. I'm Misty."

The woman's face dropped, gobsmacked. She sat down near her and started to roll a cigarette. "Oh, I know who you are now. Tom fucking despises you, so good luck with waiting about for him. He'll drag you out of here by the hair on your head if he gets his hands on you. An evil bitch you are. I've heard all about what you did to his brother and I for one hope you get what's coming to you. You had the poor man over for thousands. I heard."

Misty clenched her fist into two tight balls at the side of her legs. That was it, this skank was going to get leathered. Who was she to even comment on her past, she knew fuck all about it! Misty locked eyes with her. "You know nothing about what went on. And I'm not going to explain it to you either. Gordon was a bullying bastard and I for one was glad that he got what was coming to him. He was diseased, fucked in his head, evil, rotten to the core."

"Not what I heard," the junkie snarled.

"You will only ever hear one side of the story love. Think about it, do you think Tom would ever slag his brother off? I bet he never told you that Gordon was banging my best mate did he. Yeah, shagging her while I was with him. Shady fucker wasn't he. Tom fucked her too by the way. I bet he kept that on the low didn't he?" Oh, this was getting good now, it was a true slanging match. Misty could see she'd wounded her, put her in her place. Her jaw was swinging low. Yes, she'd taken the wind right out of her sails. Misty sat up tall and prepared for her opponent's comeback.

"Who was the girl he was shagging? He never told me anything about her and he's told me everything about his life. We have no secrets, he loves me?"

Misty gave a cunning grin and sat down properly in the chair. Fuck it, why should she hold back any information. She could have this junkie onside in minutes if she played her cards right. A bit of woman to woman talk was needed here. "Gordon was a cunt, he made my life hell and when I was seven months pregnant he wasted me." The woman's eyes were wide open and you could tell she didn't know the real story. Misty continued. "And when I say he wasted me, well, that was an understatement. He left me half dead."

"Go on, tell me more because Tom has never said anything about this. It's all new to me."

Misty continued, her voice was chilling as she disclosed her past. "Francesca was my best mate at the time. We did everything together. I thought she had my back but more fool me for ever trusting her. My son died because of Gordon. How could any man hit a pregnant woman?" The woman was on the edge of her seat, she was chugging hard on her fag, engrossed in the conversation as Misty continued. "I caught him in bed with her. That was only a few nights after I'd lost our son. So you can imagine how I felt. He ripped my heart to shreds!"

"I would have cut his balls off. I swear, how fucking shady is that. What did you do to your mate? I hope you kicked fuck out of her, you should have booted her fanny in because that's what I would have done. Yes, she wouldn't have got away with that."

"Francesca got what she deserved in the end and in fairness, she got the rotten end of the stick really. When I left them to it Gordon did the same thing to her, he was shagging anything with a pulse. I suppose that's how she ended up turning towards Tom for affection."

The woman sat cracking her knuckles. "Tom has never mentioned to me that he'd had a relationship with his brother's woman. That's sick isn't it? Wrong on so many levels. Bang out of order."

Misty reached inside her coat pocket and took out a small bottle of vodka, she pressed it firmly against her lips and swigged a large mouthful. "It was all fucked up when I think about it. Tom knew what his brother was like, yet he let it happen because he was scared to death of him. Yeah, Gordon treated Tom like a dickhead. You should have heard the way he spoke to him, he bullied him, too."

The crackhead dipped her head. "Tom always speaks highly of his brother. He never says a wrong word about him and he's always at his graveside. I swear, every Sunday he goes to the cemetery and spends hours there with him. Fuck knows what he talks to him about but he sits there on his own religiously."

Misty's eyes clouded over. Tom wasn't a bad lad, he was just mixed up in all this shit like she was. It wasn't by choice, she supposed. He was a victim of circumstance. There was a loud bang. The front door slammed shut and the whole room shook. The woman sat up straight and her eyes were wide open. "It's Tom," she spluttered. Misty closed her eyes slowly and her chest began to rise frantically. She was ready for this bastard, ready to put an end to this misery.

Tom was shouting from the hallway. "Mel, put that fucking heating on. It's freezing in this place. Honest, my balls are frozen."

The living room door swung open and Tom was stood there in his grey long-Johns and a scruffy discoloured white T-shirt. Misty bolted up from her chair. "What the fuck is she doing here Mel? Why have you let that sweaty bitch in here?"

Misty eyeballed him and replied. "She didn't let me in, I came in by myself. I don't need an invitation to see you. We need to talk. Sort shit out."

"I've got fuck all to say to you. Get your sad little arse out of here before I knock ten tons of shit out of you. And don't think I won't, because I will. Our Gordon would turn in his grave if he knew I was even talking to you. Get the fuck out of here before I spit in your eye."

Mel walked towards Tom, trying to calm him down. "Just let her say what she has come to say and then she will go."

He pushed her away with force. Mel fell over the side of the sofa. He was hysterical. "Stop licking her arse. Don't tell me you've fallen for her sob story too. She's a slag, a dirty boot who ruined my brother's life. Lies, that's all she'll tell you. A bag of fucking lies."

Misty had to think quick, she could always win Tom over and she hoped today was no different. She had to remind him of days gone by. "Are you forgetting how he treated you? You were like me Tom. You were scared to death of him. Admit it, you hated him as much as I did. We'll never know who killed him but it wasn't me for sure."

Tom froze on the spot. The colour drained from his cheeks and he was sweating more than usual. He knew who had killed his brother. That was his secret and even to this day he'd never breathed a word about the night he shot his brother. The police had closed the case years ago and, as of yet, Gordon's murderer had never been found. Maybe that was the reason he was doing this - guilt. Tom bounced about the room, she had to dig deeper. "Tom, take your head out of your arse and remember how things really were. You loved Francesca and he ruined that for you too. You could have had a normal life. Look. It's him who pushed you back into this game. He never cared about you. If he did then why did he get you back on the gear?"

Tom's eyes were wide open and Mel sat back down with her arms folded tightly in front of her. "Yeah, and you forgot to tell me about Francesca too. I thought you said I was the only girl you've ever loved?"

Tom growled over at her. "Mel, give it a break will you. Don't start all this now. It's all in the past." Misty stepped forward and looked him straight in the eye. "Exactly, it's past so why are you raking it up and ruining other people's lives?"

He was thinking about her words, digesting them. Had she finally got through to him? Tom paused, dragging his fingers through his greasy mop of hair. "My brother has two children and I am gonna make sure she knows who her dad was. It's your lies Misty, your past that you have to deal with. That cunt isn't her Dad. My brother Gordon fathered her, nobody else. Tell her the truth or I will."

Misty was thinking on her feet, she was calm. Did she know more than she was letting on? She cleared her throat and sat back down, her arms folded tightly in front of her. "I remember the night he died Tom. I was there. I remember every single detail of that night, every noise, every step everyone took."

They locked eyes and neither of them was flinching. What did she know? Whatever it was, she sure as hell was putting the fear of God in him. He was trembling, sweating and unable to look her in the eye.

"Get out of here and don't ever come back you dirty slut."

Misty tilted her head to the side and smirked. It was time to reveal her ace card. "I believe word on the street is Francesca is back in Manchester. Perhaps I need to go and bring her here so she can tell everyone just how much of a cunt Gordon really was. I wonder how you would feel if she came here to see you?"

Mel squawked, her feathers had been well and truly ruffled. "Not over my dead body is she coming here. I don't want the whore in my house. I mean, Misty has already told me how she fucked her own life up with Gordon. She's not coming here flirting with you Tom, not a cat in hell's chance!"

Tom ran over to Misty and grabbed her by her arm.

How dare she come in his house causing trouble. "Out, fucking out. Look what's happened. You've been in here two minutes and you're already causing trouble. I'm doing what I'm doing, unless…" he paused and went nose to nose with her, "…unless, we carry on like your mother did. A few quid each week should keep my mouth shut. I mean, buy my silence."

Did this man have no shame? Misty was trying to dig her hand in her pocket but it was no good, fumbling about. Whatever she was concealing it was no good, she couldn't get to it. Her temper was boiling and she was ready to explode. "You're not getting a carrot from me. My mam must have been off her head to pay you. I'll tell you something for nothing shall I. This is far from over. You want war, then I'll give it to you. Everyone has a jugular Tom and it's just a matter of time before I find yours. Yes, you know I can play ball if that's the road you want to go down."

Tom dragged her to the front door and opened it with shaking hands. "You've got fuck all on me. Do what you're doing. Like I said you daft bitch, if there is no money, then your Charlotte is going to get a great big surprise."

His words crippled her, stabbed deep in her heart. It was her shout, what the hell was she going to come back with? Misty was launched into the front garden. As she stumbled about, she dug deep into her coat pocket and pulled out a sharp silver blade. She gritted her teeth tightly together and held the blade up towards him. "So, that's the way you want to play it is it smart-arse? I swear Tom, I'll cut your balls off and make a necklace out of them if that's the way you want to roll. Remember, everything that has a beginning has an end. And," she stretched her neck long so he could hear every word she was saying, "I know it was you who done Gordon in. I sussed it years ago. Maybe I should give the police a call and tell them what I think?"

Tom froze on the spot. What was all this fucking mumbo jumbo? Was she trying to mess with his head or what? She knew nothing, he'd cleaned his tracks, she had fuck all on him. He swallowed hard and watched her as she walked towards the gate.

"Tell Charlotte, Uncle Tom said hello."

Oh, what a cocky bastard he was, he was testing her now. Misty ducked her head low and Tom craned his neck to see where she had gone. Seconds later, a brick sailed through the air and just skimmed past his head. Misty was a nutter, a maniac. She was looking for something else to fling at him. For crying out loud, this was going to cause some damage. Misty spun another brick and this time it smashed straight through the kitchen window. Tom slammed the front door shut and stood behind it, shaking in his boots. He'd opened a can of worms now and his head was all over the place. Misty was furious. She'd reacted nothing like her mother did when he'd told her he wanted money to keep his mouth shut. This was going to be harder than he first thought. He closed his eyes slowly and slid down the cold hallway wall.

Mel came to join him and bent her knees so she could look into his eyes. "She's a dangerous woman Tom. Honest, I nearly shit my knickers. She is a couple of butties short a picnic. She needs sectioning. I'm scared."

Tom dropped his head onto his knees and took a few seconds to gather his thoughts. "She's fuck all to me. It's about time she got a taste of her own medicine. How can she sleep at night knowing the secret she is keeping from our Gordon's girl? That's bad isn't it?"

Mel touched his hands with hers and nodded her head. "It's some fucked up shit Tom. But in my eyes, every kid deserves to know who their old man is." There was an eerie silence, not a word spoken.

Misty marched onto the main road. The rain was hammering down. Her head was low and her coat was zipped up tightly. She flung the empty bottle of vodka onto a grass verge and picked up speed. This was getting worse. There was no way Tom was backing down. He was a money-grabbing tosser who didn't care what he had to do to earn a few extra quid. Maybe Misty should come clean, tell her daughter the truth. No, no, it would destroy her. Too many years had passed now and it would break her in two. Misty walked up the main road and stopped dead in her tracks. The cemetery was facing her. The place Gordon was laid to rest.

Misty crossed the road and stood at the black iron gates that led to the graveyard. She peered inside, it was pitch black. Her fingers clenched the cold gates and her head banged on them repeatedly. She was pissed and not thinking straight for sure. With haste, she entered the cemetery. Her heart was pounding inside her chest and she looked slightly confused as she tried to remember where Gordon was buried. Her heels clipped along the gravel path. A small street lamp from the main road gave off a small amount of light and she could see the names on some of the headstones there. Misty walked along the thick brown mud with her feet sinking low. She pulled her lighter out from her pocket and clicked it slowly as her feet stopped dead at a grave in front of her. She held it towards the black headstone. Her eyes were wide open and as soon as she could read the words engraved there, she dropped her lighter. Here it was, his resting place - six feet under.

Her lips trembled, hands shaking as she picked the lighter back up from the ground. It was time to speak to him, tell him to back off. Misty stood tall as she spoke to the photograph on the headstone. "Look at you, you're loving all this aren't you?" she said, her fingers gripping his headstone, "listen, tell your brother to piss off and leave me alone. You've caused me enough heartache so don't carry on now you're dead. Put a stop to it, please. If you ever thought anything of me, just make it all stop, please." The wind howled past her as she looked around her surroundings. What the hell was she doing stood here on her own? She leaned on the headstone and dipped her head, looking at her ex's photograph. "I fucking hate you Gordon. I detest you for the way you treated me. Why, why did you do it? I read the letters that Francesca gave me and you tried to explain how you still loved me," she shook her head and glanced back at his headstone. "No, you never loved me otherwise you would never have treated me the way you did. Please, don't fuck with your daughter's head. You owe her that, let her be happy, please, for me." Misty swallowed hard and her expression changed. She stamped her feet on the earth beneath her and snarled. "I hope you're in hell. I hope you never rest you bastard." Misty sucked hard in her mouth and spat on his photograph. She let out a menacing laugh and started to back away from the grave. "We'll see Gordon. You won't have the last laugh on me. Not this time, trust me." Her body wobbled as the wind picked up and she started to leave the cemetery. It was time to go home, time to face her family.

★

Charlotte lay next to Rico and looked deep into his eyes, her fingers stroking slowly up and down his firm toned chest. He'd treated her like a princess all night long and the night was coming to an end. Was he going to kiss her or what?

Rico licked his lips slowly and moved in closer to her. You could tell he wasn't sure of his next move, still dithering, his arse was twitching for sure. Charlotte closed her eyes slowly and puckered up. She was lost in the moment and she was ready for the kiss. Here it was, at last he'd plucked up the courage. Their lips connected and they shared a long meaningful kiss. Charlotte ran her fingers softly through his thick crop of dark hair as he gripped the end of her chin softly. They were both aroused and perhaps this was turning into something more than a kiss. What a result for this lad, he usually had to wait at least two or three months before a bird opened her legs for him. Manchester girls were top. They knew what they wanted and they didn't waste any time getting it. Rico wasn't shy anymore. This was his chance, no more hang-ups. He knew she liked him and he started to relax. This was a perfect moment for them both; a dimly lit room, soft music playing in the background. This was nothing like Charlotte was used to. Usually it was a quick meaningless bang in an entry somewhere, knickers pulled to one side and a quick jerk and a squirt. Nobody had ever touched and caressed her body like this. Every part of her was aching to feel him inside her. Slowly, he lifted her top over her head and kissed every inch of skin, ravishing her, inhaling her fresh floral perfume. Groans of pleasure, her arched back, she was more than ready. Rico entered her slowly, looking deep into her enchanted blue eyes. He was lost in them for sure.

Not for one single second did he take his eyes from her. This was so intense, magical, two lovers entwined.

Charlotte's face changed as he started to make love to her. And this was love for sure, she could feel it in her heart. This was so weird, so unexpected. She'd never felt like this before about a guy. Mandy had talked to her about being in love in the past but until now she never really believed it existed. It was just something that happened in fairy tales, right? A guy on a white horse plodding up to a woman and whisking her away into the sunset. No, shit like this never happened to her. Love was for weak, needy people. She had never needed it and never would.

The sex intensified. He gripped her shoulders and penetrated deeper inside her, faster and faster. Charlotte eyes rolled, her body tensed as a wave of pleasure surged from her toes to the top of her head. This was the best sex she'd ever had. And with a geek too... a nerd. What the hell was happening? Rico couldn't hold on anymore, he found pleasure too and ejaculated. Once he'd reached orgasm he looked deep into her eyes and smiled. "That was amazing." Charlotte smiled softly and brushed her hair back from her face. She was hot, her cheeks were bright red. He was right though, it was a top sex session. Their fingers locked tightly together as he lay by her side. This was a bond. A bond nobody would ever break in the future. These two had passion, chemistry and from the moment they'd set eyes on each other they had fallen madly, deeply in love. Maybe love at first sight was real after all. The front door slammed shut and they both shot a look at each other. For fuck's sake, someone was here. Rico's arse fell out. If his mother caught him naked she would lose the plot. Fuck, fuck, fuck. He bolted up from the sofa, starkers. Charlotte rummaged about on the floor and found her clothes. Her voice was stressed. "Stop them coming in Reeks, for fuck's sake, don't let anybody see me like this. I've not got a stitch on." He yanked his jeans up and slid his t-shirt on. Before he opened the living room door, he twisted his head back quickly to make sure she was getting ready. The door closed slightly after him. She could hear him talking in the hallway.

"Mam, you're back early. I thought you were out for the night. Did you close the front door properly, just check it again."

He kept her talking in the hallway as she walked back to check the front door. Charlotte could hear them chatting. That was close, she straightened her hair. Francesca walked inside the front room with her son following closely behind her. She paused as she clocked Charlotte for the first time. Had she just walked in on her son having sex with this girl or what? She examined her closer, red cheeks, messed up hair, her shoes off her feet. Yes, she'd come home a bit too soon. Francesca slid her coat off and slung it on the back of the chair. Her eyes were still fixed on Charlotte. "What time do you need to be home love? It's nearly eleven o'clock. Won't your parents be worried about you?"

Rico snarled at her. "Mam, she's fine. I've told Charlotte she can get a taxi from here when she's ready. She's already rang her mother and she knows where she is so stop getting busy on us. Stop flapping."

Was that the truth though? Okay, Rico had told her to tell her parents where she was but when she tried ringing her mother, it just went to voicemail. She pretended to leave a message but in fact, she ended the call as soon as her mother didn't answer. Misty wasn't arsed where she was anyway, she never had been. Many a night she'd stayed out and her mother had never batted an eyelid. She was usually pissed up and didn't know what day it was anyway. Rico sat next to Charlotte and held her hand. Francesca clocked it straight away and growled over at them both. This was bad, she could see it in her son's eyes. He loved this girl, head over bastard heels in love with her he was. What now, what if it didn't work out, who would pick up the pieces then? It would be her, she knew it. It would be like Sandra Daley all over again. Rico just fell in love too bloody easily. He wasn't a player, he didn't know how to play hard to get. He knew fuck all about the rules of dating. Sandra had left Rico heartbroken when he was only twelve and if his mother would have had her way, she would have killed her, ripped out every bastard hair on that tart's body. Rico was her life, her boy. Nobody hurt her son while she had a breath left in her body.

Francesca studied her closer. Charlotte would break his heart for sure, she could see it in her. Charlotte wasn't a keeper, she was just another good time girl after a free ride. Francesca turned the big light on and sat in the armchair. The music was switched off and the TV was flicked on. Any love they'd planned was well and truly over. His mother was here for the night. There would be no more hanky-panky in this house tonight, no way in this world.

Rico sighed. He could have been ready to go again in another five minutes or so, she'd put a stop to that alright. Why on earth had she come home early anyway? Charlotte was on edge, she looked at the clock on top of the TV. "I'm going to get going. Reeks will you ring me a taxi?" You could tell by his face that he wasn't too pleased. He tried to make eye contact with his mother but she kept her eyes focused on the screen. What was to do with her mush anyway? She was always telling him to live his life, to try new things, travel, meet new people. And the moment he did, she saw her arse. There was no pleasing her sometimes. As soon as Charlotte was gone she was getting a mouthful. Rico walked Charlotte to the front door when they heard the taxi honking its horn outside. She stood and smiled gently over at Francesca. "See you soon." There was no reply, just mumbling. Rico was raging and felt completely embarrassed by his mother's response. She was always preaching to him about good manners and here she was being so disrespectful. What on earth was her game?

Rico rubbed at his arms as the cold night air hit him. A shiver went down his spine and the hairs on the back of his neck stood on end. He dragged Charlotte back by her arm before she started to walk down the garden path. Checking over his shoulder quickly, he made sure nobody was listening. "Tonight was cool. And, just for the record, what we just did in there was something special too. It meant something to me." The corners of her mouth began to rise. She didn't know what to say, she was speechless. He pulled her closer and kissed her for the last time. He struggled to let her go as the taxi honked its horn again. "Text me when you get home to let me know you're safe."

"See you soon and I will," she replied as she rushed to the taxi.

Charlotte walked down the garden path and climbed into the back of the car. She waved at Rico as the taxi pulled out from the street. She was in love, totally head over heels, smitten with him.

Rico marched into the front room and confronted his

mother. She was getting told, the miserable cow. "What on earth is up with you? I swear, how ignorant were you to Charlotte? Why would you act like that in front of her? You have showed me right up tonight!"

Francesca twisted her head slowly towards her son and clenched her teeth together tightly. "You two have been having sex. You've known her two minutes and you're shagging her. What does that tell you about the girl? She's a slut, a tart. If she drops her knickers for you that easily, imagine how quickly she drops them for everyone else. I don't like her. Cheap she is, a dirt bag."

This was the kettle calling the pot black for sure. Had she forgotten her past or what? This woman had had more nob-ends than weekends. No, she was getting told. He snapped at her, fuming he was. "Stop being so horrible. It's always the same when I get a new girlfriend. I'll tell you what shall I, perhaps if you got yourself a man you might not be as concerned about my sex life and concentrate on your own. I'm not a kid anymore, so stop treating me like one. It's embarrassing."

Francesca flicked the invisible dust from the top of her shoulder. "Blah de fucking blah. Listen, I've met girls like her all my life and I know she is not someone I want my son making a girlfriend of. You've done what you wanted to do with her, so cart her. Find a nice girl, one who isn't as bleeding cheap as that one. Fuck her off before I do."

It was going to kick off for sure, he was raging. He plonked down in the chair facing his mother and looked her straight in the eye. "You were like Charlotte once weren't you mother? From what you've told me you were just as bad as her. So don't sit there judging people. I like her and nothing you can do or say will ever change my mind. You can like it or lump it."

Francesca snapped and sat on the edge of her chair. Where the fuck had this attitude come from? "Oi, cocky balls. I'd shut my mouth if I was you. Charlotte is nothing but trouble in my eyes, so listen to the voice of experience or end up heartbroken again," she shot a look over at him and raised her eyebrows high. "You do remember all the nights you cried over that girl don't you? And who was the one who got you through all that, ay?"

Rico dipped his head. That was ages ago, puppy love, a daft childish romance he had with a girl from his school. He didn't know what love was back then but he did now - and there was no way his mother was stopping it. "Oh, here we go again, that's history mother. How long are you going to go on about that? Just for the record, you sat crying over my dad for years so you're just as bad me. Go on, how many people told you that he was no good for you?"

Francesca rubbed her hands together, she was fidgeting. "That was different, don't you dare rake up my past just because I've said I'm not keen on your new girlfriend. I'm entitled to my opinion that's all. All I'm saying is don't coming running to me when she carts you."

Rico let out a laboured breath. "It's always the same with you, nothing or no one will ever be good enough for you. I'm living my life just like you did. And yes I will make mistakes, just like everyone does, so chill out and leave me alone." Rico jumped from the chair and marched to the living room door. "I think it's you with the problems, so go and see someone and deal with whatever it is that's bugging you every day. I've turned my life upside down for you. Remember it was you who wanted to come back to Manchester, not me. Go on, why were you so eager to come back here?"

She sucked hard on her gums but made no reply. The room shook as he slammed the door behind him. Francesca bit down hard on her bottom lip. She debated running after him, screaming up the stairs, throwing a shoe at his head on the way up. Cracking her knuckles, she sat back in her chair and carried on watching the television.

★

Misty sat picking her toenails as Charlotte walked inside the house. She never flinched when the door opened. Charlotte kicked her shoes off and plonked down on the sofa. It was like she was in some kind of trance. Without thinking, she just started to open up. Usually, she was closed off and never told her mother anything about the guys she was dating. "He was absolutely lovely. Honest mam, I've never been treated like that before from a guy. He had manners, cooked for me he did too."

This should have been a lovely mother and daughter talk, a chance for Misty to give her some advice about the male species. Maybe tell her how special she was and how glad she was that she'd found happiness. Charlotte swung her long shiny hair over her shoulder and played with her fingers. She was still talking even though nobody was listening. "I think he's the one. Mandy will go mad when I tell her all about him but I don't care. He ticks all my boxes, granted, he's not what I usually go for, but he makes me smile and that's what matters, isn't it mam?" Charlotte lifted her head up and looked at her mother. "Did you even hear a word I said?"

Misty turned to face her and slurred her words. "Sorry,

what did you say? I was in a world of my own."

"You mean you're drunk again. It doesn't matter. I don't know why I even bother speaking to you sometimes. I can't be arsed with you anymore."

Misty sat back and folded her arms. "Oh, don't you fucking start too. I've had enough shit today without you adding to it."

"It's always the same with you, mam. No time for anybody but yourself. You'll be sorry when I stop talking to you. And that will happen, trust me. I'm sick of seeing you wrecked every night. Do yourself a favour and ring my dad. He's the only one who can get through to you when you're like this."

Misty was fuming, steam was coming out of her ears. "Shut up, just leave me alone. Do you think I'm arsed about him anymore? He's history as far as I'm concerned."

Charlotte shook her head and licked her dry lips. "You'll be sorry. You'll end up a lonely old woman you will. Nobody will give a flying fuck about you soon. See how happy you are then." It was time for Charlotte to leave. If she had stayed a second longer, it would have kicked off big time. Misty watched her leave the room and her eyes clouded over. Why didn't she just keep her big mouth shut and listen to what she had to say? Her mouth was moving but no words were coming out. Lifting her mobile up, she scrolled through her contacts and stopped at her husband's name. She just sat staring at it…

Charlotte lay on her bed and closed her eyes. She was smiling and in love. A text alert on her mobile phone caused her to open her eyes. Quickly, she flicked on to her messages. It was from Rico.

Are you home now? Let me know. By the way, tonight was

just the best.

Charlotte started to reply to the message.

Yep, I'm home. Tonight, was special, thank you.

Without any hesitation, she sent the message. Charlotte started to get undressed. Once she was tucked nicely in bed, she decided to give her best friend a ring. It was late but she didn't care, she needed to tell her about her newfound love. She held the phone tightly to her ear. It was ringing and ringing, she was getting frustrated now. Mandy must have been asleep. Typical, the only time she wanted to pour her heart out to someone and her best friend had decided to have an early night. Argghhh.

CHAPTER SIX

TOM FELL BACK on the chair as he finished tooting the heroin from the silver foil, his cheeks were sunken in at each side as he sucked up the tube he was holding. He'd not injected for months now and in his own way, he thought he was tackling his long fight with the drug that had ruled his life for so long. He was in denial, his addiction was worse than ever. Just because he wasn't injecting the gear into his arm, it was still an addiction. He was a raging baghead. Years and years of drug abuse had taken its toll on his body. He was fucked. Dark purple veins collapsed all up his arms, his groins too and in between his toes. A bleeding disgrace he was, there was no other word for him. His mother had washed her hands of him years ago. She'd tried her best. By God she'd tried everything in the book to get her lad clean from drugs but nothing worked. No methadone script, no rehab, he was a junkie and always would be. What was the point in taking drugs if it made him act like this?

His jaw was swinging and his eyes were rolling to the back of his head, he was a bleeding disgrace. Melanie sat next to him and she was off her trolley too. What on earth was going on here, they both needed help. Melanie was slavering as she spoke to Tom. "You don't still love that woman Misty was talking about do you?"

Tom stirred and his eyes opened slightly, they were heavy, like lead weights hung on each eye lid. He reached over and touched his girlfriend's hand and squeezed at it.

He had no conversation in him whatsoever. The smack circulated around his body, putting a chain on his tongue. She rested her head on his shoulder and looked up at him. "Let's get clean Tom. I'm sick of this life. Look at us, we're fucked." Tom began to move about, the truth hurt. He'd been down this road so many times before in his life, but the only woman he'd ever loved enough to change his ways for was Francesca. He had a purpose in life then, a reason to get up in the morning but she was just like all the others, she'd given up on him too. She got on her toes as soon as something better came along. So what, she was his brother's woman. Gordon didn't want her but he *did*. He would have loved Francesca with all his heart. He would have got a job, stayed off the gear and made her proud. Now, Misty had told him she was back in Manchester. For years he'd thought about her, craved her love and affection just one last time, closure for the love they shared. Maybe it wasn't too late. She had fallen in love with him once, maybe she would again?

His eyes dropped down towards Melanie and he shook his head slowly. This wasn't love. It was just two lost souls clinging onto something, trying to be loved. Melanie was as bad as him. Three kids she had, each of them living with a new family. Contact with them had ended years ago, when she failed to attend the contact centre for several weeks. The judge told her straight that she was in danger of losing her family if she didn't mend her ways, but she never listened. The only voice she heard was that of her new master, the smack, the gear - heroin. It had gripped her for longer than she could remember and in her own words, her kids were better off without her. She could never look after them, feed them and put clothes on their backs. Or love them like they needed loving. It was a shame really, she had a heart of gold and would have given you her last penny. She was just a shit mother.

Tom pushed her away, squeezed his eyes together tightly and looked at the clock on the television. "I better move my arse. We need some money. Are you going out too or what?"

Melanie was folded in two on the sofa. Her expression changed and she itched at her body vigorously as if tiny ants had been emptied all over her skin. "I'll go down Cheetham Hill tonight. There are too many girls working at this time and I'm lucky to get a look in. Forty quid I earned the other day and I was there for hours. I'm not ever doing that again. Four fucking blow jobs I had to do. Two of them were sweaty fucking Pakis too. Tom, you know how I feel about them, they stink like a sweaty ball sack."

Tom sniggered and shook his head. His woman had a way with words and sometimes she made him smile so much when he was feeling down. Tom had to earn at least eighty pounds a day to feed his addiction. If he copped lucky and got a few extra quid, he could score some crack too. Just as a treat though, he didn't smoke it every day. Tom neared the mirror hanging on the wall. He got a glimpse of himself and screwed his face up. Was this really him? He didn't even recognise himself anymore. He'd changed, he looked at least ten years older than he really was. "I'm rough as a bear's arse. Fucking hell, look at my skin, it's grey," he mumbled under his breath.

Melanie was on another planet and his words fell on deaf ears. Tom's eyes clouded over as he ran his grubby fingers under his eyes. He knew in his own heart all the bad things he'd done in his life to feed his addiction; every line and scar on his face told a story. A tale of how desperate he'd been to get the money he needed to score some smack. Through the corner of his eyes, he clocked his girlfriend in the reflection in the mirror. She was no oil painting for sure, she was minging. Piss-stained jeans, a vest top that hadn't been off her back for days and scruffy matted hair stuck in a ponytail. Everybody was right about him, he'd hit rock bottom.

Tom sat on a bench near the shops scouting the area; waiting, lurking for a quick earner. Usually it would be a pensioner who had left her handbag unattended for a few seconds or a kid who had left their bike outside a shop. He didn't care where the money came from, he had no morals when it came to grafting for drugs. Tom sat with his head hung low, every now and then he lifted his eyes up to see if any daft bastard had left something for the taking. He was a predator and when something was to be had, he was as fast as lightning. There were no flies on him. The weather was mild today, the sun just breaking through the few clouds in the sky, a pleasant, gentle breeze skimmed his cheeks. Today was market day in Harpurhey and all the shoppers were out looking for bargains. The regulars all knew the rules of shopping in this area and always held their bags close to them. Even the kids who lived on the estates close by knew the law of the land. If it wasn't nailed down, the junkies would have it away. Thieving bastards, the lot of them. If they weren't begging for money, they were lurking in the shadows ready to make a quick kill.

Tom picked the dark brown grit from his fingernails

and sat chewing at it. He could see an old woman from the corner of his eye approaching the bench. Moving over slightly, he made sure there was enough room for the old dear to sit down. What an out and out bastard he was. Surely he could see this woman was a pensioner, she didn't have a pot to piss in; frail, old, defenceless. The poor old soul looked ready for the knacker's yard. Her back was arched over slightly and you could see coming out today had been a big struggle for her. Every step she took looked painful. Tom stood up and held his arm out towards her. "Come on love, take the weight off your feet and have a rest. You look like you're going to drop." The old woman smiled, pleased that someone had taken the time to even speak to her. She was like a lot of elderly people in today's world. She'd probably been locked up in her house for hours on end with nobody to speak to. Speaking to this stranger had probably made her day, made her believe in society again. Tom clocked the bags near his legs. And the art of spotting her purse came as second nature to him. There it was, sitting on the top of her shopping within arm's reach. This man had no shame.

Tom twisted his fingers, cracking his knuckles and flexing every thieving finger on his hand, ready to strike. "It's nice today isn't it, my old queen," he sneered at her.

The pensioner smiled, glad to be having a natter before she made her journey home. "Yes, it is. I shop for myself these days. My Johnny always used to do the shopping but since he's been gone, I have no choice but to come out for it myself. I miss him, I miss him oh so much." Tom licked his dry cracked lips and leaned over. The bag was right next to him. A few more seconds and he would be gone. The old woman continued. "I wish I would have had a few children but me and my husband were never blessed with any. We have two dogs though, they're our babies." Tom wasn't listening to a word she said anymore. He was in the zone and ready to strike.

It all happened so fast and he had the small brown leather purse in his hands in seconds. Straight away he stood up and concealed it inside his jacket. Nobody saw him, he was a master at this. A true professional. "Have a nice day my lovely. Nice chatting to you."Tom swerved out of her way and headed off in the distance. The old woman smiled after him and mumbled under her breath. "What a lovely young man. They all should be like him."

Tom sprinted across the road dodging traffic, cars honking their horns at him, drivers screaming at him. His breathing was rapid and it took a while for him to calm down. He was nowhere near as fast as he used to be. His lungs were fucked and the fags he'd smoked every day didn't help his health. He was a chain smoker and he was always bumming a cigarette from anyone who would give him one. His fingers opened the purse and his eyes were wide open. For a few seconds he froze, as he looked at a small photograph on the inside of the purse. This must have been the woman's husband. A military man dressed in full uniform. Tom gripped the two twenty-pound notes from the purse and quickly searched the other compartments. There was nothing, a few coins but nothing of any real value. This was enough to score, at least this was a good start to the day. There was nothing worse than rattling. Going cold turkey was a nightmare and he knew every detail about that too; the sweating, hallucinations, vomiting, shitting his pants. Yes, Tom knew what it meant to rattle for drugs.

Walking from the shadows, he threw the purse onto a grass verge. Maybe someone would find it and return it to the victim, maybe not, he wasn't arsed. Tom headed towards the phone box on the corner of the road. He needed to score and after a quick phone call, the runners would be here with the brown he'd ordered. It was a great customer service with the dealers. One phone call to place your order, then the drugs would be passed over at a nearby destination. It wasn't rocket science and even the thickest of people could follow the instructions. Tom started to walk past a primary school on his way to score. His feet paused as he watched all the young children in the playground. He could hear them laughing and screaming as they chased each other about. He smiled and carried on watching them. If he could have turned back the hands of time he would have put himself back in this playground, made different choices, got his head stuck into education. Reading and writing and being creative. Life was simple back then, there were no problems, no worries about where his next meal was coming from. Tom edged closer to the fence and dropped his head onto the cold railings. His heart was heavy as he reminisced about the days gone by. His eyes were wide open as he spotted a familiar figure coming nearer to him. No, surely it wasn't. His heart leapt about inside his chest and his windpipe started to tighten, he was going to pass out, faint. Staggering away from the school, he wobbled to a nearby wall and twisted his head back towards the school. He had to get another look, to make sure his eyes were not playing tricks on him. Pulling his hood up, he shot his eyes to the woman stood nearby. It was her, it was his Francesca. The love of his life. Tom covered his mouth with his hands and froze. He was in a deep trance, unaware of the world around him. His mouth was moving but no words were coming out. He studied every inch of her; her hair, her clothes. Should he shout her name? Maybe whistle over to her to get her attention. No, he was a disgusting stank, his hair was stuck to his head with grease. Tom started to scurry away and kept twisting his head back. She was back in Manchester alright. Misty had been telling the truth.

His woman was home.

Misty saw the back gate swing open. For fuck's sake, this was all she needed on top of everything else. Denise was like a hurricane storming down the garden path, her cheeks bright red and her hair flying all over the place. She was a woman on a mission. Misty prepared herself. The draught from outside filled the room as Denise barged inside. The curtains flew high from the window. She let rip, holding nothing back. Not a second to waste.

"Oh, you cheeky bastard. How did I think you were telling the truth? You never stayed for your hair appointment did you? I called in there myself and the girls told me you left not long after me. What's your game, come on, fucking tell me because I don't have a clue what is going on inside that fucked up head of yours!"

The words were strong here today and these two could have come to blows if it carried on. Rob walked into the living room and took the spot where he was before he went to the toilet. He let out a laboured breath and plonked down in his chair. He was unaware he'd just walked into a battlefield. "My bowels have been up the bleeding wall since your mam has been gone. It's like parting with a child from my arse every time I need a crap. The doctor said it's constipation but I think it's something more. No one should have to wait that long to drop a load. Misty, how long have I been sat on that bleeding toilet for, come on, it's got to be at least twenty minutes."

Misty and Denise were still eyeballing each other. Rob shot a look at them both and kept schtum. The penny had dropped and he was on pins. Denise sat facing her niece and held a sour expression. "Go on, tell me what happened before I drag you around this house by every bleeding hair on your head. You must think I was born yesterday. How dare you try and have me over!"

Misty swallowed hard and brushed her hair back over her shoulder. Her auntie never messed about when it was something like this and she knew she would do exactly that. Misty had to think quick, stop any more threats. "Denise, I had stomach ache. I was sat there for ages and I swear to you, I was sweating and ready to faint. I went outside for some fresh air and threw my guts up. I couldn't go back in there, I was covered in sick."

Denise sighed, was this a load of bullshit or was she telling the truth? Rob was feeling awkward and tried to change the subject. "What time did Charlotte come home last night, it was late wasn't it?" Misty shrugged her shoulders. Rob was like the neighbourhood watch since he'd moved into the home and nothing ever got past him, he never slept. He always said since he was in the marines that you never ever sleep fully again. You had to watch your back, sleep with one eye open. "You need to get her in line Misty, there are some bloody lunatics knocking about late at night. You need to tell her to let you know where she is. I mean, where is she now, she was up and out first thing this morning? That's not like her, usually she is in bed well into the afternoon."

Misty snapped, what was his game anyway sticking his oar in? "Rob, stop going on will you. I know where my daughter is, thank you very much. So keep your beak out of her business. She's gone to see Mandy she said. I think they're going shopping."

Denise sat back and folded her arms, still pissed off with her niece. "So, have you spoken to Dominic or are you still being a smacked arse? My mate Angela said she saw him down the boozer last night, pissed out of his head he was."

Misty was alert now. Dominic was no drinker and even a couple of pints knocked him for six, she didn't understand why he had turned to the beer. This was so out of character for him. "Are you sure it was Dominic? It's not like him to even go out. What time was this at?"

Denise raised her eyes. "Fuck knows, but it was him. Angela knows him well." Misty reached for her phone and glanced at the screen. She'd had no missed calls from him, no text messages. Her heart sank and it was only now that she realised how bad things really were. She had to get her life back and deal with the shit she was facing. Dominic was her world and her backbone. For crying out loud, she loved this man with all her heart, always had, always would. Why hadn't she seen this before? It was the drink, yes, she'd been drinking that much lately that everything was oblivious to her.

Rob had a serious look on his face and made sure his voice was low. "Did you speak with Tom? I mean, all this has to be put to bed now once and for all. He's a shady bastard that one is and if I get my hands on him, I will wring his bleeding neck. I told your mam to let me deal with him months ago but she wouldn't have none of it. I have contacts you know. The bastard would have been put in a body bag if I'd have had my way."

Denise looked over at Rob and examined him further. Where had the mellow Rob gone? He was acting like a gangster, like someone who knew how the criminal world worked. Misty gasped her breath and spoke to him. Who the hell did he think he was? "Turn it in Rob will you. I've told you before I will deal with Tom. Yes, I did go and see him but he's still saying that Charlotte will know who her father is. The cunt is not blackmailing me, no way. I'm trying to work things out in my own mind and I don't need you pecking my head about it twenty-four hours a day."

Denise looked over at Rob and could tell his feelings were hurt. "Bleeding hell Misty, give him a break, he's only trying to help. And he's right, the clock is ticking and sooner or later you have to face it." All her close family members knew the secret now, it was a family affair. Misty choked back the tears. Her emotions were high and she was ready for breaking. She sucked in a large mouthful of air and started to control her rapid breathing. Denise could see her niece's hands trembling, small beads of sweat forming on her forehead. She reached into her pocket and pulled out her cigarettes. "Here get a fag, calm yourself down. It's all going to be alright, we will work something out. Everyone has a jugular and there must be something that we are missing here."

Misty looked at the clock and stood up from her chair. "I'm going to see Dominic. You're right, I've made a mess of things and I need to go and sort things out before it's too late." Rob's eyes were wide open. This was a start, at least now they might have some normality back into this house.

Denise watched her niece leave the room and kept her voice low. "Has she been drinking all night, she looks shocking? You can see the dark circles around her eyes, that's lack of sleep that is."

Rob nodded, he checked they were alone in the room and voiced his opinion too. "She's been sat in that chair there for the last two nights. I've emptied the bins and I can see all the empty bottles of vodka she's been drinking. I'm scared to say a word though, Denise. You know what she's like when she gets going, she'd rip my bleeding head off."

"Rob, you need to be my eyes and ears around here from now. I just hope she makes things right with Dominic. Once he's back he will put her in her place. God only knows she needs it."

Misty closed her bedroom door and scrambled about on the floor. She rolled under the bed and her hands stretched desperately to grip the bottle of vodka stashed there. With her eyes on the door she necked a large mouthful. Her body was trembling from head to toe and it was only now that she was starting to see how dependent she was on the alcohol. Misty sat down behind the bedroom door and dropped her head into her hands. The drink was never far from her mouth and after a few minutes, the tremors inside her body began to subside.

★

Charlotte sat on Mandy's bed and rubbed her hands together. "He's really nice Mandy. I swear to you, I know you think he is a geek but he's actually very funny. He makes me laugh and I know it shouldn't work but it does.

We're so chalk and cheese."

Mandy squirmed and shook her head in disgust. "Charlotte, the guy is so not you. Have you seen the state of the way he dresses, he's not one of us, he's a prick and I don't know why you are even bothering with him. Bin him and get someone decent."

"Don't be like that, give him a chance. I like him and we just click."

Mandy was sick of hearing about the love story, she needed to burst her bubble and bring her back to reality. "You'll click for sure when Paul finds out about him. You know that head the ball will savage him. Honest, mark my words, once he knows you've hooked up with some guy, God help him. Just saying that's all. You're playing with fire."

Charlotte's back was up now and she'd seen her arse. "Listen you, Paul will have to get used to it. He's not my Lord and Master, you know. Anyway, if he gives him any shit I'll tell him straight that my love life is nothing to do with him anymore. It's not like we were ever an item or anything is it?"

"Paul declared his undying love for you, didn't he? He has told you that he will batter anyone who comes within an inch of you. So, good luck with that. I wouldn't like to be in your shoes when he finds out."

"Mandy stop being so negative all the time. I get that you don't like Reeks but I do. You didn't hear me going on when you was with that dickhead, Nathan, did you. If we are being totally honest here, that guy treated you like a right nobhead. I was the one who sat with you all night long when you were waiting for a phone call or a text message from him wasn't I? A text message that never came by the way, so, think about that before you start judging me?"

"There's no need to bring that up is there? That was ages ago."

"Yes, there is when you're having a go at me. I told you that guy was bad news but did you listen to me? No. I told you he was banging someone else too but you were still there every night waiting for the dirty rat to ring you."

This was game set and match. Charlotte was right and Mandy knew it. There was an awkward silence for a few seconds before Mandy spoke. "I'm just saying that's all. You're my best friend and I'll always have your back no matter what but I'm just scared Paul will go sick when he finds out you are seeing someone else. Tread carefully that's all."

Charlotte patted the top of her friend's shoulder to comfort her. "Let me do the worrying. I'll be fine. Like I said, when it comes to it, I'll deal with it."

Mandy shook her head slowly and her eyes held fear. She knew Paul better than anyone and she knew once he got wind of this, he would make sure Reek never went near his woman again. This was bad.

★

Misty stood at the front door and rapped on the letterbox. She'd had a wash and tried to make an effort with her make-up and her overall appearance. She was still rough-looking though. Looking up at the bedroom window, she searched for any sign that somebody was home. Fancy curtains, sparkling clean windows, immaculate garden. Helen had always been house proud and everything about her home was tip-top. There were no weeds in the garden like, no litter scattered about the garden, it was spotless.

There was still no answer, she tried knocking again and this time she hammered on the door with her fist. Probably a bit too hard if she was being honest but she needed to let the occupier know someone was at the door. If they were inside they would have heard her by now, she nearly shook the house down. Misty stood back from the front door as she heard someone approaching. She could hear them screeching from inside. Dominic's wife licked her lips and prepared herself to meet her mother-in-law. The front door flung open and there she stood snarling at her, the smarmy bitch, hands placed on her hips, hissing.

"Misty Sullivan. What the hell do you want here? Take your scruffy little arse out of my garden and get off my property before I have you removed."

Misty rolled her eyes. She knew this was never going to be easy and she was ready to fight her corner. Her voice was calm and confident. "I'm not Misty Sullivan anymore, as you know. I took your son's name when I married him. Anyway, is he in? I need to speak to my husband. In other words, I want to talk to the organ grinder not the bleeding monkey?"

Helen closed the front door slightly and smirked over at her son's wife. "You'll be lucky, he's out. And he's been out all night, if I'm being honest. Hopefully, he's got himself a new woman and kicked your scruffy bony arse to the kerb."

Ouch, this was a cat fight for sure. Misty held her head to the side and stared at her. "Do you have to be so horrible? Stop telling lies. I know he's in, so just tell him I want to speak to him and cut the crap."

Helen stood tall. Her tone was high and mighty, she was loving every second of this. Seeing Misty suffer had made her day worthwhile. "There is one thing I'm not darling and that's a liar. Do you really expect my boy to sit in here crying over you again? Those days are well and truly over. Maybe he has seen you in your true light now. I've told him for years you were nothing but trouble and perhaps now he has seen it for himself with his own two eyes. Hallelujah!"

Misty started to curl her fists into tiny balls at the side of her legs. She was going to knock her block off. How dare she speak to her like that? There was no love lost between these two but at least she could have showed her an ounce of respect. Misty was still fighting her corner. "Helen, you've tried for years to split us two up and it has never worked up to now. Give it up. Dominic loves me and always will, so deal with it. Everyone has arguments and make up after it, so wind your neck in and tell him that I called. Please, ask him to ring me as soon as."

Helen watched her walking back down the garden path and shouted after her. There was no way this runt was getting the last word. She pulled her cardigan tightly over her big breasts and stood on her tiptoes to make sure she could see her. "Get it into your thick head woman that it's over. Don't you ever come here again you scruffy cow. You stay in your neck of the woods where you belong, you dirty trollop."

Helen was going for gold and she didn't care who heard her. Misty slammed the gate shut and turned to face her mother in law. She rammed two fingers in the air and smiled. "Fuck off you fat cunt. I don't believe you for one little minute. On my life, you need your head feeling. There is something seriously up with you. You have mental issues."

Misty marched down the street and she was struggling to breathe, adrenaline pumping around her body. Was Helen telling the truth? She wasn't sure. She'd always been a bit of a storyteller and nobody ever believed a word she said but she'd put the doubt there for sure, the seed was sown. Sitting on a nearby wall, she rummaged in her pockets and grabbed her cigarettes with shaking hands. She was gasping for a blast of nicotine to calm her down. She needed to think about this, get her head together and focus. Misty sucked hard on her fag and both her cheeks sank in at the side as the nicotine filled her body. Reaching deep into her coat pocket, she searched for her mobile.

This was it, she was texting her husband.

Ring me please

Pressing the send button, she held her head back and sucked in a mouthful of fresh air. She was boiling hot, ready for passing out. Misty scouted the area and made sure nobody could see the bottle of booze in her hands. She'd had necked a quarter of the bottle. The alcohol made her fearless, helped her forget her troubles and relax. Sitting on the wall, she kicked her legs to and fro. She needed a plan, a cunning plan to take away all this stress from her life, and she needed it fast. Was her husband really banging somebody else? Was it over between them? She dragged her hands through her hair and it was like her life was flashing right before her eyes. All the romantic gestures he'd made; flowers, cards and the affection he'd showed her. For crying out loud, she could see it all now. Misty did love her husband with all her heart. God, why hadn't she seen him drifting away? She'd always loved him, every inch of him, she always would. Gathering her thoughts together, she jumped from the wall. She stood for a few seconds and made her way to the market. Tom would be there today and she would have another crack at him, see if he would see any sense. She plodded up Rochdale road and stood near the Shiredale pub. It was situated on the front of the road. She was sweating and looked like she was going to pass out. Just one drink, just something to steady her nerves, that was all she needed. After all, she'd had a bad day and her head was mashed.

Misty walked into the pub and shot her eyes around the joint. A few regulars were sat about gas-bagging. These were the usual candidates; the Monday club, the all-dayers. It was like that in this area. Punters got their benefits and after buying the bare necessities, they would blow the rest of their cash on getting pissed. And why not? Life was no good for these people and they seemed down on their luck. They had no job, no future and no proper income to live the life they wanted to. A lot of people lived like this and the Monday club was a celebration of all those people who were in the same boat - potless.

Marj shot a look over at the woman stood by the bar. She was a friendly old soul and always loved chatting to new people. Marj loved to know their stories, their poverty, the bad luck that had led them to be in the boozer. She had bleached blonde hair and the biggest tits anyone had every seen. It was a shame her figure was just as big. It was still early and once the night progressed, she would do her usual party-piece and get her tits out for all to see. She'd rub them in the men's faces too, let them grope them and tweak her nipples. It was all good fun and the landlord was used to her ways. If she was ever getting too much, all he had to do was give her the eye and she calmed down. Marj made her way to the bar. This was the chance of making a new friend, perhaps she'd get a free drink... The more friends you made in this place, the more free drinks came your way.

Misty stood at the bar twisting and turning nervously. She had never really been confident when it came to things like this and usually it was her husband who got the drinks in on a night out. Marj could see the woman was anxious and moved in closer to her. "What's the weather like out? Is it still windy?" There it was, the ice breaker. Misty looked round, was this woman talking to her or somebody else? She wasn't sure. Marj carried on talking and she was at her side now, resting her flat palm on hers. "Bloody hell, your hands are freezing. Are you staying for a few slurps because if you are, you're more than welcome to come and join my crew over there. We're a crazy lot, but ay, we all stick together. Brothers in arms we are."

Misty swallowed hard. She could do with a friend right now and the corners of her mouth began to rise. "Cheers love, I'll get myself a drink and I'll come over to join you."

Marj had to be quick here, otherwise she would miss her chance to gain a free drink. "You'll be fine with them lot. I'd stay myself but money is tight and I've just finished my last drink. Go on love, go and join them, they will make you feel welcome."

Misty stood digesting what she'd just said. Marj turned her head slightly, waiting and hoping that her plan had come together.

"I'll get you a few drinks. You don't have to leave yet," Misty said at last.

Marj held a cunning grin across her face and didn't wait a second. "Oh, that's so nice of you. Mine's a pint of Stella." Marj headed back to her friends with a smirk across her face, she'd bagged herself a free pint yet again. Hats off to the woman, she sure knew how to play this game.

Misty carried the drinks over to the table once she'd been served. Marj patted the empty space next to her and urged her to sit down. All eyes were on her. Misty was the new kid on the block. Everyone was eager to hear her story, find out what had brought her into the pub today. Marj quickly gripped her beer and sucked the froth from the top of it, wiping her mouth with the cuff of her bright pink jumper, "Lovely jubbly, just what the doctor ordered, thanks love."

Misty sat down and reached over for her glass of lager too. She had thought about necking a double vodka at the bar before she sat down but chickened out at the last minute. A pint of lager was fine for now, just something to stop her from shaking. Marj looked directly at the group and touched the top of Misty's shoulder. "Introduce yourself then."

Misty was blushing, she was on the spot, under pressure. Sucking in a large mouthful of air she began, "Hi, I'm Misty." That was all it took, each of them in turn now started to introduce themselves. These pissheads were a jolly lot, nothing seemed to faze them. There was no misery here today, no negativity, everyone was in a good frame of mind and enjoying getting pissed. They all pulled together here, helped each other out when they were a bit short. The Monday Club was getting better by the minute. Misty could be herself here and drink what the hell she wanted. No one would judge her or start counting the drinks she had. She was among friends.

A little later, Marj jiggled over to the jukebox and slid a silver coin into it. She stood with her eyes squeezed tightly together trying to find the tune she wanted. Here it was, her anthem, as the song started she began swinging her hips to Tina Turner's "Simply the Best". Marj flicked her hair back and perked her breasts up. This was her time, her dance and her song and she was singing it to all her friends as she wiggled her arse across the room. Misty was in stitches laughing, this was going to be a long night. Fuck motherhood, fuck cooking and cleaning. This was how she was rolling today.

★

Charlotte sat at the table in the pub. It was Saturday and most of the crew went here. Mandy passed Charlotte a glass of coke and covered her mouth as she spoke through her fingers in a quiet voice. "Paul's just walked in. He's not taken his eyes off you, so watch your back, he's on the rampage."

Charlotte started to turn her head but Mandy grabbed her knee, squeezing it. "Don't fucking look yet. He's right behind you."

Charlotte froze for a few seconds and casually looked behind her. She clocked Paul stood at the bar. This guy was massive, towering over most of the other men there. He was on steroids for sure, he had bulging biceps and a thick neck with veins pumping from it. He was definitely on the juice. Their eyes locked and for a few seconds, neither of them blinked. Paul picked up his drink and made his way over to them. He was like a moth to flame where Charlotte was concerned. Any chance he got to talk to her, he was there trying to win her back. Paul's mobile phone was constantly ringing and he looked stressed as he answered another call. "Go to the bridge mate, yeah two white and one brown. He'll be there in five minutes. Don't have him fucking waiting."

This was his graft phone and most of the orders for drugs in the area came to him first. That way, he could keep track of every single penny he made. Every bag he sold. There would be trouble if there was any money down on the count and heads would roll. He'd kick fuck out of them and end their life. Paul rarely got his hands dirty now. He was too clever for that. He had runners who did all his dirty work for him. Young teenagers who knew nothing about the jail sentences that came with selling drugs. Especially class A drugs. They were kids hoping to buy new trainers, help their families out with money, vulnerable youths. Of course, he'd been a runner in his day too and it was fair to say he'd done his time as a bottom man. But it was the money that made him want more; the greed, the power that came with selling drugs. Drug dealing had given him his name back in the day. Why was he running about for other people when he could be making the money for himself?

At the age of sixteen, Paul made a name for himself in the area. Even today, people still talked about what he was capable of doing if his cage was rattled. He was twisted, a head the ball who knew no boundaries when it came to making people suffer, he was sadistic. The night he challenged the then Mr Big to his title had gone down as one of the most brutal fights anyone in the area had seen in a long time. It was a bloodbath. Paul had chewed off his opponent's ear in a long hard fight that went on for over twenty minutes. Bottles were hurled at each other, knives were pulled, everything was at stake and the winner was taking it all. Paul was never going to give up, he had fuck all to lose and everything to gain. When the fight finally ended, Paul screamed at the onlookers with the other guy's ear still hanging in his teeth, bright red blood oozing from it. Nobody ever treated him like a dickhead again. He would no longer be anyone's runner. He was the boss, end of. This was his manor now and he was willing to take anyone down who crossed his path, no matter what it cost.

The sound of a chair scraping across the floor filled the room as Paul plonked his pint on the table and smiled over at Charlotte. "Smile, it might never happen." He poked a finger into her waist.

Mandy darted her eyes at her friend and she could see she was ready to give him a mouthful. She stopped her dead in her tracks and replied before it got out of hand. "Bleeding hell that phone of yours never stops ringing does it? It would do my head in."

Paul chuckled and nodded slowly. "Every time it rings it's money love, so I don't mind answering it." He never took his eyes from Charlotte. He was examining her, digesting her, lusting after her. "You look pretty today," Paul said after a pause, "have you dressed up for me or what?"

Charlotte nearly choked on her drink. The cheek of this man. "Have I fuck, why would I get dressed up for you? Get a grip will you and take your head from out of your arse. You fucking idiot. We're done, get over it."

Paul cracked his knuckles and bit down hard on his bottom lip. She was making a fool out of him, knocking his confidence. This girl made his blood boil, he wanted to strangle her, stop her breathing. He leaned over and looked her straight in the eye. There was no way this bitch was getting the better of him today. "Cut the shit, bitch. No need for the attitude, it doesn't suit you. It costs nothing to be nice. So keep it shut."

Charlotte twisted her body away from him and snapped. "Why are you even sat here? Fuck off over there with your mates and you won't get any attitude. Why do you always feel the need to cramp my style?"

Paul examined her closely and Mandy was on standby just in case he snapped. He was more than capable of shutting her up. He'd done it before and wouldn't have thought twice about doing it again. Paul swallowed hard and smirked at her. He whispered in a sexual manner. "It turns me on when you're nasty to me anyway. That's why you do it. Why don't you let me take you out?"

Mandy was on pins as she watched her friend sit up straight in her chair. Don't do it, keep your fucking mouth shut girl, she silently pleaded. You can see he's ready to snap, just ignore him.

Charlotte's eyes danced with madness and you could tell she wasn't going to hold back.. Who did this wanker think he was? She wasn't scared of him and he was getting told. "I've got a new relationship, so fuck off and leave me alone, you stalker. You're like a fart that lingers. Move on and stay out of my life."

Paul's ears pinned back and his nostrils flared. His chest rose rapidly and his cheeks were bright red. Was she fucking with him? Was she telling him lies to wind him up? He gritted his teeth and looked her straight in the eye. "Yeah, right. You always say stuff to hurt me just because you still love me. As if I'm falling for that old chestnut."

Mandy closed her eyes and shook her head, this was getting worse by the minute. Charlotte was in the zone and ready to embarrass Paul good and proper. Deliver a knockout blow. This would floor him for sure. "I've been seeing him for a few weeks now. And let me tell you something for nothing, it's the real thing, he treats me like a princess. In fact, I'm in love."

She had him now. Paul was stuttering, small beads of sweat forming on his forehead. "Who is it then? Go on! If you're not chatting shit, tell me his name?"

She could have just left it there... but oh no, not Charlotte...

"He's called Reeks."

Paul stretched his hands over his head and closed his eyes slowly. A vein at the side of his neck was pumping with anger and he now seemed capable of anything. You could see it in his eyes, he was bubbling with rage. His hands gripped the edge of the table and he flipped it over with one quick flick of his wrist.

The landlord stormed over straight away to try and calm things down. He knew Paul was a crank and many a night he'd carted him out of his boozer for taking liberties with his punters. "Whoa, chill the fuck out, pal. What's going on here?"

Paul snarled over at Charlotte who was wiping beer from her coat. "It's that daft cunt over there thinking she can play me. She thinks she's smart with her mouth. I swear, if she carries on, I'll knock every one of them bastard teeth out. I swear I will, you just watch."

Charlotte smirked over at him, she had no fear. Mandy stepped in front of her mate as Paul came charging towards her. He was raging, ready to one-bomb her. Bob, the landlord, was all over this now. He dragged him back by his jacket. "Paul, I'll ring the police if you so much as touch a hair on that girl's head. For fuck's sake man, sort your napper out. Stop being a bully. It's a woman you're thinking of hitting here..."

Mandy was holding Charlotte back, she was game as fuck and ready to rumble. She had her father's genes for sure, she was ruthless. "Go and crawl back under the rock you came from," Charlotte shouted, "you dirty cunt. As if I would let you with within an inch of me again, you rat."

Mandy dragged her away to the other corner of the room as Bob and a few of the other punters dragged Paul to the door. This fucker wasn't going anywhere. It took a few more of the regulars to make him budge. "You'll see" he shouted over his shoulder, "just you watch now, you daft bint. I'll have the last laugh."

Charlotte rammed two fingers in the air. "Jog on, Mr Nobody. As if I'm arsed about a plastic gangster like you."

There were crashing noises, a loud commotion. Paul booted the door before he left. He was furious and this beef was far from over. This girl was living on borrowed time. Mandy's eyes were wide open as she heard him screaming outside. She was shitting it, the colour drained from her cheeks.

"She's getting it. Mark my words, that slag will be in a body bag when I get my hands on her," Paul screamed.

Mandy rubbed at her arms, goose bumps appearing, the hairs on the back of her neck were on end. She shot a look over at Charlotte.

"Now that guy scares me. How can you just stand there like you're not arsed? Charlotte, he said you are going in a body bag. Aren't you even a little bit worried?"

"He doesn't scare me. The guy is a prick. I've heard all his threats before. I'm not arsed. Let him do what he's going to do."

Mandy shook her head and kept her eyes on the

window near by. She was edgy and half expected a missile to be hurled through it any minute. Charlotte walked back to the table and picked it up her drink. Bob was on his way back inside the pub now and he was sweating. "I'll tell you what, love. That guy needs sectioning. You should have seen the performance out there. He's booting cars, attacking lamp posts... If I was you I'd stay in here for a bit until he's calmed down. Better still, ring the police and warn them about him. Otherwise, leave Manchester for good."

Bob rested his hand on the bar and sucked in a mouthful of air. He wasn't as fit as he used to be and if he was being honest, this man would have floored him with one blow if the other men weren't there to back him up. Mandy sat down next to Charlotte and for a few seconds, there wasn't a word spoken. They were shell-shocked. "Why the fuck did you tell him about Reeks? He'll find out who he is now and you know what a sick bastard he is. He'll make him suffer, make sure he never sees you again."

Charlotte gulped, now she was seeing the error of her ways. She could handle this wanker but to think of Reeks being hunted down by Paul was another matter. Mandy was right, she needed to warn her man about the prick. He was a dead man walking.

CHAPTER SEVEN

DOMINIC SAT AT THE KITCHEN TABLE reading the newspaper, he wasn't really taking anything in, he was just passing time really. He was lovesick for sure and even his mother had to admit that he wasn't looking good. He was unshaven, his hair was stuck up, he had a grey complexion and he looked totally depressed. Helen came to his side and rubbed the top of his head with a flat palm, she had to try something, he was all doom and gloom. "I'll make you a Full English if you want son; bacon, egg, mushrooms, fried bread - the full Monty. I'll do your bacon just the way you like it too, crispy at the edge."

Dominic raised his eyes from the newspaper and shook his head slowly. "No, I'm not hungry. I can't seem to taste anything anymore. My palate is dead, just like my heart." He dropped his head into his hands and let out a deep sigh, he was desperate. "Mam, why hasn't she been here for me? I've had a daft text message from her saying she wanted to talk to me but I need more than that. I want her to show me that she loves me. I mean, how hard is it to come here, knock on the bleeding door and tell me how she feels? I'm no angel but at least I tried to make our marriage work!"

Helen's eyes were wide open. She didn't know where to look, the conniving bitch. She walked over to her son and touched his shoulder. This woman had more front than Blackpool. She licked her lips slowly as the lies rolled off her tongue. "Sometimes you just have to walk away, son. If a woman really loved you then she would be hammering at that front door to sort things out, wouldn't she? Maybe you have to face the facts, it's over."

Dominic nearly choked. How dare she say that? Here he was just wanting a bit of sympathy, a friendly ear, and all she was doing was making him question his wife's love for him. She was sending him under. Misty loved Dominic, he knew that, she was just a stubborn cow. Their love was deep, they were soulmates who understood each other. They were bigger than this and even now, he was kicking himself for bailing on his wife when she needed him most. Helen rested her hand on the kitchen side. "Son, I know you don't want to hear this but if I was you, I'd get myself ready and head to the nearest bar. The women would be all over you like a rash. Look at you, you're bloody gorgeous. You don't need her, you can have the pick of the bunch. You've got a home here forever. There's no drama here and you know I will always look after you, don't you? So dust yourself off and get back out there. Women are ten a penny!" How could she kick him when he was down? Helen was lonely herself, I think she'd even talked the plants on the window ledge half to death, by the look of them, they were withered liked her and in desperate need of attention.

Dominic tried to set the record straight. "Mam, I love my wife with all my heart. Get it into your thick head that I don't want anyone else. Just because my dad left you and hooked up with another woman straight away, don't think I'm the same as him. I adore that woman."

This was a low blow. As if Helen needed reminding about that bastard she married. Her eyes clouded over at the mention of his name, the memory of how she was treated. It all came flooding back to her. She rolled up her sleeves and sank her hands in the sink. Pots clashed together, water spilled over the sides of the sink, she was raging inside, her face blood red. "Oh here we go. Listen, I'm trying to help you that's all. You know how I feel about your dad, so why would you even mention his name? He makes my skin crawl, he's diseased in my eyes. So keep him out of it. He's a dirty, no-good bastard and you know that as well as me." He'd done it now! Helen was going ballistic and there was no way she was stopping for love nor money, she'd seen her arse. She started to retaliate, spitting her dummy out. "Piss off back to her then if that's what you want to do, see if I care! If you want to be treated like a bleeding skivvy, then so be it. That one will always be a slob in my eyes. Whatever possessed you to take her back after that Gordon fella anyway, she was damaged goods and you know it!"

Did this woman ever let up? Helen was taking liberties, she'd crossed the line for sure. "For the last time mother, I love her and I'll always love her. You don't even know her properly, you've never given her a chance. And why?" He was up in arms and fighting his corner, "Go on, ask yourself why!" He looked at her with his eyes wide open as he continued. "Yeah, because she had no money. Because her family were on benefits, that's the reason you never gave her the time of the day. You're all about money, you are. And if we are putting our cards on the table here, you wouldn't have a pot to piss in if it wasn't for my father. He was the one with the money, not you. Go on, tell me the truth, you married him for his money didn't you?"

Helen dried her hands on the tea towel at the side of her and launched it over at him. Here they were, her true colours. "Fuck off out of here! Why do you speak to me like that! I helped your dad build his empire and when we divorced I got what he owed me. What I deserved in fact. So before you put your mouth into gear, get your facts right. Who told you that anyway? Him?"

"I heard him telling you whenever you got above your station with him. You made that man's life a misery and I'll be damned if you think you're going to do the same with me. You're the one who ruined your marriage. Don't try and do the same to mine. I love Misty, you will never stop it, ever. True love never dies."

Helen slammed her palm on the side of the table. Her eyes were all over the show. "Have you heard yourself, grow a pair of balls and stand up to her you big fairy! You've always been the same, you've no backbone. At least with your father I fought back. I didn't lick arse like you always do with your wife."

Bloody hell, it was kicking off big time now. These were hurtful words. Dominic swigged the last bit of coffee from his cup and stood up. He grabbed his jacket and snarled over at his mother. "I don't know why I even bother coming here. You're bitter and twisted. I'm going to see my wife to see if I can patch things up. But one thing is for sure, I won't be staying here with you. I'll call back later for my clothes."

Helen's bottom lip quivered. She'd fucked it now. She stood in front of him and blocked his exit. He was all she had, she couldn't lose him too! "Stop being so angry. Okay, I've said some bad things, but so have you. I'm sorry for my part in it."

Dominic looked at her and knew she was on the verge of breaking down. She always played this card when she'd upset him. It would be tears next. The story of how much she loved him, all the chances she'd missed to bring him up, she was holding nothing back. "Mam, just move out of my way. I've had enough shit today to last me a lifetime so don't be adding to it. My head will fall off if you do. Is that what you want?"

"No, son. I just want us two to be happy again. Don't leave like this, it's all too much for me. The doctor has told me to avoid stress. I never told you that did I?" She pressed her hand over her heart and closed her eyes slowly. "The doctor said it's my heart, he said I might not last the year." Wow, this woman was unbelievable. She had a few cholesterol tablets, that's all. Why on earth would she lie to him about the time she had left?

Dominic was gobsmacked, she'd knocked the wind right out of his sails. Helen watched him cunningly and started to back off. She knew her boy would never leave her now, not now she'd told a whopping big lie about her health. "Mam, why didn't you tell me? Bleeding hell, when did you find this out?"

Helen sat down and fanned her hand in front of her. "No son, you go and sort your life out. Don't you worry about me. You have your own problems without me landing this on you."

She watched from the corner of her eye as she dabbed a white cotton handkerchief into her eyes. Dominic sat next to her and reached over and touched her hand. "I'm sorry too. It's just that, I need her back. I just want things to be back to normal. I can't function without her by my side. I'm weak."

"I know son, go and see her, just leave me here. I'll be alright on my own." What the hell was she playing at now?

This was dangerous ground, fancy telling someone you're going to die when there is nothing wrong with you. The woman deserved an Oscar.

Dominic looked at his wristwatch and sighed. "Yeah, I'll nip round and see Misty and I'll see how the land lies."

Helen let out a laboured breath and nodded her head. "I'm going to have a lie down, son. If you get a chance later, call back and check on me. I've not been feeling well for days and I think I've being doing too much." Helen stood and kissed her son's forehead. Her steps were slow now as she headed to the door. "I just want you to be happy. That would be my dying wish, all I want is to make sure you're okay before my time is over."

Dominic watched her leave the room and sat staring at the floor. Had he been that caught up in his own life that he'd never seen how his own mother was suffering? She was right, all she had was him. He had no brothers or sisters. Helen was a loner.

Misty finished hoovering and collapsed on the sofa. The housework had taken it out of her today and already she was exhausted. Usually she would have blitzed this house clean in a few hours but today she was struggling. It was taking forever. Everything had got on top of her lately, there was dust everywhere, stained glass, stale smells throughout her house, manky walls, it was a shit tip.

This was the first morning in a while that Misty had not touched a drop of alcohol. It was only because there wasn't a drop in the house, otherwise she would have been drunk. She'd been edgy all morning and on more than one occasion, she'd gone upstairs looking for anything that would take the edge off her withdrawal symptoms. She was a mess. This woman was having a battle with her addiction for sure. Misty turned the television on and flicked through the channels, maybe this would help her calm down, take her mind off the drink. Rob came into the room whistling. He was happy today and not full of his usual doom and gloom. She shot a look over at him and you could tell she wanted to rip his head off. The sound of his whistling drilled against her brain, flooding her eardrums, she'd had enough. She couldn't stand it a second longer, he was chirping like a bleeding budgie. She shot a look over at him and sneered.

"Rob, can you stop making that fucking racket? Honestly, my head is banging and you're pushing me over the edge. Shut the fuck up and sit down for God's sake."

Rob raised his eyebrows. For crying out loud, the man was whistling a melody not knocking a bleeding wall down. She was overreacting. Maybe it was a bad idea him moving in with her after all. At first Rob thought it would help him but now he was having second thoughts, this woman was a nutter, she was too unpredictable. At least in his own home he could do whatever he wanted, when he wanted. Since when had whistling been a criminal offence anyway? Rob sat down and started to roll a cigarette. He could feel her eyes still watching his every move like a sniper. She was gunning for him for sure and he was more than aware of it. He looked over at her, trying to calm the situation down. "Do you want me to roll you one too?"

Misty cringed and shook her head. She was ready to blow and she was on a short fuse. "No, since when have I smoked that shit?"

In fairness, he could have answered her back and

fought his corner but he played it cool. He didn't need to remind her that when she was pissed out of her head and her own fags ran out, she smoked roll-ups all bleeding night. Oh yes, when she ran out of cigarettes she was always pestering him to roll her a few. Bleeding hypocrite she was. The smell of his Golden Virginia tobacco filled the room as he sat back in the chair relaxing. There was silence, not a word was spoken for a few minutes. Misty was fidgeting, unable to concentrate. She was itching her skin constantly and every now and then she tugged at her hair, stressed. Was she cracking up or what? Rob clocked her but never said a word about her strange mannerisms. "I might go and take your mam some flowers later if you fancy a walk to the cemetery?"

Misty turned to face him and sucked hard on her bottom lip. "It's not for me all that Rob. I get no comfort from it whatsoever. I mean, she's snuffed it and that's it. Nothing will ever bring her back to life so save your money, go and have a pint or something instead. Save yourself the heartache of going there."

"That's a bit harsh love. Lisa loved flowers. I go and talk to her all the time. I feel like she listens to me too, it helps clear my head when I'm feeling down. She gives me inner peace."

Misty snorted and sat gawping at him. Was he for real or what? How can a dead person listen to you? When someone pops their clogs that's it, game over. No second chance, no coming back. Was he losing the plot or something or was this just the way he was coping with Lisa's death? She wasn't sure. "Rob, do whatever makes you happy. I'm just saying it's not for me, that's all. Tell her I was asking about her if that makes you feel any better. Tell her she's left a bleeding mess down here too, interfering cow she is."

She snarled and sat playing with her feet, which were tucked underneath her bum cheeks. Rob sat up in his chair as he heard the back gate swing open. He peered outside and shot a quick look over at Misty. "Hey up, it's Dominic." Her heart stopped for a few seconds and her cheeks went bright red in seconds. For Christ's sake, she wasn't even dressed properly, she was still in her scruffs. What the hell did he want this early in the morning, had he shit the bed or something? The back door swung open and there he was, her husband, the love of her life. Misty looked over at him and raised her eyes. She had to be nice, not kick off. "And to what do I owe the pleasure? I thought you would have still been out with your new fancy piece?"

Dominic looked blank, what the hell was she going on about? Rob stubbed his fag out in the ashtray and made a quick exit. "I'll see you two later, I'm off for a few pints and to see my Lisa. I'll be back when I'm back. Don't wait up."

Dominic smiled over at him as he replied. "I might join you later if you're still in the boozer when I've finished here. We could have a few scoops together and catch up."

"Smashing, lad. I'll look forward to that," Rob chuckled, glad of the bit of company, someone to open up to.

Misty folded her arms tightly across her chest and started to watch the TV. Her husband could fuck right off if he thought he could just walk back into her life after sleeping with another woman. She was probably a tart anyway. Misty had new friends now and little did he know that she could just waltz into the pub anytime she wanted to as well. What's good for the goose is good for the gander. The front door slammed shut. Dominic stretched his arms above his head and yawned nervously, where did he start, how to begin? He looked over at his wife and knew this wasn't going to be easy. "So, are we going to sort this mess out or what? Surely you must be missing me. Well, you went as far as sending a text message so I presume you want to sort this mess out too?"

Misty was never one for backing down and her pride always stood in the way, even when she wanted to make friends with her husband. Rage bubbled inside her, an anger she couldn't deal with right now. "Piss off, what's up with your new slapper, ey? Has she carted you or something? Or have you realised now just how good I am?"

"What the hell are you going on about? I've not been near another woman since I've been gone, trust me!"

"Really? Well it's not what that old hag is saying. According to her, you're hooking up with someone new."

Dominic scratched his head. He sat down near his wife. "Hold on, I'm confused now, who's said what?"

Misty sat up straight and flicked her hair over her shoulder. "Oh fuck off acting like you don't know what I'm going on about. Your mother's already told me everything, so don't act like you don't know. Come on, give me a bit of credit at least. I'm not daft. That's probably the reason you couldn't wait to get out of here in the first place. You probably had her all set up in the background."

His voice was loud and he was getting angry. "What, have you spoken to my mam?"

"Yes, didn't she tell you that I called round to her house to see you? She couldn't wait to tell me that you were out banging some new bird!"

Dominic punched the arm of the chair, specks of dust rising in the air. "I'll bleeding kill her! She's never mentioned a word to me. Honest, on my life, the conniving bitch never told me anything!"

Misty looked at him closer, he was telling the truth, she could tell. No raised eyebrow, no itching the end of his nose. "So she's not even told you I came to speak to you? I swear, that woman needs shooting. I've told you how many times before, she needs sectioning that one does! But do you listen, do you fuck."

Dominic let out a laboured breath and held his head in his hands. "I'll have a word with her. I'm sorry, you know what she's like. Anyway, why did you come to see me?"

Misty stuttered, she was on the spot now. Could she open up, confess all and tell him she loved him from the bottom of her heart and that her life wasn't worth living when he wasn't in it? She twiddled her hair and looked around the room. He was waiting on an answer. Praying she would say she loved him more than anything. "It doesn't matter why I called now does it." Here it was, the wall she built around her, her stone heart pretending she didn't care about him.

Dominic swallowed hard, he knew her of old and tried to make amends. "Listen love, we still love each other don't we? We're just going through a rough patch that's all. Most couples go through it. We just need to stay strong and help each other through it. I'm sorry if I've not been as supportive as I should have been. I'll try harder. I promise."

Dominic sat cracking his knuckles, waiting, hoping she wanted to fix this mess. "I'm not sorry for grieving for my mother. You don't know how hard it is to lose a parent, it cuts deep, drags your heart out. I have a few drinks to help take the edge off it all and you declare to the world that I'm a bleeding alcy, a pisshead."

"I never said you were a pisshead love. That's you putting words into my mouth again. I just think you were drinking too much. I'm entitled to have an opinion, bleeding hell, shoot me for even caring."

"Well, you should keep it to yourself then shouldn't you? You even started on me about cleaning the house, nitpicking, finding anything you could to moan about. It grinds me down, tears me apart you know."

"Misty, I just want you to be normal again that's all. I was coming home from work every night to a drunken wife who didn't know what day it was. Come on, admit it. You never cooked, you never cleaned, what did you want me to do, ignore it?"

So much for making up, building bridges, they were at loggerheads again. Misty sat forward in her seat, ready to scratch his eyeballs out. "Do I need all this? What, did you wake up early this morning and think I know what, I'll go and see Misty and fuck her head up again? A tormenting bastard you are, nothing more."

Dominic ran his fingers through his hair. This was the last thing he wanted, he needed to turn this around before they were back to square one again. "I want to come home. I need to help you, support you."

"I'm not a cripple. I need understanding, a bit of compassion that's all. Not a bleeding carer."

"Can I come back home then? We can get through this if you want to sort it out."

Misty changed the subject, kept him hanging on. "Charlotte is like a new woman. That Reeks or whatever his bleeding name is has calmed her right down. She's being nice to me, honest, you won't believe it, it's a miracle."

Dominic rolled his eyes. He'd never believe it until he

saw it with his own eyes. Charlotte was a bitch, all for herself and wouldn't do a tap for anybody unless she was getting paid for it. "I've missed you both," he lied, "Charlotte has sent me a few text messages but I've not seen her."

"You and me both. She comes in late in the evening and then she's out at the crack of dawn."

Dominic sighed, this was hard to believe. Usually his step-daughter was in bed all day, it was very rare that she climbed out of it until late afternoon. "Well, as long as she's away from that nutter I'm not arsed. There was something not right in that guy's head, he worried me, seriously, he has issues."

"She never listened to a word we said about Paul either. The more we told her to stay away from the crank, the more she wanted him."

"Like mother like daughter then?"

Misty rolled her eyes and the corner of her mouth started to rise. "I was a mixed up kid that's all. Rebellious, looking for an adventure let's say."

Dominic looked at her and his heart melted. There she was, the woman he fell in love with all those years ago. His voice was endearing and each word he spoke came from his heart. "Misty, let's make up. You know I can't stand being away from you. I don't sleep or eat and I just feel dead inside. My head's all over the place. I can't function without you by my side."

She swallowed hard and closed her eyes slightly. Her head turned towards him and a ball of emotion packed up her throat. He was her world too, the man she had always loved, the man she'd married. For better or worse, till death do us part. Looking deep into his eyes she remembered him in his younger days. Her hand touched the side of his face and all her defences dropped. Her eyes clouded over and the words just rolled from her tongue. "I love you too with all my heart. I've just been a little bit lost lately. I'm sorry, I just got caught up in the drinking and before I knew it, I was drinking more than I should have. This Tom saga has been doing my head in too. Dominic, he can ruin our lives with his evil mouth. I've been to see him and he's still saying he's going to tell her."

Dominic's ears pinned back. "I'll go and see him. I'll take a few of the lads from the gym round. They'll put the fear of God up him."

Misty squeezed at his arm desperately. "No, it's no good. You could kick ten tons of shit out of Tom and he'll say anything you want him to say. Honest, the minute he's on his feet he will do whatever he set out to do. He has no emotions, he's heartless."

Suddenly Charlotte barged in the back door and stood gawping at her parents. "Please tell me you two have sorted it out. It's gone on for too long now. I need some harmony back in this house, calmness."

Misty looked at her husband and rested her head on his shoulder. "He's coming back home. You're right, we are idiots for falling out."

Dominic smirked over at his daughter and winked. "Hey, your mam has been telling me about this new guy in your life. She said you're in love."

Charlotte blushed, she smirked and her body was filled with a warm glow. "It's early days yet, but, yes, I think he's the one. Honest dad, he's heaven sent. He's the complete opposite to me but he gets me. Is that weird? Do you know what I mean?"

Misty nodded her head and snuggled closer to her

husband. "Yes, I do. He's your soul-mate. When I first met your dad he was the biggest geek ever but he just won my heart."

Dominic nudged her and chuckled. "I wasn't a geek. I was a cool kid, you just never saw it."

Charlotte folded her arms tightly across her chest. "I've just had murders with that Paul in the pub. The clown tried to attack me. Bob the landlord had to cart him. I swear he wanted to do me in."

Misty sat forward in her seat, she hated this guy and he reminded her of a man she used to know in her past. She gritted her teeth tightly together and spoke to her. "Paul Jones is a cunt. I've never liked him from the start. From the second you brought him home I had a gut feeling about him. He's a wrong-un. Rotten to the core in fact. He's a right smarmy bastard. Didn't I say to you Dominic that I hated him?"

Her husband chewed on his fingernails, he was thinking. He remembered this lad too. He was a menace and after doing his homework on him, he realised that he was nothing but trouble. The day Charlotte had told them they were over it was a Godsend for them all because this man could turn nasty at any given time. He held a look of madness in his eye and he wasn't to be trusted. Charlotte started to head to the kitchen door. "I'm going out with Reeks and Mandy tonight. We're going to the pictures to see a film. Well, Mandy is on a date too with Jason, that's Reeks' mate. Mam, she was proper funny when I told her she was on a double date. You know she doesn't date as such, already she's flapping." Misty smiled, her life was happy again, no more dramas, her husband was home and all that was left to do was to silence Gordon's brother.

★

A little later, Dominic left to go collect his belongings from his mother's house. She was getting told too. What a lying cow she was! There he was, heartbroken, and she didn't even have the decency to tell him his wife had been round to her house to sort things out. What was wrong with her? She was on another planet for sure.

Misty watched her husband leave and licked her lips slowly. She sat playing rapidly with her fingers. There was the craving again, the urge to get off her face. Standing to her feet, she rushed upstairs and into her bedroom. She listened carefully, Charlotte was talking on her phone in the other bedroom. Misty sat on the edge of the bed, head in her hands now, sweat pouring from her brow. She remembered where she'd stashed some booze. It was in the same room as her, under her bed, calling her, making her mind race. She had no control, it was drawing her in. Misty fell to the floor and dipped her head under the bed. Her hand stretched long until the cold glass was in her grip. Sitting up at the side of the bed, she drew her knees up to her chest and closed her eyes. Just one last drink, nobody would know, call it one for the road. Her fingers quivered as she unscrewed the lid from the vodka. There was no more thinking now, the decision was made for her. She gulped a large mouthful and then another. With a quick flick of her wrist she wiped the corners of her mouth. This was a secret that no one could ever know, this was the last time she would get drunk, honest, never again...

Dominic marched into his mother's house. His voice shook the room. "Mam, get your arse down here. I want a word with you. You're in big trouble this time. Get your arse down here." He walked up a couple of stairs and shouted again. "Mam, are you in bed? Don't pretend to be asleep because you know what you've done and you are going to pay for it you evil demented woman."

There was silence.

He climbed up another few stairs and gripped the banister tightly. His mother's bedroom door was open slightly. Once he reached the top of the stairs, he popped his head inside and he could see her body under the duvet. "Mam!" he shouted. Still no response. Walking closer to the bed, he could see her foot sticking out from the edge of the covers. He tweaked it with all his might, hoping to wake her. His eyes shot to the bedside cabinet and his eyes opened wide.

Tablets, empty bottles, a small bottle of gin.

Panic set in and he ran to the top of the bed. "Mam, wake up, come on mam, stop pissing about!" His hands gripped the tablet bottle and at that moment he realised his mother had tried to end her own life. He picked her lifeless body up from the bed and started to shake her. "Mam, come on, don't do this to me! I'm sorry for shouting at you. Open your eyes! Talk to me! Fucking hell mam, open your eyes!" Dominic was a mess, he ran one way then another. He was talking to himself. "Phone, I need to get help, ring an ambulance." He stampeded down the stairs and ran into the living room. Once he got to the phone he picked up the receiver, his head was all over and he pressed the wrong digits for the emergency services

"Hello, I need an ambulance please, my mother has taken tablets," he paused as he listened to the voice at the other end of the phone. "I'm not sure. I'll go and check." Dominic dropped the phone and sprinted back up the stairs. Helen was still in the same position, she'd not moved an inch. How would he know if she was alive or not, how did he check her pulse? He placed his head on her chest, was there a heartbeat, he wasn't sure? Lifting her heavy body up, he rocked her to and fro. "Come on mam, you're not dead. Wake up. It's not your time yet mother. Open them eyes, come on, don't you dare leave me!" The tears came now, his grip on her tightened, knuckles turning white. Kissing the top of her head, he inhaled the fragrance from her hair. This could be the last time he ever smelled her locks or held her in his arms like this. His heart was beating ten to the dozen, he was having a panic attack. He could hear the sound of sirens in the distance and then voices inside the house and the sound of feet running up the stairs.

Dominic never flinched as the medics ran into the room. He was in shock and not a word left his mouth. The medics hurried to the bedside and quickly removed him from his mother. They were examining Helen, checking her breathing, her pulse. Dominic sat in the corner of the room and drew his knees up to his chest. It was all happening so fast, everything seemed to be happening in slow motion. He needed some fresh air, his airwaves were closing up, suffocating him. Gagging into his hands, he ran down the stairs straight out into the front garden. One of the medics came running after him and started to calm him down. Dominic sat on the grass verge and looked him straight into the eye.

"Tell me she's not gone! Is she going to make it, don't say she's dead please?" The medic didn't answer, he was more concerned about sorting his breathing out. He lay him in the recovery position and asked him if there was anyone he could phone to come and sit with him while all this was going on. Dominic patted his pocket. "Take my phone and ring Misty, she's my wife, she'll come over. Yes, please ring her!"

The medics had been in the bedroom for ages now. Misty was there with her husband and Charlotte had come along to support him too. They were all waiting on the news, nobody had said anything yet, there was still hope in his heart. Misty cradled her husband in her arms as they sat in the front room awaiting the verdict. She kissed the top of his head and whispered into his ear. "She'll pull through love, just you watch. She's a soldier that one is." Dominic wasn't digesting anything anyone was saying to him, he was in a trance, nothing was making sense anymore. Guilt had taken over now and the words he'd spoken to her before he left that day were lying heavily on his mind. Had he pushed her over the edge? She had told him he was all she had, he told her some home truths too, stuff she'd wanted to forget about. His mind was racing and if he could have turned back the hands of time, he would have.

Dominic bolted up from his chair and marched to the door. Misty stood up behind him, fear in her eyes. "Where are you going love, just sit down and let them do their job. If there is any news they will let us know."

He snapped at her, eyes dancing with madness. "No, I need to know what the hell is going on! I can't just sit here doing fuck all."

Charlotte flicked the curtain back from the window and her eyes were wide open. "Dad, the dibble are here. A van and two cars, team-handed they are."

Misty let out a laboured breath. This was the last thing they needed. Nobody was causing any trouble here so why were they even sticking their noses in? Dominic never made it upstairs. The medic came to the door and asked him to sit down. Misty quickly hurried to his side. She held his hand and squeezed at it with all her might. Surely not, no way had Helen died. The medic gulped and prepared his words. This part of his job was never easy. "I'm afraid it's bad news." Dominic closed his eyes, pain stabbed deep into his heart, emptiness flooded his whole being. Misty burst out crying and hugged her husband. Even Charlotte joined them and they both held Dominic in their arms. This was family time, they needed this.

His shoulders were shaking, he was snivelling...

Two male officers walked into the room and to add insult to injury, they were there to make sure there was no foul play. This was now being treated as a crime scene. Another police officer came into the room and sat next to the family. Everything was being explained now. This was the protocol when a body was found at a home address. As far as the police were concerned, Helen could have been done in. Maybe killed for the inheritance money, the police had to be sure. Dominic pushed Misty away from him and snarled at the officers. His eyes were wide open and he could barely get his words out. "What, you think I've done her in? That's my mother up those stairs. I want to see her. I need to see her. For fuck's sake, is nobody listening to me here? I want to see my fucking mother!"

The officers stood behind the door and he knew if Dominic wanted to get out of the room, he had to get past them first. They were ready to twist him up, put him on his arse if they had to. Charlotte stepped forward and gripped her father by the side of the arm. Somebody had to talk some sense into him before he ended up getting nicked. "Dad, come on, sit down for a minute, calm down. Let the officers do their job. They won't be long and then we can all go and see her together."

She led him back to his seat, he was in a strange mood and nothing was registering. The neighbourhood was out in full force now. Gossiping bastards, the lot of them. Women trying to peer through their windows to find out what was going on. Oh yes, the neighbourhood would be talking about this for months to come. Misty looked out of the window and she could see the gossipmongers congregating outside the house. What on earth did they think was going on? She would have loved to have been a fly on the wall. Helen was as clean as they came. She never once stepped on the wrong side of the law. Even when there were knock-off clothes and handbags going round the estate for cheap, she always turned her nose up at them. She was whiter than white.

Charlotte snarled at the neighbours through the window. She rammed her two open fingers in the air at them. "Should I go outside and tell them to piss off? Look at them all, like vultures waiting on any scrap of news," she hissed.

Misty stood back from the window. Her heart was low and she was also on a guilt trip. Maybe she could have been nicer to her mother-in-law, invited her over more for tea, gone shopping with her every now and then. She was searching her soul. Why was it that when a person died, everyone who knew them had some kind of regret? If that's the way they felt, why on earth didn't they change that when the person was alive? Life isn't a trial run, it's the real thing and when you're gone, you're gone. Maybe the human race had a lot to learn about their time here on this earth.

A police woman sat taking statements from all the family members. Dominic had to go through every detail of what he'd witnessed. From the days before to the minute he found her dead. The police were nitpicking here, trying to catch him out, making him go over and over it again and again. He was a prime suspect.

Rob turned up soon after. The heartache of losing Lisa was visible on his face. The emotion stuck in his throat, the need to burst out crying. It was bringing it all back to him. This family was falling apart and his heart was low, he needed to do something.

Charlotte had been on her mobile for the last five minutes talking to Reeks. He'd wanted to come round but she told him there wasn't a thing he could do. Rob sat next to Dominic and started to speak. "I'm here for you, son. I know no amount of words will heal your breaking heart right now, but just remember, I'm here for you. I'm going nowhere." The two of them held a look and Dominic knew these words came from the heart.

It was late now and the doctors had been and pronounced Helen dead. Her body was being carried down the stairs by the undertakers. Dominic couldn't hold back the tears. He'd had his heart ripped out. He fell to his knees and no words at this moment could have taken away the hurt he felt in his heart. One by one, the officers started to disappear. There were no further investigations for now. This case seemed cut and dried: suicide. When the last officer finally left, the family sat in silence. Should they spend the night here or should they lock the place up and go home? What the hell were they supposed to do? It was Dominic's shout and they were all waiting on him to say something. Misty walked to the drinks cabinet and poured her husband a large brandy, of course she had a nip too. No one seemed to care who was drinking what, they just all needed something to take the edge off it all, to escape what had happened here today. Misty passed her husband a drink as he walked out of the room. She was going to follow him but Rob held her back. "Leave him love, he needs to say goodbye in his own way." Was this family cursed or what? It was just one thing after the other.

Dominic walked into the bedroom and froze. Goosebumps appeared all over his arms. The hairs on the back of his neck stood on edge. He shot a look around the bedroom and his eyes flooded with tears. His mother had lived in this house for as long as he could remember and all his childhood memories were here. This was the bed he first made love to his wife in. When they were teenagers he took her into his mother's double bed when she was out, they had sex here on more than one occasion. This was also the bed he'd sat on when his world fell apart years earlier, the bed he poured his heart out on when Misty had left him for Gordon. The bed held so many happy stories and sad times too. This was the bed his mother laid in for months when her marriage fell apart. Dominic edged closer to the bed and bent his knees slightly. His hand glided across the white cotton duvet, stroking it, slowly moving across it. It was Egyptian cotton, not that cheap shit, it was the best that money could buy. His eyes looked around the room, was she really gone, had she really taken her own life? He was in misery, his heart stuck in his throat.

You never really know the minute do you? One minute everything can be rosy in the garden and the next, boom, gone, never seen again. Helen had always come across as a strong woman, a fighter, independent. Suicide would never have been predicted for this woman, it was so out of character for her. Maybe she never meant to take her own life, perhaps she just wanted to scare her son. Perhaps it was a cry for help. Dominic's mother had left a letter too, but the police had taken it for evidence. They had to get inside this woman's head, retrace her last steps, her last lonely thoughts. Helen stated in her letter that she'd had enough of being lonely. Even in a room full of people you love dearly, a person can still feel lonely and Helen was one of them. It seemed she'd given up on love a long time ago. After her husband, she'd never really loved again. She was bitter and hated seeing anyone in a loving relationship because she no longer had one. When Charlotte was born, Helen was a devoted grandparent and spent hours with her granddaughter. But as she started to grow, the hours she spent with her became less and less. She needed to be needed if the truth was known. Throughout her last words in her letter, she declared her love for her son. Every second word was telling him how special he was and that he would never be far from her thoughts, no matter where she was. Helen spoke of inner peace in the words she wrote, the need to feel normal again, the craving to be loved.

Dominic lay flat on the bed and dragged the duvet over his head. He could smell her perfume all over the pillows as his nostrils flared slightly. Digging his head deep into the duvet, he sobbed his heart out. Today was a sad day, a time he would never forget. The day he lost his mother.

CHAPTER EIGHT

TOM LOOKED FRESH, he'd had a wash and a shave today, he looked top notch he thought. He was lurking in the car park so no one could see him. He'd planned every move, every last detail of how he would first meet her. Surely it was time for her to be here now. It was nearly eight o'clock in the morning. The children from the school had started to arrive for breakfast club so he knew his wait was nearly over. Tom sat cracking his knuckles, biting the edges of his grubby fingernails. What was he going to say to her when he finally got his chance to speak to her, would she even want to talk to him after all this time? It was a do or die situation.

A black car pulled up and Tom stood on his tiptoes to get a better look at the driver. His eyes squeezed together tightly, his vision blurred. After focusing for a few seconds, he clocked that it was Francesca. His heart was beating now, his mouth was dry. This was it, showtime. Tom stepped out from the corner of the car park and stood where she could see him, fidgeting, anxious, pulling at his clothes. Francesca looked smart today, a white cotton blouse and a navy knee-length skirt. This was nothing like she used to dress. In her day she was all tits and teeth; sexy mini skirts and low-cut blouses. But she was a teacher now, prim and proper. The sound of her heels clipped on the pavement, getting nearer. He had to say something before she passed him. He stepped forward a little and sucked in a mouthful of air.

"Hello there, long time no see 'ey?" Tom smiled at her,

showing his brown stumpy teeth. Francesca paused and turned around slowly.

She squirmed and was about to tell this scruff to piss off out of her way. How dare this junkie come into school grounds begging for money, some people had no shame, no shame at all. She paused and examined him further. Her eyes opened wide, her mouth still open. She knew who he was now, her jaw swung low. She stuttered, heart in her mouth. "Tom, what on earth are you doing here?"

He'd planned his answer all night long and the words came flying from his tongue. "I've come to see you. It's been years hasn't it?"

Francesca gulped and remembered where she was. No way did she want her collar felt for talking to some drug addict in the school car park. She wanted no connection with him whatsoever, he was her past and he was staying there. He reminded her of a time she was trying to forget. She kept her voice low and tried her best to be nice to him. "Yes, it's been a long time, Tom. Why are you here, do you have kids who go to the school?"

This was just friendly talk, nothing more. He was happy now she was having a conversation with him. He was in with a chance, maybe she still loved him too. "No love, I don't have any kids. How's our Rico doing anyway? I'd love to see him. I've not set eyes on him since he was a nipper. Can we arrange for me to come and see him?"

Francesca's eyes clouded over, was this really the man she thought she'd loved all those years ago? He was a walking wreck, stinking. Tom looked like death warmed up, dark circles under his eyes, sunken cheekbones. Checking her surroundings, Francesca led Tom to a corner just outside the school grounds out of sight from the public. For crying out loud, if anyone would have seen her there with him they would have thought she was scoring some drugs or something. It was on top, shady. Once she had him out of sight, she began to speak. He needed telling straight from the off, no cutting corners. "Tom, you can't just turn up here like this. I work here and people will start to talk if they see me with you. I've got a decent job here so don't try and fuck it up. I'm not the same person I was years ago. I've grown up, turned my life around, unlike you."

Tom looked down at his clothes and it was clear he wasn't too proud of himself. Maybe he should have worn his white shirt, splashed a bit of aftershave on his body, upped his game to impress her. He knew where this was heading and there was no way he wanted to be blackballed. He'd always loved this woman and had often imagined the day he saw her again. He could make her love him again, he just needed a chance. He chuckled, trying to take the edge off her last blow. "I can get some new clothes and scrub up. Let's meet up later and I'll take you out on the town. We can paint the town red, just like old times. I swear, I'll have my hair cut and have a good wash. What do you think? I'm pretty sexy when I make the effort you know?"

Francesca screwed her face up and she knew she would have to stop him getting his hopes up. Did he really think she was going to sleep with him again? No way, not a cat in hell's chance. He repulsed her. She would rather stick hot pins in her eyes than have this junkie on top of her body again. He was lower than low, a messed-up heroin addict. Francesca had been mixed up when she was sleeping with Tom all those years ago. Maybe he was just a shoulder to cry on at the time, someone to hold her when she was at breaking point. She looked at him closer. He made her skin crawl. Francesca had to tell him the truth. Stop him dead in his tracks before he started to get any big ideas about them rekindling their relationship. She looked him directly in the eye and her voice was firm. "Tom, you know there is no 'us' anymore. Me and you were a long time ago and it's something I would go back to again. We were kids for crying out loud, we were both fucked up in the head, not thinking straight. I mean, do you really think me and you would have ever been a couple? It was a one-off, a stupid mistake. Come on Tom, even you're not that thick."

Tom gulped and fell back onto the wall, slaver hanging from the corner of his mouth. What a low blow, he wasn't expecting this, she'd knocked him for six, wounded he was. His heart was smashed, he was gutted. "Yeah, I know that. I just want to see my nephew that's all. I've got a decent bird anyway, I was only having a crack with you. You know I've always been a bit of a joker." Tom took a few seconds to compose himself and rubbed the end of his nose as he continued. He had to stand tall now, he couldn't show her that she had smashed his heart into a thousand pieces. "Rico's my brother's son and all I have left of our kid. He's my family, my bloodline. Does he look like him or what? Is he hard as fuck like Gordon was? Can he have a good fight?"

Francesca growled at him. Why on earth was he bigging his brother up? Gordon was a bully who terrorised everyone, a control freak. Her son was the complete opposite to Gordon, he was calm, loving, gentle and didn't have a bad bone in his body. "Tom, fuck off will you. Rico is a good kid, don't you think it's hard enough bringing a kid up with no dad around, without you turning up and raking up the past? Rico cried for months when I told him his father was dead. Honestly, he was heartbroken. Stay out of his life Tom. I don't want you stirring things up. I know that sounds harsh but it would do his head in."

Tom hung his head. This wasn't going to plan. What about the first kiss they shared, her hot cherry lips pressed firmly next to his, why didn't she feel the same anymore? Why wasn't she hugging him, declaring her undying love for him? The penny dropped and he snarled over at her. No more Mr nice guy. "What about Tigger, how did that pan out with Mr Lover Boy? The one you carted me for, may I add?"

"You don't need to ask Tom. He was just another wanker at the end of the day. A womaniser just like your brother. A prick who promised me the world but got on his toes the second another woman took his eye. He's lucky I never cut his nob off and shoved it up his arse."

Tom sniggered, there she was, the girl he remembered. "I never had an eye for the ladies did I? My eyes were only for you sweetheart. I gave it all up for you Francesca and you just fucked off and left me on my tod," his voice was desperate now but they were words spoken straight from his heart. He sucked hard on his lips as a single bulky tear slid down his thin cheekbone. "I loved you with all my heart. I got clean for you, knocked the drugs on the head so me and you could make a go of it. I loved you then and I love you now. Please give us another go. I swear I'll get sorted and we can have a good life together."

His words fell on deaf ears, she'd switched off. This was a life she was trying to forget and if she had never seen this man again, it would have been a blessing. She had to treat him with kid gloves though, try not to hurt his feelings. She started to backpedal. "Tom, I think it's best if you keep out of Rico's life. He's been through a lot and I don't want to mess with his head. Gordon is my past too and if I'm being honest with you, I'd rather not be reminded about the time I spent with him either. Tom, you know what that man did to me, to both of us, so don't defend him. He was a bully, a bleeding nutter. I just think it's for the best."Tom reached over and touched her hand. His grubby fingers were all over her, she felt sick to the pit of her stomach. She backed off and squirmed. "Tom, I'm going to be late. School starts soon and I need to be there before the children arrive. Please, just leave us both alone. Gordon is dead in my eyes and I never want to have to mention his name again if I can get away with it. His name on my tongue makes me feel sick."

Tom felt the cold shoulder from her and his heart sank. He'd imagined in his head that she would hug him, kiss him and tell him she still thought about him every minute of every day. This was a big kick in the balls for him and one he'd not expected. His face changed and his tone did too. He had nothing to lose anymore. "Listen, Rico is my blood and I want to see him, perhaps a kick-about on the park if he wants. But one thing is for sure, I'm going to be in his life. I promised my brother I would always look out for him and I never go back on my word. Unlike some people." Tom sneered at her, reminding her of the false promises she'd made with him.

Francesca was backed into a corner. She flicked her eyes around the area again, she just needed to get away from this baghead before anyone clocked her. She knew what made him tick to get him off her case. She reached inside her handbag and pulled out her purse. She quickly pulled out a ten pound note and wafted it in front of his eyes. "Here, go and score. But fuck off and leave me and my son alone. You're forgetting I know how to deal with rats like you, Tom. I'm from the same mould as you, so give your head a shake before you think you can bully me. I'm still Francesca under all these clothes you know and I'll eat you for breakfast if you think you can fuck with me. My son's my life and I'll die to keep him safe. Did you hear that, you pest? Yes, I'd die for him. So take the money and go and do what you do best. If I see you here again, I'll report you. I'll say you're a known kiddy-fiddler. You know I will, so for your own sake stay well out of my way."

Tom snatched the money out of her hand and growled. "So, war it is then. Good luck with that if you want a battle with me. I'll find Rico myself. Maybe I can tell him all about his mother too, tell him all about the coke whore she was. The baggy-fannied bitch who ruined my life. Yes, you remember don't you?" He was in her face now.

Francesca stood her ground and didn't flinch, their eyes locked and neither of them blinked. This guy was sick in the head, his eyes were vacant. Tom started to smile and shook his head. His mood switched again. "I'll see you soon love. Tell Rico Uncle Tom will be in touch with him soon. Send him my love from his family."

Francesca's heart leapt about in her chest, she was finding it hard to breathe and she had to suck in a few mouthfuls of air in before she turned towards the school building. This was the last thing she needed. Tom was an out-and-out bastard and by hook or by crook, she was going to make sure this prick never stepped within an inch of her son. She needed a game plan and quick. Francesca marched away from Tom. She didn't look back at him. The nightmare she thought she'd left behind all those years ago was back again. Tom was still shouting abuse behind her as she carried on walking and her fists curled into two tight balls at the side of her legs. "Bastard, you want war, I'll give you war."

*

Rico sat on the wall with his mate Jason. There were a few other people there and they were just chilling. The girls were making dances up, twerking and slut-dropping, anything to ease the boredom. They were loud and starting to draw attention from passers-by. Jason checked his phone and nudged Rico. "That Mandy hasn't text me for hours. I sent her a message and look, nothing. Why hasn't she replied to me yet?"

Rico glanced at the screen and sniggered. "Stop being a beggar, buddy. Mandy is too cool for school and girls like her don't text back straight away. Just relax and see what happens."

Jason pulled a sour expression. "Since when have you been a player? You were a geek when I met you and now you're trying to give me some advice. Are you having a laugh or what?"

Rico tilted his head to the side and smirked. "I've learned a lot since I've been in Manchester and I think I'm on the level now. I'm a true Manc."

Jason burst out laughing. "For fuck's sake, I've created a monster. Welcome to the real world our kid."

They chuckled as a silver car pulled up not far from where they sat. Jason covered his mouth with his hand and whispered under his breath. "Fucking prick, look at him thinking he owns the gaff. I swear, I wish someone would knock him down a peg or two. He's one cocky cunt." They watched as a teenager rode over to where the car was parked and passed the driver a parcel. Jason lifted his head up and kept his voice low. "Look at the prick. That must be the money being passed over. It's fucking broad daylight and he doesn't give a toss who's watching. If the dibble had him on lockdown he would have been nicked by now. I mean, we can see what's going on over there, so why can't they?"

Rico shot a look over at the car and tried to get a better look at the driver but the tinted windows limited his view. "Who is it anyway?"

Jason jumped from the wall and straightened his tracksuit bottoms. "Paul Jones. The main head around here. The guy's a liberty taker. Look at John over there, doing all his graft for him and he's probably paying him next to nothing. It's the kid who'll take the rap for him though if it comes on top. He'd get years in the big-house if they got onto him. I swear, selling class A drugs comes with a right jail sentence. I bet at least four years would be rammed up his arse if he's caught dealing drugs."

"So why doesn't someone tell John to fuck him off? Tell him he's just being taken for a ride, doing the guy's dirty work."

Jason kicked his foot against the wall and made sure nobody could hear him. He wanted no comebacks from what he was about to say. "Nobody will say a word against Jones. The last person who stuck his nose in his business was in hospital with a nil by mouth notice hanging over his bed for weeks. He's a cunt, a bully. I swear, one of these days I'll stab the fucker up. I will you know. He doesn't scare me. We can all be sick and twisted if we want to."

Rico looked at his friend closer and couldn't make up

his mind as to whether or not he was chatting shit or he was the real deal. Jason had always been a bit of a bullshitter and he took most of the stories he told him with a pinch of salt. Jason liked to big himself up, tell his mates about jobs he'd been on, people he'd knocked out with one blow. Yes, Jason was a storyteller for sure. Rico twisted his head and from the corner of his eye, he could see Charlotte and Mandy approaching. There it was again, his heart beating faster than normal, his palms becoming sweaty, his smile as big as ever. This was his true love and even watching her walk towards him gave him butterflies. He was smitten. Jason was still more concerned with Paul Jones and when he saw him drive off, he shook his head.

The young teenager came riding past him and he shouted over to him to stop. John skidded his bike and smiled over at Jason. "What's up bro, what you after a bit of weed?"

Rico was listening in now. Did Jason really care enough about this kid to warn him about selling drugs and the prison sentence it carried? Jason walked over to the youth and softly kicked his tyre. "Nice bike, are you selling it?"

Rico sighed, what a letdown Jason was, no balls, no backbone to say the words he wanted to. Charlotte was here now and nothing else mattered. He could only hear her voice and although there were other people around him, he could only see her. Rico reached forward and grabbed her by her hand. "Come here and sit next to me. I've missed you."

Mandy squirmed and let out a laboured breath. She was never one for keeping quiet and she voiced her opinion. "You two knock me sick. Why don't you just go and get a room. I hate all this lovey-dovey shit."

Charlotte blushed and dropped her head onto her boyfriend's shoulder. "We're in love that's all."

Mandy stood with her hand on her hip and watched Jason talking to John. She turned her head back and spoke to Rico. "What's he doing talking to him?"

Rico shrugged his shoulders and didn't want to say anything, it was none of his business in his eyes. Mandy marched over to Jason as soon as she saw John riding off. "What were you two talking about?"

Jason tapped the side of his nose with a single finger and started to spin her a load of lies. "Ask no questions and I'll tell you no lies. Just a bit of business. You know, something to earn me a few quid."

Mandy scowled, since when had Jason been able to earn a few quid? He was potless. She knew without even asking that he was chatting shit. "Listen Charlie big spuds, cut the crap. You know as well as me that you don't do anything like that. It's up to you if you want to tell me the truth but please, don't insult my intelligence by lying to me. You are probably the most honest, law-abiding citizen I know around here so please don't lie."

Jason went beetroot, for fuck's sake this girl was clever. Nothing ever got past her, she was on the ball. He had to come clean before she made a show of him. And she would have done exactly that, she would have named and shamed him. His cheeks were beetroot and he kept his voice low. It was time to come clean, no more games. "I was just asking if he was selling his mountain bike that's all. Did you see it, it was mint?"

Mandy grabbed him by the collar and pulled him closer. "If me and you are ever going to have a chance of any kind relationship, you need to cut the bullshit out. I've downgraded to have you as my boyfriend, so show me a bit of respect and don't embarrass me with your big gangster stories because it doesn't wash with me. It's embarrassing to watch."

Jason wanted the ground to open up and swallow him whole. This girl held nothing back and he knew if he wanted to keep her, he had to sort his shit out. His arm draped loosely around her neck. "Sorry babes. I just get a bit carried away every now and then. Water under the bridge now though isn't it?"

Mandy held a stern look and opened her eyes wide. "So we agree, no more bullshit?"

He looked around and made sure no one could hear their conversation. "Yes, I promise you. I cross my heart and hope to die." Phew, that was close. Imagine his street cred if anyone would have heard him bowing down to his bird. He would have been a laughing stock. The four of them were together now and they were chatting away. Charlotte noticed a man stood in the distance watching them all, she focused and then looked over at Rico. "That guy has been there for the last ten minutes. He's just sat gawping at us. Have a look and make sure it's not me being paranoid."

Rico tried to get a better look at him. Jason was on his tiptoes now and the onlooker knew he'd been clocked. He zipped his coat up and kept his head low. "Look, he's going now we've seen him. I bet he's a paedo or something. It's been on the news that a few kids have been snatched from round here. Do you think we should report him? Imagine if he takes a nipper from the street, we would never forgive ourselves."

Mandy stepped up and licked her lips slowly. "No, he's fucked off now. We don't even know who he is or what he was doing. You can't just phone the Old Bill and say someone is watching us. If he comes back I'll run over to him and see what his game is. You know me, I'll just twat him. No questions asked." Rico studied Mandy and backed off. She was a livewire for sure and he didn't want to get on the wrong side of her, not now, not ever.

Charlotte looked worried, she was spooked. Jason found his voice again and he was bouncing about next to them. "So, let's go to the pictures. Mandy, would you do me the honour of accompanying me to the flicks tonight?" Mandy smirked and you could see she was warming to this guy more and more each day. He just ticked her boxes, made her laugh. But there was no way she was telling him that, no way in this world. If he wanted her love then he would have to earn it. And just for the record, it would take more than a few trips to the cinema to win her heart, she wanted the full shebang. The four of them started to head to the bus stop. Rico and Charlotte were holding hands. Love's young dream they were, besotted with each other.

Tom hid away in the shadows. He was watching his nephew's every move. It didn't take long to find out where he was either. As soon as he asked a few local lads where he chilled out, he made his way there. It was just a matter of time now before he found him and started the ball rolling. By his own admittance, he thought it would have taken a few days at least. But luck was on his side today and he got a great result. Tom's heart sank low when he first laid his eyes on Rico. He spotted him straight away. Tall, dark and handsome he was, a pretty boy. He looked nothing like his brother if he was being honest. Tom was low today and now Francesca had broken his heart all over again, he had nothing to lose. He was sick to death of people walking all over him. It was time to put the record straight and show these bastards what he was about. He had a promise to keep and the clock was ticking. It was just a matter of time. Tom had other things on his mind at the moment and his addiction reminded his body it was time to pay the price..

CHAPTER NINE

DOMINIC STARED OUT OF THE WINDOW. His mother's death had hit him hard and he couldn't see what was going on right in front of his eyes. His wife was forever filling his glass up with vodka. The crafty bitch. Numbing the pain she called it. Was this situation real? Dominic was numb anyway, his emotions dead inside. Reality was kicking in. He'd never see his mother again, never kiss her cheek. Never listen to her moaning about everything that was wrong in her life. The buried regrets inside him surfaced and the guilt was weighing him down, crippling him. Was he the best son he could have been? Helen hated his wife and he never once listened to her opinion. He shot a look over at Misty, examining her, weighing her up. Was his mother right about her, was she really the woman for him? It was debatable really.

Misty came to his side and passed him the glass. "Get one of these down your neck, love. It helped me when I lost my mam, it just takes the edge off it all. It will help you sleep."

Her husband struggled to raise a smile, his heart had been ripped out. He was trying to hold it together without breaking down. "Thanks love. It means a lot that you are caring for me. I'll be alright soon. I just think it's shock. Her face…" he paused, "…I just keep seeing her lying on that bed." His head sank onto his chest, his eyes clouding over. "Why do they say the word 'lost' when someone dies?

They're not lost, otherwise you would be able to find them again wouldn't you?"

Misty looked over at him and necked a large mouthful of her drink. She looked confused, had he lost the plot or something? Rob walked into the room and just caught the end of the conversation. He inhaled deeply and his chest expanded as his own heart revealed itself. "If my Lisa would have been lost I would have searched high and low for her, never ever given up looking for her. Being lost would have given me hope, death leaves nothing, no hope, no second chance, no nothing."

Bleeding hell, this was going from bad to worse. The three of them were grieving. Morbid really, it was dark and depressing. Misty sat back and twiddled her hair as she listened to her husband. "My mam had her faults and at times she did my head in but to end her life just like that, what the hell was she thinking? I never had her down for anything like that, never in a million years."

Misty choked up and her bottom lip quivered as she spoke. "They say there's five stages of grieving. I saw it on a programme on the television. I can't remember them all, but anger was one of them. And, to tell you the truth, I feel angry every bleeding day; angry that she opened her big trap, angry that she told one of our family's biggest secrets."

Rob screwed his face up and sat cracking his knuckles. No one was putting his woman down in front of him. Not now, not ever. He defended his woman. "She made a silly mistake, Misty. She would never have done that intentionally. We will get through this. We just need to be careful Charlotte doesn't get wind of it."

Misty slammed her hand down hard on the arm of the chair. She was on one and the vodka was talking now.

The rage inside her bubbled and her grip tightened on the cushion she held on her lap. "Rob, stop sticking up for her, you interfering old fart. You know as well as me that she fucked up. Tom will spill the beans no matter what. So don't you sit there telling me things will be sorted out. I've lied to my daughter all her life and you think she's just going to take that lying down? There'll be blue murders. Do you think she will ever forgive me for something like this? All she's ever known is Dominic being her dad. This will break her in two, fuck with her head. So please, don't sit there preaching to me about stuff you know nothing about."

Dominic closed his eyes, the noise crippling his ears. The abuse once again being hurled by his other half. He was sick to death of it, sick, sick, sick, of it. Why should he be quiet anymore? He had to put her in her place. His mother had told him to do it years ago and he should have listened to every word she said to him. "Just be quiet will you? I'm heartbroken here! My mother is dead and that is all I can think of right now. It's driving me nuts. I feel like I'm going insane here and all I can hear is you two bleeding bickering. Please, let me deal with this first before you two start piling more shit on me," he shot a look at Misty and shook his head. "Listen to you with your horrible, vile mouth again. Turn it in." Misty picked up the bottle of vodka as her husband continued speaking to her. "And don't think I haven't noticed you with the drink. From now on you're on the wagon. Every time I look at you, you're filling your glass up."

Misty flipped and retaliated. "Don't fucking start with me. I'm here trying to help you that's all. It's him over there who's starting the arguing. I think he should go back to his own home. We have enough of our own shit happening here without this old codger sticking his nose in."

Poor Rob, all he'd said was the truth. His face changed and he gritted his teeth over at her. "I'll go home now if you want. You asked me here, remember that. I never asked you to stay. You've always been trouble you have, no wonder your mam kept her distance from you. Evil your mouth is, bleeding terrible."

Misty smirked over at him. Rob shook his head in disbelief, there was no way he was getting into this now. He'd said his piece and felt much better knowing he'd fought his corner. He directed his words towards his son-in-law. "Dominic, I'll go in the morning if that's alright with you? It's late and my legs are playing up. It's the gout you know, puts me out of action every time I have a flare-up."

Misty let out a sarcastic laugh. "Oh, don't give me that old chestnut. My mam might have swallowed it but I won't. It's laziness it is. Nothing else. Just something you have self-diagnosed to get a bit of sympathy."

Rob was champing at the bit. He did have gout, he could take her to his doctors right now and show her his medical records. For years he'd suffered with it. The medical condition had stopped him doing a lot of stuff he loved doing. Walking, riding his bike. "Misty, you just get another drink and do what you do best. Dominic," he paused, "I'll leave in the morning as I said before. I don't know why you even bothered coming back here. She doesn't deserve you. Listen to the way she speaks to you. What's up with you lad, just walk away and leave her to it."

These were strong words from Rob, he'd never once said a bad word about anyone, she'd rattled his cage for sure. Misty gripped the neck of the bottle. For fuck's sake, she was going to launch it over his head, she was weighing him up and down. Dominic clocked her and caught her just in time. "Whoa, you crazy cow. What the fuck do you think you're doing?"

Rob hurried out of the room before he lost his temper. Misty shouted after him, fighting, struggling to break free. "Go on, fuck off to bed now you've caused world war three down here, you interfering old bastard. We were fine until you opened your big mouth. I've never liked you anyway. You're not my dad and never will be. My mam never married you because she saw you were a wanker too. You're a dickhead, not worth a toss."

Dominic had heard enough, he gripped the side of her face and squeezed her cheeks together with all his might, skin turning white. "Shut the fuck up. I'm sick to death of hearing your gob every bastard day and night. Button it, before I lose my rag with you. I mean it, carry on and watch what I do."

Misty was shocked, her eyes were popping out from her sockets. He'd never laid a finger on her in her past. She always knew he had a dark side, and here it was raising its ugly head. Her natural instincts were to attack him, defend herself, scratch his eyeballs out. But her hands were secured and she couldn't move a muscle. She'd underestimated him, he was as strong as an ox. "Let go of my hands you fucking nutter. Get off me."

His words were calm, slow and meaningful. "Calm the fuck down. Stop it, honest Misty. I've had enough." She was like a wild woman, he'd crossed the line.

Who the hell was this man? She didn't know him anymore. "Take your filthy hands off me. You'll never ever lay a finger on me again. Go back to your mam's house. Go and live in misery just like she did."

This was way below the belt, for crying out loud he'd just buried the poor woman. Dominic realised what had just happened and froze as his fingers slowly unfolded from around her cheeks. Sweat on his forehead, pouring down the sides of his head. "Misty, I'm–" she never let him finish.

"Just go, you're not welcome here anymore." Just at that second, half a brick come crashing through the window. Sharp blades of glass spun in the air. Dominic ran to his wife's side, covering her body with his. There was a silence in the room. Footsteps running about upstairs.

Rob was shouting from the landing. "It was him. I just watched the dirty rat with my own eyes through the window. It was a drive-by."

Dominic ran to the back door and yanked it open. His feet sprinted down the garden path. Everyone could hear him now, he was loud and ready for whatever was waiting for him. His eyes shot one way, then another. He could see a car in the distance driving off. A man with his head sticking out of it, laughing. "Oi, plastic dad, tell my niece I'll be coming to see her soon."

Dominic could see Tom, he was blatant. What a cheeky bastard he was. Who did he think he was, just blurting stuff like that out for all to hear? His blood was boiling and he motored towards the moving vehicle.

"Come on then. Get out of the car and let's have a straightener. A one on one, me and you." The large vein at the side of his neck was pumping with rage. Dominic ripped his t-shirt off and stood there like a bare-knuckle fighter, a gypsy. Tom was gone. He'd done what he intended to do. They got the message alright and knew this smackhead would be back sooner or later. It was D-day, there was nothing else left to do. They had to tell Charlotte who her real dad was.

Rico walked Charlotte home. It was late and he'd planned to do some coursework when he got back home. He'd let things slip lately and exams were just around the corner. It was time to knuckle down and get the grades he needed to make his life complete. Standing on the corner of the street, he watched Charlotte go inside her house. He waved his hand above his head and turned on his feet to set off home. This lad was in love. Every minute of every day she was all he thought about. He couldn't think straight anymore. Love was a strange emotion and until he'd met Charlotte, he never knew it could be so intense. The weather was bad tonight and the wind was howling past his ears. Zipping his jacket up, he dropped his head. The roads seemed quiet, not many cars about. It was after midnight though. Most normal people would be tucked up in their beds by now getting some shut-eye. Rico cut across the grass verge that led him near Tavistock Square. The place was still alive with drug dealers and kids who had no homes to go to. There was music playing loudly and motorbikes skidding about. Without any hesitation, he started to walk across it.

Rico kept his head low, aware of the activities going on at the side of him. A voice, shouting, causing his heart to beat faster. "Oi, cocky balls. Get over here while I have a word with you." Rico twisted his head to the man not far from where he stood. Did they want him, had he misheard them, he wasn't sure? Rico looked behind him, there was no one else there. He took a few more steps forward. The voice again and this time it was angry. "Do I have to come over there and drag you here you daft wanker?" Okay, now he knew they were talking to him. He swallowed hard and dug his iPhone deep into his coat pocket. There was no way they were having that away. It was his pride and joy and something he treasured. Rico walked to the dark corner of the square. There were two men stood there smoking weed. The smell was strong and he coughed a few times as the ganja filled his lungs. A hand reached over from the shadows and gripped him by the throat. "You've got some front coming on here. Did you think you could just take her from under my nose and fuck all would happen to you?"

Rico was confused, surely this was a big mix up. "I don't know what you're going on about."

"Smash his fucking head in Paul. Go on, I'll keep dog and make sure no one hears the wanker screaming," his sidekick shouted out.

Paul went nose to nose with Rico, his warm stale breath in his face. "She's mine, do you hear me? Mine!"

Oh, the penny had finally dropped now. Charlotte had mentioned this guy to him before. Paul's arse fell out and words failed him. Could he strike a blow and hope for the best? Maybe break free and make a run for it. No, he would be caught within seconds and twisted up. He had to face it. Paul headbutted Rico, there was no more talking, it was time to get down to business. He'd show this muppet what he was about once and for all. Rico fell to the ground like a lead balloon. His attacker's feet were swinging hard into his body, booting fuck out of him. Why was nobody stopping this? There were people stood about just watching as if this was an everyday occurrence. They were shitbags, every single one of them. They should have been on the blower to the dibble instead of just standing there looking like spare parts. Paul Jones picked Rico up by the back of his jeans and drop-kicked him for the last time. His body fell to the ground with an almighty thud.

Paul dragged his head up so he could see his eyes and spat into his face. "That's just a warning, next time I'll make sure you don't see the daylight again. Keep away from my woman! Do you hear me? Keep well away."

Rico was barely conscious, his eyes rolling to the back of his head. Deep red claret oozed out of the side of his mouth. Feet started pounding the pavements from behind them. It was Tom. "Leave it out, lad. Come on, he's had enough. Awww, look at the state of him. No need for that, seriously, fucking liberty-taker you are Paul."

Tom bent down and cradled his nephew in his hands. Paul Jones stood over them both and let out a menacing laugh. He licked the bright red blood from the edge of his finger. "Fuck me, a junkie with feelings. What's the world coming to!"

His mate chuckled and patted the side of his arm. It was job done, there was no need to hang about anymore. Paul took a few deep breaths to calm down and scratched the end of his nose. "Take the wanker home and clean him up. One word from him to the Old Bill and his family will have their door boomed in. You know the crack, so sort it out."

Tom was licking arse now. There was no way he was getting on the wrong side of this head the ball. "Yeah, sorted. I'll make sure he keeps his mouth shut."

Paul dug deep in his pocket and threw a small wrap of smack over at Tom. "Good lad, you know it makes sense."

The attacker walked off. Tom clutched hold of the drugs and rammed them into his pocket. He slapped the side of the victim's cheek.

"Rico, wake up! Can you hear me, wake up."

There was no response, the kid was sparkled. Once Paul Jones was out of sight a few of the other kids came running over to fill Tom in. "He wasted him, mate. Honest, twatted him all over the show. He didn't stand a chance. I swear, a few knockout blows he gave him. He'll be lucky to breathe again after that. You better book an undertaker."

Tom growled and shook his head. He was always tooled up and half of him wanted to run after this bully and stick his blade deep into his back. Dig it deep, dig it into his lungs so the cunt never breathed again. Tom lifted Rico to his feet, he was coming around now. His words were slurred, he didn't know where he was. "You're alright pal. Uncle Tom is with you. I'll sort you out, don't you worry about that. You just take good deep breaths." Rico draped his arm around Tom's neck and his legs wobbled. This was a bad attack. Paul had half-killed the poor sod. One of the lads from the square helped Tom get his nephew walking. He agreed to walk all the way home with Tom too. He was only knee-high to a grasshopper too. A small kid with a big heart. Rico was coughing blood, white as a ghost.

Melanie was hysterical when she first caught sight of Tom at the front door. He was covered in blood. Rico was bleeding from a few places but as of yet, he'd not worked out where it was coming from. "Oh my God Tom, what the hell has happened? Who is he?"

Tom just barged past her, gagging for breath. "Close that fucking front door. Go on, before anyone comes in."

Melanie waddled to the hallway, she was white as a

sheet. "Tell me what is going on Tom! Who the fuck is he? Please tell me the front door is not going to come flying off its hinges any second now? I'm shitting it here, fill me in please?"

Tom was flapping. Had Paul seen where he lived now? What if he wanted to finish this lad off? Nothing would stop him once he'd got a beef with someone. He was a mental bastard and it was well known in the area that he liked his victims to suffer. Twisted in the head he was. "Get me a cloth or something to wipe this claret from his head. I need to see where he's bleeding from."

Melanie looked concerned. "Tom, I think he needs to go to the hospital. He's in a bad way."

He growled at her. "Just get a towel or something. Fuck me Florence Nightingale, since when have you had any medical training? It probably looks worse than it is. Move it then, don't just stand there like a gawp! He's fucking bleeding half to death here. Hurry up!"

Melanie sprinted about the living room like a headless chicken. She gripped a grey, stale-smelling bath towel from the side of the sofa and ran back to the injured man. Tom didn't look at it twice, he just swiped it across Rico's head. "Come on son, you're not that bad. I'll look after you just like I used to look after your old man when he'd come unstuck."

Melanie stood picking her black leggings out of the crack of her arse. She turned her head to the side and got a better look at the lad. Even with all the blood over him, she could tell he was a looker. "Get him a cup of water, in fact, get me one too."

Melanie followed orders and off she went into the kitchen. Tom held Rico up and patted the wet towel across his head. "I've had bigger scratches on my arse, lad. It's only a little cut. Fuck me, I thought you was a goner. What the fuck have you done to Jones for him to do this to you?"

Rico was helped to his feet and sat on the sofa. He hadn't clocked who Tom was yet or even processed the fact that he'd been attacked. Melanie handed him a cup of water. Her eyes were fixed firmly on him. This guy was sexy, handsome. Rico's hands were shaking as he tried to take a sip and Tom had to step in to help him. Rico was in shock. "Just take a few gobfuls. Water always helps when you've had the living daylights beaten out of you." Maybe he was right.

After a few sips, his head might start to return to normal. He studied Tom and his girlfriend. His eyes were wide open now and panic set in. Had Tom assaulted him, where the hell was he? He was having a full-blown panic attack, he tried to stand to his feet but stumbled. "I want to leave, I want to go home."

Tom stood near the living room door and blocked the exit. "No way mate. You're in no condition to go anywhere. Just sit back down and chill. I'm not letting you move until I know you're alright. You're not safe out there anymore."

Melanie could see the fear in his eyes and spoke in a calm tone. "Tom didn't do this to you. He helped you. He brought you back here to sort you out."

"Yeah, that's right. Paul Jones attacked you, not me. He fucking wasted you too from what I witnessed. I swear on my life, I was going to run after him and stab the cunt up."

Melanie covered her mouth with her hand. "This isn't your fight Tom. We have enough troubles of our own without you bringing shit to our door. Jones is a fucking lunatic."

Tom's nostrils flared. "This is my nephew we're talking about here. I have to protect him. Our Gordon would have shit a brick if he was alive. Do you think he would have just sat here and let this go by without doing something? Nah, not a cat in hell's chance. He would have had the prick by his balls now. Shot him up."

Melanie reached over and grabbed a fag. Before she lit it, she snarled over at Tom. "Well, Gordon isn't here is he and I don't want you getting involved. Send the kid home, let him deal with his own shit."

Tom sighed and stared at Rico who was starting to calm down. "Yeah, I remember now. Paul Jones, he said to keep away from his woman."

"Oh, I might have known there would be a woman involved in all this. For fuck's sake Rico, you took a good hiding for a bit of skirt. Cart her and tell him he's welcome to her."

Rico needed to sit down, he felt lightheaded again, he thought he was going to spew his ring up. "I'm not giving Charlotte up. She's not been with this guy for ages or so I believe. No way, I love her. I'll fight for her too."

Tom blew a laboured breath and held his head high, looking proud. "Yep, you've got your father's blood running through your veins alright. You tell him kid, tell him to get to fuck."

Melanie growled as she watched Tom from the corner of her eye, he was doing her head in now. "Stay the night here, Rico. If that Paul is on the rampage then don't be a sitting duck for him. Keep your head down for a few days and tell no fucker where you are." Rico was in the moment now, listening to every word his uncle was telling him. He was scared, his insides churning at the thought of another beating. Tom continued speaking. "I'll nip around to see your mam tomorrow and tell her you're spending a bit of time with me, she'll be cool with that."

"Over my dead body are you going to see Francesca. You two have history and from what I can gather, I don't think you ever really got over her."

Rico's mouth dropped. He looked over at Tom and squirmed. Was this true, had his mother really slept with this hobo? No, he needed some more information. But, not now, it could wait until he was alone with him. Melanie sucked hard on her cigarette and you could see she was insecure. After a minute or two she sighed, "he can get his head down on the sofa then. Tom, get him a few coats from the hallway to throw over him to keep him warm. The gas has gone again and I'm skint so he'll have to make do like we have to."

Tom started to relax. Here was his chance now, time to spend with his blood, his nephew. But first he had to sort himself out, inject the poison into his body yet again. He dug his hand deep into his tracksuit bottoms and pulled out the drugs. Melanie's eyes lit up. She was on the verge of roasting too. She snatched the small bag of brown powder from his hands and went to the corner of the room. Tom started to tie a shoelace around his arm, getting ready for a hit. Rico's eyes were heavy and although he wanted to go home, his body was too weak to move, his head was pounding and his eyes were closing. His body fell onto the sofa and it took seconds before he was ready for sleep. His eyes misted over and he could see the shadows of Tom and Melanie not far from where he lay.

CHAPTER TEN

MISTY LAY IN BED and her eyes were red raw. Dominic was at the side of her and both of them were still fully dressed. It had been a long night for sure and after hours of arguing and name-calling, both of them had come to bed to get some rest. Dominic reached over and touched her hands. She moved him straight away. She wasn't ready to make friends yet. "We need to tell her Misty. Let's just be open and honest and tell Charlotte about Gordon. She'll understand, she has to."

Misty swallowed hard and the hairs on the back of her neck stood on end. "How can I tell her something like this? She'll never forgive me."

"I'll be with you every step of the way, just like I've always been."

"I can't face it. It will break her heart in two."

Dominic rolled over on his side and looked deep into her eyes. "We will get through this. We've been through so much together and we need to support each other. Misty, I want you to get help. You can't deny this anymore. You have a drink problem."

Misty swallowed hard and now she was ready to make friends. She stroked a single finger across his chest. "I know. It's just got a grip of me and I thought I could handle it but I can't."

Dominic pulled her closer to his body and kissed the top of her head. "We'll get through this together. I'm here to support you. I'll never walk away. I love you too much."

Misty held back the tears. Why was this man so nice to her? He never, ever, saw the bad in her and he looked at her with rose-tinted glasses. He was her world, her knight in shining armour. "I'm sorry about last night, love. I hate myself for treating you like that. My emotions just got the better of me and I lost it."

"No, it's me who should be apologising. I know your head has been all over the place and I pushed you to the limits. I need to say sorry to Rob too. I bet he's sick to death of the way I've been treating him lately. He just always seems to be there when my head goes. I'll say I'm sorry later and hope he can forgive me."

Dominic brought her fingers up to his mouth and kissed her fingertips. "It can all be fixed, we can come through this together. When Charlotte comes home tonight, we can sit her down and go through it all."

Misty blew her breath and closed her eyes. "Alright, I'm scared. So bleeding scared."

Charlotte looked at her screen on her phone again. She'd sent Rico so many messages and not once had he replied to her. Had he gone off her, found somebody new? Mandy watched her friend with eager eyes, she could see something was bothering her. "Why the sad face, what's up?"

Charlotte rammed her mobile phone back into her pocket after reading a text from her mother. "Nothing, just a bit pissed off really. My mam and dad want a serious word with me tonight. Apparently it's something that we all need to sit down for and be adults."

"Bleeding hell, it's a bit late to be telling you about the birds and the bees isn't it? Talking about bees, where is Rico today? He's usually buzzing around you by this time?"

"I don't know. He's not texted me all night and nothing this morning either. It's not like him at all."

"I told you that guy was a player. He's got the gift of the gab too. I've heard all the sloppy stuff he says to you and it makes my stomach churn. Honestly, you mark my words, I bet he's got another woman on the go."

"Fuck off Mandy. Don't be saying stuff like that."

"It's true, I say what I see I do."

"Well you can see how distraught I am so don't rub salt in the wounds."

"Charlotte, I've never lied to you ever and that's why we have a great friendship. I seriously think he's banging someone else. Go on, why hasn't he texted or rung you?" Mandy had a serious expression and opened her eyes wide. "There you go, I rest my case."

Charlotte folded her hand tightly across her chest, she was in a strop. Her class was about to start soon and even now she was still scouting the area, looking out for Rico to appear. Mandy stood up as one of the lads she knew from the estate came rushing past her. "Alright Mandy, did you hear about Reeks getting wasted last night by Paul Jones? One of the clan who was there told me. I swear he fucking murdered him. Word on the street is that Reeks is dead. No one has seen sight or sound of him. Jason is going mental."

Mandy gripped hold of his coat as he tried to walk past her. "Whoa, hold your horses! Who told you what? Take your time and tell me properly."

Charlotte was there with them now and the colour drained from her cheeks. The youth blurted it out again, exaggerating every word he spoke. "He kicked fuck out of

Rico. Headbutted him, the lot. Even now there is all blood stains on the floor in the square where he dropped him." Charlotte held the bottom of her stomach. The food inside her stomach was churning, she was ready to spew up.

She spoke directly to the lad now herself. "Who did it to him, tell me who done him over?" For fuck's sake, shoot the messenger or what. Here he was just telling them both a bit of gossip and he was the one getting a good old bollocking. Mandy held Charlotte back. "Just hang on. Mark is going to tell us what he knows. Hold your bleeding horses and let him tell me again so we can take it all in."

Mark was sorry he'd opened his mouth. He took a deep breath and made sure no one was listening to him chatting about stuff that had gone on the night before. "Paul Jones left him for dead. Fuck knows what for but my mate told me he knocked him straight out with one killer punch."

Mandy carried on talking to the informer as Charlotte ran to the nearest toilet. How could he do this to him? Rico was no match for Paul. He was no fighter, he was gentle. Charlotte kicked the toilet door open and fell to her knees, she was gagging into the toilet bowl. Mandy rushed in behind her and started to rub the middle of her back. "What a big daft bastard he is. Rico is a nobody, why would he do that to him the evil bastard?"

Charlotte wiped her mouth with the cuff from her blouse and started to inhale big mouthfuls of air. "I need fresh air. My body is on fire. Help me up, get me outside please before I curl up in a small ball and die." Mandy helped her up from the floor. Fuck education today. This was a code red and she needed to find out how her boy was. No wonder he hadn't texted or rung her. Why did she ever think he'd binned her, their love was strong. Charlotte's head was working overtime. Maybe he was lying in a hospital bed barely conscious, maybe he'd forgotten his name. What if he hated her now? This was all her fault. "I need to go to his house," she gasped.

"Paul will go sick at you if you turn up there kicking off."

"I mean to Reek's house. I'm not arsed about Paul yet. He can go on the backburner. I've got plans for him. I'll shoot the cunt. You just watch, I'll take him down. Who the fuck does he think he is!" her head dropped and her eyes flooded. "I just need to see my boy. Help me out. Ring a taxi or something before my head falls off. I just need to make sure he's alright." Mandy rang a taxi and stood out on the road looking for it, she was edgy and in a panic. Charlotte was texting, her head was all over the place. She was in a world of her own. Would he blame her for the attack now, hate her, cart her? Was this the end for them both?

★

Francesca was wide awake, sat at the kitchen table nursing her cup of coffee. She'd throttle the little shit when she got her hands on him. Fancy not even letting her know he was staying out! She bet he was with her, lay in her bed without a care in the world for his poor mother's mental health. He knew she would have been worried to death about him. Anyway, the minute he walked through that front door he was getting told, put right in his place. Clipped around his ear. She'd stood by long enough now and there was no way in this world she was letting this tart lead her boy astray. Maybe it had been a bad decision to come back to Manchester. He was settled where he was, he had nice friends who wanted to make something out of their lives, not layabouts, or thieving bastards like he was mixing with now.

A knock at the front door shocked her. She slammed her mug of coffee down on the table and marched into the hallway with a face like thunder. Where was his key, was he having a laugh or what? She rolled her sleeves up and was ready to bite her son's head off. He'd had a few clouts in the past when he got a bit lippy but this was something way out of character for him. Francesca opened the front door ready to go ape. She looked at the two girls and stepped outside the front door. Her son must be hiding. What a shitbag he was! Fancy sending these two first to make sure the coast was clear. Francesca stood next to Charlotte with both hands placed firmly on her hips. She hissed over at her. "Tell him to come out of his hiding place before I start shouting. He knows what I'm like if he doesn't come home all night. Not a wink of sleep I've had. I hope he's happy now! Go on, shout to him to get his arse over here before I snap."

Mandy looked at Charlotte and shrugged her shoulders. She was going to say something but decided at the last minute to keep her mouth shut. This wasn't her war, it was Charlotte's. Mandy nudged her friend in the waist to say something. "He's not with us Francesca."

"Well, I suggest you go and get the dickhead and tell him to come and face me. I mean, you know what I'm like. I thought you would have had the decency to ring me at least and let me know he was staying at your house. Look at the state of me, black circles under my eyes, eye bags the size of pillows. All night long I've tossed and turned worrying about him. But you won't give a flying fuck will you, when your knickers are down on the floor."

Bleeding hell, that was a bit strong. Charlotte snarled at her but kept her calm. "He's not been with me for your information. And as for my knickers being down, I think you're cheeky even saying that. I'm no slapper you know."

Francesca walked closer to her and tilted her head slightly. Did these two think she was wet behind the ears or what? She knew the score, she was a wise head. "I hope you're not sticking up for him here. He knows the rules, so stop fucking about and tell him I want to see him now."

Charlotte swallowed hard, her words jittery. She had to tell her the truth, get it out before she lost her bottle. "He was involved in a fight last night. It must have been after he walked me home."

Francesca froze, blood draining from her face. She digested the information. Not a sound, no movement. Mandy stood biting her fingernails. This was about to kick off, she was sure of it. If this woman so much as laid a single finger on her bestie she'd one-bomb her. "Did you say he was involved in a fight?"

"Francesca, I didn't know a thing about it until this morning. I came here to see if he's alright?"

"So, where the fuck is he if he's not with you?" Francesca ran inside the house and they could hear her screaming and shouting from inside.

Charlotte made her way inside the front door and Mandy dragged her back by her arm. "Don't be going in there on your own. She'll attack you. You just seen her, she's a madhead. Just hang fire and see what she's up to. If need be I'll put her on her arse if she starts with us."

Charlotte struggled to break free. She twisted her body and growled at Mandy. "She's just in shock that's all. He's her world and she's a bit overprotective with him. She won't lay a finger on me. And if she does I can handle myself."

Mandy backed off and sighed. "You can say that again. He's like a fucking big baby."

"Mandy, shut up will you. Come in with me and let's see if we can get to the bottom of it all."

Francesca was putting her trainers on. She shot a look at Charlotte as she entered the front room. "I swear to you now, if my boy is hurt, heads will roll. Who has done him in? I'm not scared, tell me now because when I get my hands on them I'll cut the fucker up?"

Mandy was eager to tell this woman anything she knew, she didn't want to get on the wrong side of her either. "It was Paul Jones. He's one of the main heads around here. You need to know he's no dickhead and he wouldn't think twice about hitting an older woman. He twatted my mate's sister once, busted her lip, five stitches she had."

Francesca gritted her teeth together and shot a look over at Mandy. She could fight with the best of them. Gordon had leathered her for most of their relationship so she knew how to protect herself, to strike a blow. "Like I'm arsed if he hits a woman or not. We can all be sick in the head if we want to. I swear, I'll cut his balls off when I get my hands on him. Where will he be now?"

Charlotte shrugged her shoulders. There was no way she was admitting he was her ex-boyfriend either, not yet anyway. Mandy jumped into the conversation. "He'll be chilling on the square. If he's not there now, he'll be there later. He's always there at some point during the day."

Francesca marched around the front room in a panic. "My car keys, where the fuck are they?" Both the girls started to help her look for them, she was a mess and on the verge of a nervous breakdown.

"Here they are," Charlotte shouted.

"Right, you two can come with me and show me where this clown is."

"Do you think we should ring the police? Rico could be anywhere, he could be lay in a ditch for all we know," Charlotte said.

Francesca looked over at Mandy and then back at Charlotte. This girl could be right, her poor son, her poor innocent son. Was it time to ring the Old Bill or what?

★

Tom stretched his arms over his head and yawned. His breath was stinking as he slid his furry tongue along his dry cracked lips. After sitting thinking for a few seconds, he remembered his nephew was downstairs. He had plans now, he had him in his grip. Nobody fucked with him, he was going to have the last laugh for sure. Tom stretched over to the side of the bed and looked at Melanie. God she was ugly. A right porker. He squirmed as his body touched hers. He froze, no way did he want to wake her up, she was a sex maniac. Two or three times a day she wanted a shag, there was no pleasing her, she was a porn queen, sick twisted stuff she was into. But she cared for him, helped him out when he was on his arse. Helped him feed his habit. That's why he was still with her. Slowly, he lifted the duvet up from his body and slid out of the bed like a snake. Melanie was dead to the world and didn't stir. This man was all skin and bone, you could actually see his ribcage, every single bone in his chest. He was underweight and ready for the knacker's yard for sure.

Tom opened the living room door slowly and peered inside as he blew his hot breath into his cupped hands. The room was dark and he could just about see the body lying sprawled on the sofa. Nipping into the kitchen, he started jumping up and down on the spot trying to keep warm. This gaff was freezing, it was like the Antarctic. No heat had passed through these pipes in a long time. It was usually a choice of buying some gas for the heating or scoring. The rest was history, drugs always took priority over anything else in his life. Tom made two cups of coffee and walked back into the front room with the mugs hooked around his fingers. Steam rose up, hitting his face. Placing them both down on the table, he walked to the window and yanked the curtains open. The light was bright and he squirmed as the daylight hit his eyes.

Another day, another dollar.

Tom had a ritual every single morning. Cig and a brew. Nothing ever really happened until he'd had both. He usually sat there for half an hour planning out his day's graft. Drugs, drugs and more drugs. All he ever wanted was to get twisted, off his trolley so his mind was numb and nothing from his past crept up on him. The more he earned, the more he scored. His eyes shot to Rico and he was studying him. Tom launched a pillow over at the sofa, hoping to wake him up. "Come on lad, wakey-wakey. Rise and shine."

Rico stirred and when he turned to face him, Tom's face creased at the sides. This kid was fucked up big time. His eyes were swollen, every inch of his face was bruised, dark purple, and he had bloodshot eyes. The wanker had gone to town on him for sure. Kicked the fuck out of him. Tom sucked hard on his cigarette and blew a thick cloud of grey smoke out in front of him. He held a cunning look in his eyes as he spoke. "Listen pal. You'll have to stay here until all this blows over. Word on the street is, he's not finished with you yet and there is a price on your head. I'll nip and tell your mam where you are later but for now, you need to lie low. That means tell no fucker where you are. No phone calls, no text messages, fuck all. I swear, if that pricks gets wind that you're here he'll boom the front door in and finish you off. I'm putting my neck on the line here for you, so you need to show me some respect and stick to what I've told you. I wouldn't do this for anyone else, but you're my blood, part of me. So, I'll make an exception." What the fuck was he going on about? He was lying for sure, he'd made the whole story up. There was no such thing. Nobody had put a price on this kid's head, nobody.

Rico moaned as his body crippled with pain. Every inch of him was aching, every movement caused him pain. "Thank you Tom. Just let my mam know I'm safe that's all. She'll be out of her mind with worry if she doesn't know where I am."

"I'll do that as soon as. Give me your phone. I need to switch it off before anyone rings you. Tricky cunts they are and we need to make sure every area is covered. It's bad news this, fucking bad news. The last thing anyone needs is that crazy fucker on their trail." Rico was caught up in the whole affair and followed his orders without any hesitation. He passed the handset over to his uncle. Tom examined it with cunning eyes, the pound signs registering in his mind. He placed the iPhone down the front of his boxer shorts and chuckled over to Rico. "No one will find it there. Not even Melanie. I mean, come on, we both know I'm only banging her out of goodwill don't we? Rotten she is, but 'ey, don't ever repeat that. She'd cut my dick off if she heard me."

Rico started to smile but as he did his cheekbones were flooded with pain. "Ouch, what the hell has happened to me?"

Tom looked concerned. "I'll get Melanie to sort you out some strong painkillers. Once that swelling goes down you'll be sorted. I've been worse than that, trust me. I was on death's door once when I got done in from a few guys from Blackley. Four of them mashed me up good and proper. For fuck all might I add," his eyebrows raised slightly before he continued. "Mistaken identity it was. They said I robbed some gaff but I never did. I have morals. I would never stoop that low. What do people take me for?"

What a lying, cheating man this was. His criminal record was living proof that this thug was a house thief, a burglar. He was a sneak thief too. Tom prowled the area late at night and looked out for windows that had been left open, doors that were left unlocked. Once he was inside he would take anything of value, he didn't care how sentimental anything was to the occupiers. He'd never admit that though. No, Tom made out he was a grafter to everyone, that he stole only from factories, shops and rich businessmen. Everyone knew the truth though, nothing was safe when he was around. His own mother had banished him from their family home years ago. He robbed her blind and she didn't trust him as far she could throw him. He could never be trusted, ever. He was a wrong-un.

Rico lay on the sofa and there was no way he was moving. He could have done with a hospital visit but Tom had told him it was too dangerous to take him outside. He'd pumped him full of tablets, some of which he didn't even have a clue what they were used for. But he made sure of one thing though, sleeping tablets were present. He wanted Rico out for the count, like a zombie. For crying out loud, he was drugging him up, knocking him out any chance he got. Tom got ready and sneaked a peep over at Rico. He could see his eyelids flickering. The sleepers were kicking in and he knew he would be asleep for at least the next four or five hours. Tablets like this were easy to obtain. A few quid here and there and you could get enough sleepers to knock a large animal out for days. All the junkies sold their medication for a quick earner. Tablets were neither use nor ornament to them. They wanted the hard stuff, the brown, the smack, the crack. Tiptoeing out from the living room, Tom zipped up his coat. This iPhone would get him a good few quid and take the pressure off his criminal activities for at least a few hours. There was no way he wanted to get nicked today, especially when a plan was unfolding in his mind. The front door slammed shut and shook the house. Rico could barely open his eyes, his eyes were rolling and his mouth was slightly open, slaver hanging out of the side of it, dribbling.

Melanie walked into the room scratching her head. "Tom, where are you?" Nothing, no reply. She plonked down on the sofa and shot a look over at Rico. There was something in her eyes that wasn't quite right. "Rico, are you awake, have you seen Tom?" She sat forward in her seat and watched him carefully to see if there was any response. Nothing, he was away with the fairies. Her hand stroked up and down her neck slowly, and her breathing quickened. She was acting weird. Standing to her feet, she took small steps to where Rico lay. With her body bent slightly, she started to click her fingers in front of his eyes.

"Yo, are you still alive, are you awake or what?" Rico never flinched. She poked a single fat finger into his shoulder and pushed his body back slightly. Nothing, he was dead to the world. Melanie licked her front teeth slowly and quickly looked around the room. What on earth was going on here, something was not right. She blew her warm breath onto her hands and rubbed them together with speed. She slipped them quickly down the front of Rico's tracksuit bottoms and rummaged about. Her cheeks were flustered and her nostrils flared as she touched him up. This was one sick bitch, twisted in her head. What the fuck was she playing at? Rico never moved a muscle as she sank her thin scabby lips onto his. She was getting off on him for sure, her hand tweaked her nipple and she started to groan as she touched her private area with fanned fingers. What a dirty, scruffy, horrible bastard.

Francesca screeched into the car park opposite Tavistock square. Charlotte and Mandy were in the back of the car and for most of the journey they never said a word, they were shitting it. Francesca was raging and she cursed all of the way. She was going ballistic. "I'll show this cunt what I'm about. How the fuck did he think he could hurt my boy and have no comebacks? Things never change around here and I can call some favours in to get this bastard shot up in two fucking minutes. In fact, let me ring somebody now."

Charlotte nudged Mandy in the waist and opened her eyes wide. She covered her mouth with her fingers and kept her voice low. "This is bad. I don't think she knows who she's messing with. It will be like a lamb to the slaughter."

Francesca looked back at them through the rear view mirror and started to speak on her phone. "Hiya, it's me. I need a big favour." Francesca listened to the voice at the other end of the phone and her fingers started to squeeze hard at the steering wheel. "You owe me, remember what I know about you. I need help, do you hear me, I need you to help me?"

The call ended suddenly and Francesca's head crashed onto the steering wheel. She was alone now, she had no backup, there was no one to watch her back. "Are you alright? Is there anything I can do to help?" Francesca twisted her head over her shoulder and her eyes were dancing with madness. She was gunning for Charlotte, trying to grip her, reaching her hand into the back of the car trying to slap her.

Mandy moved forward and as always, she protected her friend. "Whoa, what the fuck are you playing at? Charlotte isn't to blame for this, so take your hands off her before I start. If you want beef love, I'll give you some fucking beef."

Francesca wriggled about in her seat and she was still going for gold. Mandy was trying to restrain her. "Get your fucking hands off me. It's her fault my son is missing. I knew she was trouble the minute I set eyes on her."

Charlotte found her voice now and there was no way she was letting anyone talk to her like this, no matter who it was. She was loud and holding nothing back. "Nah, it's not my fault. I've not been seeing Paul fucking Jones now for ages. So don't be blaming me. The guy is an idiot, he's a crank. He just thinks he's a law onto himself, nobody can stop him. Not even you."

"I'll fucking stop him. You mark my words. We can all

be sick when we want to be."

Mandy pushed Francesca back in her seat and made sure she couldn't get grip of Charlotte again. She tried calming her down, making her see sense. "Don't go rushing in. He's a nutter and he wouldn't think twice about twatting you all over the square. Don't you listen woman. No one will help you either, if you're thinking that will happen. Trust me, everyone will turn a blind eye where he's concerned. We're not stepping a foot on the square either, so you're on your lonesome. We know the score, obviously you don't."

There was an eerie silence, just the sound of kids shouting in the distance. Francesca sucked in a large mouthful of air and gripped the door handle. "Like I'm arsed. I'm going to see him myself. You two stay where you are. I've never needed anyone to help me and I don't plan to start asking for any help now."

Francesca was gone. Mandy rested her head on the cold window and banged it slightly. "As I said before, she's a fucking lamb to the slaughter. Oh well, she was told so it's her own fault."

Charlotte was watching her march across the square. "I should go with her. I can't just sit here watching. She doesn't know the crack around here and Rico will go mad if he knows I've done nothing to help his mother."

"Be it on your own back then. There is no way in this world I'm getting involved in this shit and if you know what's good for you, you'd stay well away too."

"I'm going Mandy. I have to."

"Dickhead you are, don't get involved I said." It was too late now, Charlotte had already opened the car door and started to follow Francesca.

Francesca's heels clipped along the concrete flags,

she was raging inside and balls of sweat started to trickle down the side of her head. This was the girl she used to be; ruthless, ready to attack anyone who stepped in her way. She was fearless, her eyes flicking one way, then the other. Where the fuck was he? She gripped a teenager who was riding past her on his mountain bike and roared into his face. "Paul Jones, where is he. Tell me where the prick is?"

The young male scuffled about and removed her hands from him. Who the fuck was she, thinking she could just tackle him like that? "Oi, touch me again and I'll put you on your arse! Wow, if you wasn't a woman you would have got spat at in the face."

She repeated herself. "Where can I find Paul Jones, just tell me where he is?" The youth chuckled loudly and pointed over to a silver car on the other side of the road. This was probably just another woman he'd been banging, had over, or had their child selling drugs for him. It was just the normal everyday shit that someone was gunning for the main head in the area. "Go and ask them over there, they should know," he flicked his eyes to the other side of the square as he continued, voice low. "But lady, do yourself a favour and lose that cocky attitude because if you carry on like that, you won't last two minutes round here. Trust me, lose the attitude before you land up in hospital."

Charlotte had caught her up now and she knew the lad, she smiled at him. "Alright Marco, what's happening?"

Marco nodded over at her and smiled. "Is this crazy bitch with you or what?"

Charlotte smirked and knew she had to play this down to get any further. "Yeah, she's just a bit pissed off. You know what it's like when you see your arse. Just ignore her, she means no harm."

Marco nodded and mounted his bike again. "She's looking for Jones. I've told her to go over to the runners, they'll know where he is."

At last, a bit of information to go on. See, it was all about who you knew, not what you knew. "Cheers for that Marco. I'll catch up with you sometime. Sorry about her, as I said, she's a livewire." That was enough for now and the conversation ended there and then. Francesca stood frozen, her body quivering. She had to find her inner strength, show no fear if she was going to come face to face with this monster.

Charlotte walked to her side and patted the middle of her arm in the hope of calming her down, to show she cared. "Have you thought about this properly? I know you're not behind the door or anything but this isn't the way to do things around here. I'm as worried as you about Rico but if you go over there shouting and bawling at that prick, he will make you a laughing stock. Trust me, I know. He's got no respect for anybody."

Tom could be seen in the distance making his way towards them and he seemed in a hurry. As he met them he could see something was wrong with Francesca. "What's going on here then. Why the sad face?"

His grubby fingers touched the side of Francesca's cheek and she squirmed and came back to the moment within seconds. "Tom, listen, fuck off I'm in no mood for you today. Rico has been done in and nobody has seen him. My head is all over the place so fuck off unless you can help."

He acted shocked, concerned. "When, who done him in, why? Give me a fucking name and I'll chop the cunt up."

Here he was, her knight in shining armour, here to save the day. Francesca had to relay everything she knew now, anything to try and find her boy. "Paul Jones gave Rico a belt last night, that's all I know. He's not been home all night Tom, where the fuck is he?" She broke down crying and the tears flooded from her eyes. Tom looked over at Charlotte and raised his eyes as he comforted Francesca.

His nostrils flared as he inhaled her sweet perfume, the smell that took him back to when he was her man, her lover. His eyes closed slowly as he sucked in every ounce of her feminine fragrance. "Ssssh now. I'll help you sort stuff out. Since when have I ever let you down. I'll always be here for you, no matter what."

Francesca rested her head on his chest and sobbed her heart out. She was desperate and all she wanted was her boy back home safe. Charlotte looked uncomfortable as she felt the glare from this man. It was more than just a look, he was looking deep into her soul, it was spooky. She stood fidgeting. She didn't know where to look. "I'll go back to the car Francesca. In fact, me and Mandy will go and have a word with a few of the lads on the estate to see if they've seen anything of him. If I find anything out I'll ring you, or I'll come straight round to your house."

There was no reply, she was still crying. Tom answered her. "I'll tell her what you've just said when she calms down. What's your name sweetheart, so I can make sure I get the message right.

"I'm Charlotte, her son's girlfriend."

Tom looked over at her again, scanning her from head to toe. He looked surprised and squirmed. "Yeah, I'll tell her. Don't you worry about a thing, I'll make sure she's alright. I've known her for years. She's my family, so to speak."

Charlotte gulped and didn't know where to look. Was this scruff really a blood relation of Rico's? He'd never mentioned anything before about having family in the area. Mind you, no one would be shouting it from the rooftops if this guy was part of their family tree would they? He was a lowlife, a social reject, a down-and-out. No, he would have been kept a secret, a very dark secret at that. Tom led Francesca to a nearby wall and sat her down. Her legs were buckling from underneath her and if she would have carried on walking, she would have fallen flat on her arse. Wiping the tears from her eyes, she looked directly at Tom. "He's all I've got. He's my life, my world. Help me find him please."

Tom gulped and choked back the tears. His heart broke in two to see her like this. He squeezed at her hand and lifted it up slowly to his mouth, kissing her fingertips. "I'll search high and low for him. If anyone can sort this, it's me." There was hope now, someone to help her in her quest to find her son. Tom twisted his head over his shoulder and sucked hard on his lips. "You just wait here and I'll nip over to them lot over there and see what I can find out. Please stay put. If you come over there, they'll put two and two together and we'll get nowhere. We'll have to be crafty if we want to find anything out. Promise me you'll let me sort this out?"

Francesca agreed and yanked her coat tightly around her body, she was shivering, her teeth chattering together. "Please be quick then. I can't just sit about when my lad is in danger."

Tom didn't waste another second. He jogged over to the silver car parked on the opposite side of the square.

"Alright lads. Can I have a bag of brown?" Tom stuck his head in the car window and cunningly passed them the money over. He was biding for time now, trying to keep them talking for as long as he could. Francesca was on pins, her body rocked to and fro as she watched Tom talking to the runners. What was he talking about, was he threatening them to tell her where her boy was? He was a kind soul when he wanted to be and without his help, she knew more than anyone she would get nowhere. The only other person in the area she thought she could count on had let her down, fucked her off, Tom was her last hope. The streets were a bad place to be when you had no connections. She watched him jogging back to where she was sat. He was gagging for breath, sweating.

At last, some news. He rested his hands on his knees and tried to regain his breath. "Nah, nobody knows nothing. Paul Jones is out and about and I've just told them fuckers that if my nephew isn't found, I'll be back to shoot the lot of them. They know I mean business as well. Yeah, they know about me when I'm pissed off. Nobody fucks with me you know. The lot of them shit it, their arses fell out." He was lying through his front teeth of course but she fell for his cock and bull story. "Do you want me to take you home? You can't just walk the streets looking for him. I bet he's got his head down at one of his mate's gaffs or something. He won't want you to see him mashed up will he?"

Francesca agreed. Maybe she was too protective and Rico knew if one mark was on his body, his mother would have investigated it without a shadow of doubt. He was a man now, living in the big bad world. He had to learn to fight his own battles and not run home to mummy all the time telling her his problems. Even when he was at school, Francesca protected him. Once, when a bully ripped his shirt, she made it her business to face him herself. She told nobody what was about to happen and just waited with the other mothers to pick their children up from school. The moment her son pointed the kid out who'd been giving him grief, she marched straight up to him and skull-dragged him to his mother. "If your kid so much as touches another hair on my son's head, I'll be doing the same to you. Get your kid in order before I do it for you." The other mother was mortified and from that day on, nobody ever messed with Francesca or her son for that matter. They were a team and his pain was hers.

Tom helped Francesca up from the wall and led her back to the car. "You can't drive like this. I'll drive you home and make sure you're sorted out before I go out looking for him. I care about you too, you know that don't you?"

Francesca was numb and not responding, his words just floated over her head and she just let him take the lead. Tom sat her in the car and rushed back round to the driver's side. What a great result for him. This woman was now talking to him, he was next to her again. In her life. It was a dream come true for him. Tom flicked the ignition and reversed out from the car park.

★

Mandy walked behind Charlotte as they walked along the road. She was pissed off and fed up of talking about Rico. For crying out loud, he wasn't the first person to get his arse kicked around here, so what was the big fuss about anyway? He was a mard arse, he should have just taken it on the chin like any normal man would have done, instead of causing a scene and going on the missing list. He had no balls whatsoever. Charlotte twisted her head back to Mandy. "I'm going to ring Paul, he'll tell me what happened last night."

Mandy hurried to her side and screwed her face up. "Fuck me. Now you've lost the plot. What the fuck are you involving him for, keep well away."

"No, I need to know where he is. If that prick has battered him for fuck all then he's going to get a mouthful from me."

"Good luck with that. Are you for real or what? What do you expect him to say, 'oh sorry darling. I didn't mean to half-kill your new boyfriend'. Like that's going to happen."

"Mandy, I've got to do something. Reeks is in trouble and I need to find him. It's my fault."

The two of them found somewhere to sit down and Charlotte pulled out her mobile from her pocket. There were six missed calls from her mother that she ignored. Searching through her contacts, she found Paul's number. Mandy rested her head on her shoulder and made sure she could hear every bit of the conversation. "It's me, Charlotte. What the fuck have you done to Reeks?"

Mandy shook her head as she heard Paul laughing down the other end of the phone. What a complete wanker he was. Charlotte snapped. "Listen, you cocksucker. I swear to you now, if you don't tell me where he is I'll ring the police. Oh yes, believe you me. I'll stitch you up good and proper. I know stuff about you, are you forgetting that?" Charlotte held the phone away from her ear as she heard the roars of anger being blasted into her ear. She ended the call and booted the wall near her. "He's a tosser. He's saying that Reeks came on the square and attacked him. He's declaring he was just protecting himself. As if he would do anything like that. He's as quiet as a mouse. He couldn't fight his way out of a paper bag."

Mandy rested her head in her hands. Nothing was making sense here. If someone got done in on the square everyone would be talking about it but nobody knew fuck all. Things weren't adding up. Maybe Rico had another bird somewhere and was now being nursed by her. Mandy had always spoken openly and she just blurted out her thoughts without thinking. "I bet he's with his other chick. Because why isn't he here with you or at his mam's? The guy only knows a handful of people in Manchester and you know all of them, so it all makes sense now. He's banging someone else."

Charlotte went white, she gritted her teeth tightly together and went nose to nose with Mandy. "Fuck off, he's not with anyone else. Don't you think I would have known if he was cheating on me? I'm with him all the time, so give your head a shake. Sometimes you just talk out of your arse, you do."

Mandy wasn't backing down and a few home truths needed to be stated here. "Since you've been with him your head has been in the clouds, he's pulled the wool well and truly over your eyes. You think he's whiter than white don't you. But I've had a gut feeling about him from the start. He's a wrong-un. Just another dirtbag having you over. If I was you I'd wash my hands of him and find someone new. He's a geek anyway. He's not one of us."

"You're just jealous because he loves me. All you're thinking about is yourself. That's all I've heard from you since I've been with him, pure jealousy. Just because Jason treats you like a nob, don't start trying to plant seeds in my head to fuck my relationship up." This was bad, they were ready to scratch each other's eyes out. Neither of them were backing down. Mandy clenched her fists into two tight balls at her sides. She was getting ready to launch a blow right into her best friend's face. She was a hothead and once she was in the zone, there was no going back. This girl had anger issues and no matter how much she tried, she only knew one way to fight her corner and that was with her fists.

"Come on then if you fancy your chances," Mandy bawled.

Charlotte was debating her next move, she'd seen this girl in action and didn't know if she could walk away from this without an injury. She stamped her feet in temper. "Mandy, if you're not supporting me here then do one. I thought you were my mate. I don't need this now!"

Mandy dropped her guard and backed off. "Don't throw that at me. I'm saying what I think that's all. Come on, fucking think about it. Where the hell is he if he's not with some other bint?"

Charlotte's eyes clouded over and she swallowed hard as her emotions started to get the better of her. It could be true, maybe she trusted him too much. Had she been that much in love that she couldn't see the woods for the trees here? What a crafty bastard he was. Her heart sank low and she dropped her head, biting hard onto her lips to hold the tears back. Maybe Mandy was right after all. "Come on, let's not fall out over a guy. We're bigger than this. We go way back. Just put it down to experience and learn from it. I'll chin the cunt myself when I see him. What a piss-taker he is." Mandy hugged Charlotte and for now the friendship was repaired. They both headed back to Francesca's in the hope that Rico had turned up. Charlotte wanted a serious word with him, if he was cheating on her then she would be giving him a mouthful.

Tom sat gawping at Francesca. He shot his eyes around the living room and nodded his head. He could live here for sure, shack up with this woman for a new start, a new life. He'd get clean, off the gear and live happily ever after. This man was off his rocker. What on earth was he thinking, there was no way she'd ever have this skank anywhere near her, let alone in her bed sleeping beside her. He spoke in a calm tone, licking arse, creeping. "Francesca, stop crying love. I've never let you down before and I won't start now. I'm true to my word I am. Me and you go back years and you know I still have feelings for you don't you?" Was he right in his head or what? This woman was hurting here and all he could think of was getting his end away, the selfish prick. She let out a laboured breath and rubbed her flat palm on her forehead.

"Tom, all I can think about now is Rico. I'm going to ring the police. I should have done it earlier. They'll find him."

He panicked and gripped her hand before she stood to her feet. "No, if you get the dibble involved you'll be making a rod for your own back. I'll sort it out, just give me a bit of time. I'll just sit here with you for a while to make sure you're alright and I'll be all over it. Manchester is a big place and I know all the hideouts and all the people around here. Someone knows where he is and mark my words, I'll find him for you. He's my flesh and blood too, are you forgetting that?"

Francesca sat back down and dragged her fingers

through her hair. "I need a drink, something to calm me down. My head's all over the place. I can't think straight."

Tom stood up and shoved his hands down the front of his crusty tracksuit bottoms. "You sit there, I'll get it, where is it, in the fridge?"

"Yeah, get me a glass too from the cupboard. Get one for yourself if you want one. Bring the full bottle in. I need it."

Tom plodded into the kitchen and rubbed his sweaty palms together. She was drinking now and he knew she always got a bit frisky when she was pissed. Maybe he could hang around for a while longer and see how the land lay. A bit of slap and tickle with his ex was something he'd always craved. Tom opened the fridge and looked inside. This was the first time in ages he'd seen so much food in one place. Checking quickly over his shoulder, he gripped a small pork pie and shoved the lot into his mouth. What a greedy fucker! He hardly even chewed it. His tastebuds were alive and the hunger pains inside his body started to subside. Cakes, fruit, cheese, he was spoiled for choice. Tom went back into the front room with a cream cake hanging from his mouth. Fresh cream and jam oozing from it. "I hope you don't mind. I grabbed a cake. You know me and my sweet tooth. I love my sugary snacks."

Francesca reached over and took the bottle of wine from him. With eager hands, she filled her glass and placed the bottle back on the table. "Get a drink Tom if you want one. You still drink don't you?"

"Fucking dead right I do. You know me, I always down a few cans each day so I can get my head down each night. It helps me relax."

Francesca kicked her shoes off and pulled her legs

under her bum cheeks. His eyes were all over her, craving her, needing to be inside her. "You still tanning the gear then?"

He wasn't ready to answer this question. His addiction was something he always struggled to talk about. In his eyes he was just a social user but if you spoke to anyone who knew him, they would have told you he was a raging baghead, a lowlife. Tom couldn't look at her directly. He lied. "I'm getting off it. I've cut down loads in the last few months. I'm sick of it, I want my life back."

This man was so full of shit that he was even starting to believe his own lies. The words he chose were the ones he used when he went to see his drug worker. Bullshit really, empty promises. He always had his script ready when he needed it, especially when he was getting his medication. The professionals always thought they could help him conquer his addiction, save him. And when he needed his tablets upping, he used this spiel to get what he wanted. "Francesca, I don't see myself being a junkie anymore. I'm worth so much more and I can turn myself around with just a little bit of help. I can see a light at the end of the tunnel. It's just every now and then that life gets the better of me and I fall off the wagon. You know yourself, how much you need something to take the edge off when you hit rock bottom. I mean, look how you was addicted to the sniff. You was tanning it every day."

Francesca opened her eyes wide. This was her past, something she had put behind her a long time ago. She had turned her life around and having a bump was something she'd not done for a long, long time. How dare he bring this up, bring her down to his level? She was educated now, a pillar of the community. A teacher. "Tom, my cocaine use was just something I did when I was younger. Everyone experiments with drugs when they are growing up. I've not had a line for years. That stuff can get a grip of you and I watched so many people around me ruin their lives because of it. I was never on the hard stuff like you. If I'm being honest Tom, you look shocking. You've aged years, you're haggard-looking."

Tom growled at her. How dare she put him down like that when all he was doing was helping her look for her son, the cheeky cow. "A leopard never changes its spots," he replied in a cocky tone, "you're bang into the drugs just like I am. A party girl you are, a coke whore some people might say." Oh, he was giving it back to her now. Who had died and made her captain of this ship anyway? She needed a gentle reminder that she too had made choices in her past that she wasn't proud of. "Our Gordon treated you like a skivvy and you let him. We had something special and as soon as Tigger come along flashing a bit of cash, you dumped me and left me to rot."

This was the conversation they should have had years ago. The questions that played on his mind, the answers he needed. So here it was, closure. Tom gripped the bottle of wine and swigged a large mouthful. He needed a bit of Dutch courage if he was ever going to get this out. He stared at her before he began. "I loved you and I gave up the drugs for me and you to have a life. Once Gordon came home from the slammer, you let him get back into your head and fucked me off. Do you know he was the one who got me back on the gear? Yes," his eyes opened wide and he rubbed at his scrawny arms as he continued, "he knew I was weak when I could see you slipping away from me and he left temptation there for me to get back on smack. You were my saviour Francesca. The woman who I would have changed my life for. When you left me I sank so low and I did things that I'm not proud of. You caused that. You, nobody else."

His eyes clouded over and he was going to say something more but stopped at the last minute. She studied him for a few seconds and twiddled her hair at the side of her cheek. "We would never have worked Tom. I had a child. Gordon would never have left us in peace, he would have done you in. You know that as much as me."

"I would have done whatever it took to have you on my arm. You were the best thing that ever happened to me."

This was all getting a bit out of hand. For fuck's sake, she slept with him a few times and maybe filled his head with some shit. She had been messed up back then and just needed a shoulder to cry on. Looking at him, she shuddered and wondered how on earth she'd ever let him stick one up her. He was hanging, a bleeding disgrace. "Tom, me and you were there for each other at a time when we both were lonely. It should have never happened."

This was a low blow and you could see the pain of her words in his eyes. How could she just blurt it out like that, say he never meant anything to her? He let out a laboured breath and sucked hard on his gums. "Anyway, I bet you've had hundreds of cocks stuck up you since me. I'm probably just one name in a long line of men."

"Cheeky bastard. I'm not a slut. I've had my fair share of men but if I'm being honest, Gordon has put me off men forever. I'm used to being on my own now. Just me and my boy."

Her face dropped and she covered her mouth with

her hand. Here she was chatting away when Rico was still missing. What kind of mother was she, she should have been searching high and low for her son, not sat here reminiscing about the days gone by. She changed the subject. "Tom, I'm giving you two hours and that's it. I swear, if he's not found I'll take matters into my own hands and involve the police."

So that was it, no more talk of their relationship, the kisses they'd shared, the words she'd spoken to him when they were having sex. She was still the same girl she had always been in his eyes, selfish and all for herself. She could have said something nice about the time they had together, pacified him. Told him he meant something to her. But, no, she destroyed him all over again. Maybe it was a good thing that she'd told him he meant nothing to her. This would make his job a bit easier now. He could carry on with his own plans, payback for his brother against the woman who'd hurt him. There was no point in sitting with her anymore. He wanted to rip her head off and shit down her throat, fucking slut, a prick teaser she was, nothing more, nothing less. She could rot in hell for all he cared now, he was done, he was over her.

CHAPTER ELEVEN

MISTY WAS CLOCK-WATCHING. All day long she'd been trying to get in touch with her daughter. She'd bleeding strangle her when she got her hands on her for having her worrying like this. She knew the rules about answering her phone when her parents called her. Dominic sat biting his fingernails as he watched Misty pick up the phone for the last time. "Is she answering?"

"No, is she hell. Where the fuck is she Dominic? It's past midnight and I'm beginning to get worried."

"Try Mandy's phone, she might be round at her house. If she doesn't know where she is then I'm going in the car to look for her." Misty scrolled through her contacts and found Mandy's phone number. She held the phone to her ear. "Hello, Mandy, it's Misty. Is our Charlotte there with you?" Dominic was on his feet now, pacing around the front room. Tonight had just been one disaster after another. They'd decided to tell Charlotte the truth about her real father - for the first time ever they were going to sit her down and explain everything about Gordon and the man he was but it had all gone to pot now. The moment had gone and they were having second thoughts about revealing the truth. Misty ended the call and shot a look over at Dominic. "For fuck's sake. Mandy said she left her about half an hour ago. She said she was upset about that Reeks guy. I'll wring his fucking neck if he's made her cry."

Dominic's ears pinned back. He snatched his car keys

from the table. "I can't stand this, I'm going to look for her. If she turns up, ring me and let me know she's home." She didn't have a chance to say another word to him, he was gone and the door slammed behind him. Misty was edgy, trembling inside. Okay, she'd promised her husband that she wouldn't drink anymore. But this was a drama, her daughter was missing and surely a drink was called for by anyone's rules. She hurried to her secret stash and her hands shook as she unscrewed the lid from the vodka. No glass, no small sips. Misty gulped and gulped until she couldn't swallow any more. The warmth, the calming feeling it gave her, that was all she needed. Instead of putting the bottle back she carried it about with her, concealed under her jumper. Every now and then she brought the bottle to her mouth and gulped some more. Misty stood at the living room window and rubbed at her arms. The night was cold and the wind was howling. Where was her baby, she needed her home and safe in her arms.

Dominic was driving like a mad man. He'd cut his balls off when he got his hands on him. Everything was going through his mind. He'd probably forced himself on her, made her have sex, done sick twisted things to her. Threatened to end her life maybe. His blood was boiling as he went through every scenario in his head. He'd always promised his daughter he would die for her. No man would ever hurt her as long as he had a breath in his body. He would die for her. Yes, fight until the end, until her attacker sucked in his last breath. The car came to a halt as he stopped just a few yards away from Tavistock Square. He knew more than anyone how daunting this place was. He'd grown up around here too. And if his memory served him right, Misty used to chill there too in her wild days. His fingers gripped the steering wheel and his nostrils flared, some cunt was getting it for sure. He yanked the key out of the ignition and jerked his body forward to get out the car. It was showtime. Dominic was game as fuck and he slid a small metal bar down the side of his jeans. This was so out of character for him. Usually he was laid back and wouldn't say boo to a goose. What the hell had happened to him?

He zipped his coat up and turned his head one way, then the other. As always, the square was alive with activity. He was a fish out of water here for sure. These weren't his kind of people, they were from the hood, streetwise. Dominic stormed over to a group of youths who were sat on the wall smoking a joint. "Any of you lot seen our Charlotte?" There were giggling, snide remarks whispered. He gritted his teeth and asked them again. This time he got answers from the youngest member of the group, who looked scared to death. "She was here a few hours ago with Mandy then she done one. Why what's up?"

Dominic looked at the young male with his blood boiling, he was ready to waste him. "Fuck all is up. I'm her dad and I'm looking for her, that's all." The group carried on talking and Dominic marched over to another group on the opposite side of the square. This time his blood was really boiling.

There he was, the troublemaker, Paul Jones. "Oi, bollockhead, where is our Charlotte? If it's you who's made her upset, God help you lad, because I'll cut your bollocks off and ram them down the back of your throat."

Paul dropped his head low. There was no way he was being disrespectful to Charlotte's family. He'd always portrayed himself as a nice guy, husband material. Everyone there was gobsmacked and they looked at Paul, waiting for him to kick off. "I've not seen her Dominic and why would I upset her? You know that girl means the world to me."

What had happened to this thug, he was actually being nice. He showed no disrespect whatsoever. Dominic went nose to nose with him and made sure he could see the whites of his eyes. If he was lying, he'd see right through him and bang him right out. "So you've not spoken to her tonight?"

"No, on my life I'm telling the truth. She won't speak to me since we split up. If you can, will you have a word with her please? You know how I feel about her."

Dominic hissed, did this clown think he had come over on the last banana boat or what? The clock was ticking, where the hell was she? If Charlotte wasn't with him, then where on earth could she be?

Charlotte sat on a park bench and swigged at her bottle of brandy. Like mother, like daughter. As soon as a problem came up in her life, she hit the bottle and tried to block it out of her head. What was the point anymore? She was better off being a twat, a bitch, telling the world to fuck off and do her own thing. At least then she was better thought of. Reeks had opened another world up to her though, and she craved that world of love and tranquillity if she was being honest. That was the real person she was and not the one she liked to portray. Life had made this girl hard. How could she wear her heart on her sleeve when there was so much hurt around? Nobody believed in love anymore and most relationships she knew were violent, involving lies and deceit. She thought her boyfriend was different, the real deal. She'd even spoken about marrying him one day. Yes, she'd even looked in the thick glossy magazines at wedding dresses and felt a warmth riding through her body at the thought of one day walking down the aisle to marry the man of her dreams. That was all gone now, no second chance, no nothing. She could never forgive him for treating her like this. She may as well have gone back to Paul Jones if she wanted to be treated like that. At least he adored her, bought her anything she wanted. She had another drink to kill the pain in her heart, swig the lot, fuck it, get pissed and move on with her life without him.

Charlotte sat watching the cars drive by in the distance, yellow lights flashing past her eyes, the sound of engines ticking over. She was singing to herself now, humming a tune. Maybe she should start to head home. It was cold and lonely where she was sat. It wasn't safe for a young girl to be in a park on her own at this time. There were sick people about, men who wouldn't think twice about whacking her over the head and having their evil way with her. Charlotte launched the empty bottle on the grass verge behind her and staggered towards the park gates. At this rate she would take hours to get home, one step forward and two steps back..

Misty stood at the window smoking her head off, chain-smoking. Denise was with her now and was stood behind her, peering out through the window. She could see her niece was upset and tried to calm her down. "She'll come home when she's ready, Misty. Remember what you were like at that age. For crying out loud, you drove your poor mother crazy."

Misty smirked and sucked hard on her fag. "Yeah I did, didn't I? But come on, I was doing her job for years when she gave up on life and left us to fend for ourselves."

Denise snarled and was ready to shut her up. "Take that back, my sister never ever gave up. Lisa was a fighter. She just got a bit lost that's all. When your dad left, her world fell apart. She tried her best, God knows she tried."

Misty turned around to face her. "Denise, let's agree to disagree. Ask Max if you don't believe me. I kept this family afloat for years while she went out on the piss. No wonder my head is a mess. I was a young girl and saw things I should never have seen at my age. I was the one who found her when she tried topping herself, remember? What would have happened to us if she would have died? She thought about nobody but herself that woman, selfish."

No way, thought Denise, this was lies – she had to set the record straight. "Have you heard yourself? You can stop right there. You lot were a handful and if you would have been my kid, I would have slammed the lot of you into care. A cheeky mouthy bitch you were. Remember your mother stood by you when you came home pregnant at the age of fifteen. Never once would she let a bad word be said about you either. And let me tell you something for nothing, there were people who were badmouthing you all over the place. She had a lot on her plate, trust me." Denise straightened her blouse and continued. "No, our Lisa stood proud and told the lot of them to fuck off and mind their own bleeding business. And then you had Max coming out with the news that he was gay. Did she kick up a fuss about that? No, she stood by him too. Like I said. She was in a bad place." Denise opened her eyes wide and made sure Misty was looking at her. "So, unless you want a slap lady, keep your mouth shut about my sister. I don't know where you get it from sometimes. She was a good mother and I won't have a wrong word said about her."

Misty stubbed her cig out and licked her lips. She needed a drink. She'd already necked the last bit of her vodka and there wasn't a drop of left in the place. Denise sat down. Pissed off she was, angry that Misty would ever speak about her mother like that. Things had been hard in the past and her niece didn't know the half of it. Her sister was a strong, caring woman and God help anyone who tried to blacken her name. Denise was thinking, playing with her fingers.

"I wonder if Charlotte is pregnant. Maybe she's too scared to come home to tell you. I mean, why else is she dodging coming home?"

"Is she bleeding hell up the duff. I made sure when she started seeing Paul that she was on the pill. We are open and honest about sex and she knows she can tell me anything regarding her sexual activities."

Denise raised her eyes and her nostrils flared. "Maybe you've been so tied up in your own problems that you've let things slip. She might have been in trouble and wasn't able to come to you."

Misty was on the verge of crying, breaking down. This could have happened, she'd not been herself for months and maybe her daughter had got herself in trouble and didn't know which way to turn for the best. This was truly a groundbreaking moment, finally, the penny had dropped. "Have I been that bad Denise?"

There was no holding back this time. "If you want the truth, then yes. Even Max has been worried about you and that's saying something. He normally takes everything in his stride and doesn't give a door a bang. But yes, your drinking is a problem. A big one at that."

Misty rubbed hard at her skin, scratching at it, tearing at it. The truth hurt and Denise had hit a nerve. "I've not been that bad. Charlotte knows she can always come to me with anything. We're close, we talk all the time about stuff."

"When was the last time you sat down with her then, because all I've ever seen for the last few months is you getting off your face and chatting shit to anyone who tries to get close to you?"

Misty stamped her feet and pounded her clenched fist onto the table next to her. "I've had pure shit going on Denise. Every day stuff has been piled on me and sometimes I feel like climbing the walls. That's why I drink. I have a few just to take the edge off all the crap that has been going on in my life."

Denise was never one to hold back her words and she opened fire. "You drink all the time anyway. Don't blame anything on dramas in your life. You're a pisshead, face it. Your mam struggled with the booze and so do you. So it's in your blood, just like it was in hers."

"Fuck off Denise. You always blow stuff up and make it sound worse than it is."

"Okay, when was the last time you had a drink? And don't say you don't know because I can tell you're off your face tonight with it. Go on, tell me if I'm wrong." Here it was, the moment of truth. There was no running away from it anymore. She had to face it.

"My daughter is missing. I needed a drink to calm me down."

"Oh, Misty. Come on, don't insult my intelligence. You were pissed before you knew she wasn't home. You always have a reason to drink, just like your mother did. It's bleeding history repeating itself here."

"I've had loads of baggage. My marriage has been falling apart and Tom is threatening to tell Charlotte about Gordon being her dad."

"So come clean and tell her then. You should have told her when she was old enough to understand, if you ask me."

"We planned to tell her tonight but as you can see, she's not bleeding here."

"Don't you dare start getting stroppy with me. Sort your shit out Misty once and for all. You're a mess, a total fuck-up."

Misty chewed hard on her bottom lip. Tears flooded from her eyes as she dragged her fingers through her hair. "I know you're right and I'm going to get some help. See, at least now I've admitted I have a problem."

They could hear the sound of the back gate opening. Both of them looked at each other and stood frozen waiting for the door to open. Dominic stormed inside and threw his car keys onto the table. "Nothing, nobody's seen sight or sound of her. Try her mobile again."

Misty started to rummage around for her handbag. Denise walked over to Dominic and patted the top of her shoulder. "She'll turn up soon. You know what she's like."

He plonked down on the sofa and dragged his hands through his hair. "I'll bleeding strangle her when I get my hands on her. Fancy not even ringing us. One phone call is all it takes to stop us worrying."

The back door opened again and Denise let out a sigh of relief. "Bleeding hell, here she is! Where the hell have you been? These two have been worried out of their minds about you. Out of order you are."

Charlotte staggered into the living room and struggled to take her coat off. Misty was by her side trying to help her. "Where have you been love? Your dad has been searching high and low for you!"

Dominic was on the edge of his seat and he was waiting on her reply before he added his twopennorth. "He's just the same as all the others mam. I thought he was the one but he's had me over."

"Who has?" Misty asked, nothing was making sense.

"Reeks, that's who. I thought he loved me but he's been seeing someone else behind my back." Tears now flooded from this young girl's eyes. She fell into her mother's arms and was crying like a baby.

Dominic shot a look over at Denise and cracked his knuckles. "I'll fucking waste him when I get my hands on him. I thought he was an alright lad. He's pulled the wool over our eyes too. I swear to you, don't ever bring that lad into this house again because I'll put him on his arse."

Denise was shocked, what the hell had got into Dominic? Since when had he become a fighter, usually he was quiet and never got involved with any family drama. Misty held her baby in her arms and kissed the top of her head. There was pain in her eyes and she broke down too, knowing her little girl was hurting and there was nothing she could do about it. But what now? There was no way she could hurt her anymore and tell her about her father. This would have to wait, go on the back burner until the time was right. Misty rocked Charlotte in her arms, stroking her head, wiping every tear away that fell from her eye. This was a wake-up call for sure. Her family needed her and she was going to make sure that her problem with the drink was sorted sooner rather than later. Dominic came to join Misty and he too held Charlotte in his arms. It was all a mess.

★

Tom rushed into his house and Melanie sat waiting for him with a face of thunder. "Fuck me, where have you been I'm dying here! Did you get some gear or what?"

Tom kicked his shoes off and peeled his wet jacket from his body. "Yeah, I've had a nightmare. Nothing has gone right. How's he been?"

Melanie looked over at Rico and started to pick her nose. "He's been asleep for ages. He's not budged. I've given him some more sleepers to knock him out."

Melanie fidgeted about and something in her eyes wasn't right. "Well, he's going to have to move. He can't stay here, he's not safe. I'll wait until later and shift him."

"Why can't you just leave him here, I'll look after him?"

"Paul Jones has got wind that he's here," Tom roared at her, "and word on the street is that if he finds him here with us, we'll get done in too. Honest, heads will roll. Do you want that 'ey? That fucking nutter coming through the front door?"

Melanie had other things on her mind and scoring took preference to anything else. Tom dug deep in his pocket and launched the drugs over to her. "You get that sorted out for us. I just need a shit, my nerves have been shocking all day. I'm going to fill my pants if I don't get on that shitter soon."

Rico flinched on the sofa and Tom paused before he left the room. He touched the top of his nephew's head and held it there for a few seconds. "Sssh, son. Go back to sleep.

Sssshhh." Melanie was flying about the room and nothing else mattered anymore, only drugs. She'd been roasting all day and her head was all over the place, she needed a hit.

Tom sat on the toilet, tracksuit bottoms round his ankles. In his hand he held a bundle of cash. The dirty lowlife had sold the iPhone and made himself a few quid. He wouldn't declare this money to his other half though. No way, she could get off her fat arse and go and earn some cash herself. He was sick to death of feeding her habit as well as his own. She could get to town tonight and sell her body. Melanie didn't earn much money but anything was better than nothing. It's not like she was a looker. What did anyone expect, she was rotten. The type of punters she got were the dirty old bastards, the kinky ones who wanted to shove their dicks up her arse or just abuse her. Twenty quid was her price and for that fee she would do anything they wanted, literally anything. The men never kept her more than fifteen or twenty minutes anyway, so in her eyes it was well worth the money. It was better than minimum wage anyway. Tom pulled the bath panel back and stashed the cash there. He had plans for it and needed every single penny of it. He held his ear to the door as he heard Melanie shouting him from downstairs. "Right, for fuck's sake I'm coming now."

Tom lay on the sofa and his eyes were rolling. Neither of them were moving, they were like zombies. They were always like this after a hit, lifeless. Rico was stirring and he could see them both lying on the floor. "Tom," he whispered. His voice was weak and you could barely hear him. This lad was in big trouble, his head was rolling in sweat and the gash on his head oozed thick green gunge.

Tom stirred and tried to focus. "What's up lad?"

Rico licked his dry cracked lips, dehydrated. "I'm not too good. I feel sick."

"Just chill for a few minutes, kid. I'll sort you out soon."

Rico held the bottom of his stomach and twisted and turned on the sofa. He was white, gagging. Too late, projectile vomit surged from his mouth all over the floor. Melanie lifted her head up and fell back down. "Help me, please. I need my mam." His words fell on deaf ears and nobody cared that he was spewing his guts up. Ever since being a small child, Rico had had a fear of being sick. He would panic, run around the room and nobody could calm him down except his mother. He needed her, he wanted his mother. Rico's head sank back onto the sofa. His words were low, he was weak, he had no strength. "Just get my mam. I don't care what happens to me, just get my mam."

Tom rolled on his side and got up on his knees. Digging his hands into his pocket, he pulled out two white pills. "Here, get them down your neck, get your head down for a bit and I'll sort you out soon."

Rico's eyes were rolling, he was sweating like a camel's arsehole. He needed to see a doctor and fast. He had a temperature. Tom gripped the sofa and pulled his body up from the floor. "Rico, I'm going to have to move you from here. I've got a nice little bang-up where you can go and no one will ever know you are there. You will be safe as houses there." His words were never heard. Rico was asleep again, out of it. This was getting worse by the minute. The lad would be lucky to see the night through.

CHAPTER TWELVE

MISTY LAY ON THE BED next to her daughter, Charlotte's eyes were red raw. "Come here baby and give me a hug. No man is worth your tears, trust me I know."

Charlotte snuggled deep into her mother's chest and her voice was low. "It hurts so much. Every time I close my eyes I can just see him with someone else. Kissing her, saying the words he used to say to me."

"It happens, Charlotte. I was where you are once, so you don't have to explain anything to me. I know it hurts."

Charlotte pulled back from her mother so she could see her face. This was news to her, shocked. "Mam, I thought you and dad were like forever. I didn't know you had even had any other boyfriends."

"Yes love, there was one other. I don't really like talking about him but I think it's time for me to be honest with you. Hold on, let me get my cigarettes before I start." Was this really happening, was the slate being wiped clean once and for all? Misty sat on the edge of the bed and reached down for her cigarettes. Popping one in her mouth, she sucked hard on it as she got a light from the yellow flame. Charlotte sat up on the bed and folded her pillow behind her head. This was news to her, no way did she know her mother had had any other relationships than her dad. What a dark horse she was. Maybe she was a player, a slut, she just didn't know. Misty moved back onto the bed and reached over to hold her daughter's hand as she spoke. She needed to pick her words wisely. This was a big conversation and she needed to tread carefully. "So I'll start at the beginning. I don't want you to judge me. I was young and, well, foolish."

"Mam, I would never judge you. Shit happens in people's lives and sometimes you have to do what you have to do to survive don't you."

Misty sighed, where should she start? The story of her dark past started to unravel. "I had a good friend once, just like you and Mandy, we were inseparable. That's how I was with my best friend. We did everything together, told each other all our darkest secrets, everything. I trusted her with my life." This was lovely, a special mother and daughter moment, endearing. Misty took another blast from her cigarette and blew the smoke out from her mouth with force. She had to do this, get it all out in the open. Her nerves were shattered today and this was the first day in a long time when she'd not touched a drop of booze. "I've never really had a best friend since if I'm being honest. I struggle with trust because of her. I'll never trust anyone with my secrets again."

This was getting good and Charlotte's eyes were wide open, she was engrossed in it all. It was like watching a chick flick. "Go on mam, tell me more."

Misty sucked in a large mouthful of air and looked deep into her daughter's eyes. "Charlotte, I've always loved you from the moment I set eyes on you and that will never change. Whatever I tell you here today will never ever change that. Me and your dad would do anything for you."

Charlotte held a blank expression. What the hell was going on here, it was getting serious now. "I was young when I met Gordon. He was older than me and he was there at a time when I needed somebody. My home life was crap and well, he gave me comfort. I thought he loved me. Everyone told me he was bad news but I never listened to them. You know like you do when someone tells you something is wrong, you just do it anyway." Her daughter understood this for sure and smirked. Her mam was having a sly pop at her because that's how she acted all the time. These two were so alike in many ways. Much more than any of them knew. Misty was fidgeting, eyes staring down at the floor as she continued. "It was a horrific relationship and maybe one day I will explain things to you more in detail, but not now. I can't face it."

Charlotte bit hard on the corner of her fingernail. "Mam, I never knew any of this. You don't have to tell me anything because I can tell it still hurts you to speak about it."

Boom, here it was, the juicy bit. "I had a baby when I was younger too. I carried him until I was seven months pregnant but he was born early, a stillborn. He never made it. He died." Charlotte didn't know what to say, she was digesting all the information she was receiving. She looked at her mother in more detail. She didn't understand. Why now, why was she telling her all this now? "My ex-boyfriend battered me the night before I went into labour and that's the reason he never lived."

Charlotte's eyes clouded over. This was so sad, how had her mother ever got over something like this? It was heartbreaking, especially at the age she was. "Did you give the baby a name, did you have to bury him?"

Misty closed her eyes slowly and her expression changed. Painful memories from her past were coming to the surface. She swallowed hard and tightened her grip on her daughter's hand. "He was called Dale. I remember every little thing about him too, little fingers, little toes, he was perfect."

This was a sad moment and Charlotte knelt up on the bed to hug her mother. But she needed to move on with the story, get it off her chest. She pulled her daughter back down onto the bed. "The night I gave birth, my best friend was in bed with my boyfriend. It was only a few weeks later that I found out they'd been seeing each other behind my back."

Charlotte gritted her teeth together. "I hope you punched her lights out, kicked the living daylights out of her. I mean, that was no best friend. The girl is a slapper, a slut. I swear to you now, if Mandy would have done anything like that to me I'd never speak to her again. I'd put her six foot under."

Misty swallowed hard. The words on her tongue were diseased. The lies, the truth she'd kept hidden away for as long as she could remember. "I got rid of them both. I lost my best friend and my boyfriend in the same night. And after that I got back with your dad. We still loved each other and to tell you the truth, he saved me in more ways than one. Your dad fixed me and showed me a different way of life. He did, he repaired my heart and made me believe in love again." Charlotte smiled, she loved a happy ending and lay down on the bed. Her parents' story was special, true love conquering all, fate. Misty turned to face Charlotte, looking straight into her eyes. It was time for the biggie.

Misty cringed, there was pain in her eyes, her stomach was in knots. "Just before I went to move in with your dad, something bad happened. Gordon got out of jail and he broke into my house while I was sleeping. There was nothing I could do. He wanted revenge for me leaving him. He always told me he would kill me if I ever met anybody else. He had a gun to my head and he was demented."

"Wow, this is some sick twisted shit, mam. Why have you never told me all this before?"

"I know love, I know," she paused, her beating rapidly in her chest. She had to get this out, to tell the truth. Here it was, the truth at last. "Gordon broke in and," she took a big deep breath before she continued, "he, erm, raped me. A neighbour alerted the police after hearing my screams. They came straight away and arrested him. The bastard got sent down for years for what he did to me and I'm glad, I'm happy, he got slammed, he should have rotted in hell for all I cared. He's a dirty no-good bastard, a bully. I'm glad he's dead. I'll spit on his grave, dance on it. I hate him." Misty was hysterical.

"Mam calm down, why are you telling me all this? You don't have to go through it all again, I can see how much it upsets you."

"I do love. I do." Misty paused and she knew it was now or never. She moved closer to her daughter and tapped her fingers on the end of her knee. "My best friend got pregnant by Gordon too. Yeah, at the same time as me. I was pregnant to a man who raped me."

Charlotte's jaw dropped low and the colour drained from her cheeks. "Bloody hell, what did you do, have an abortion?" Misty wanted the ground to open up and swallow her. She was nearly there now and the truth was seconds away. "Charlotte, no. I didn't get an abortion. Your dad stood by me and we decided that I would keep the baby and bring it up as both our child. Your dad has loved you ever since he held you in his arms. You're his baby and he'd never let anything happen to you."

Charlotte held her head to the side. She must have heard it all wrong. "Mam, I don't know what you mean. I'm confused."

"Gordon is your dad."

Charlotte was hyperventilating, windpipes tightening. She was frozen, there was no expression, no words. Was she the baby her mother was talking about? The baby that was conceived after the rape?

Misty climbed closer to her on the bed and tried to hug her in her arms. Charlotte wasn't confused anymore. The truth hit her with an almighty bang. She bolted up from the bed and stood facing her mother. "Move, take your hands from me! Don't you ever touch me again! How could you have kept something like this from me?"

"You never needed to know, love. Gordon's brother has been bribing our family for years threatening to tell you."

"This is some fucked-up shit. So my dad is not my dad and I'm the daughter of a fucking rapist?"

Misty sobbed, her daughter was right. "I love you and your dad loves you too."

"He's not my fucking dad though is he?" Charlotte marched around the bedroom. She was throwing clothes, hairbrushes, anything she could get her hands on. "It's a fucking joke. No wonder I've never felt part of this family! Is that why you get pissed all the time 'ey, so you can forget about me and my real dad? You should have got rid of me. How could you have a child to the man who raped you? It's sick, fucking sick! I wasn't made with love, I was made with evil! It's a sin."

Dominic pushed the bedroom door open and stood there. Misty was holding her head in her hands and he knew something bad had happened. Charlotte eyeballed Dominic. "I know the truth. I'm not your daughter."

He wobbled and nearly fell backwards. He choked up as he spoke. "You're my princess and always will be. I was the one who picked you up when you fell down and I was the one who sat with you every night when you were teething. That's what a real father does. Nothing has changed in my eyes."

Charlotte stood with her back pinned to the wall. Her hands dragged at her hair, pulling at it, twisting it. She was breaking down, her legs buckling from underneath her. "But I'm not your blood. I'm not a part of you. I belong to my mother's ex-boyfriend. I can't deal with this. I need to go out. I'm suffocating, I can't breathe."

Dominic came inside the room and gripped her in his arms. "You're not going anywhere. We need to sit down like adults and talk this through. Me and your mother love you more than anything in the whole wide world and nothing will ever change that. Please Charlotte, just calm down and let's talk this through."

"No! There is nothing to say. You two lied to me for years and you expect me to sit down and talk about it. I can't do this. I'm off. Fuck the both of you. Liars you are, the pair of you. Go and rot in hell, you sick twisted bastards." Charlotte picked up her black bomber jacket from the side of her bed and struggled to put in on. Misty stood up and tried to stop her from leaving. The two of them eyeballed each other and Charlotte spat in her mother's face. "You lying bitch. I hate you for this. I loathe you. You make my insides crawl. Go on mother, go and get pissed. Go and do what you do best."

Misty wiped the spit from her eyes and Dominic was

raging at her side. "Don't you ever do that to your mother! That's horrible. She doesn't deserve it."

"What and I deserve a fucking rapist as a father? She's not the victim here, it's me. It's my life you two have fucked up, not yours. How could you keep something like this from me?"

"Sometimes things are better left unsaid, trust me I know."

She barged past her father and slammed the bedroom door behind her, nearly taking it off the hinges. Misty was trying to run after her but Dominic held her back. "No, let her go and cool down. You know as much as me she won't talk to you until she's had time on her own. It's done now Misty. No more lies. The truth is out and that bastard can no longer hurt us. You just watch. She'll be back soon and we can all sit down and sort this mess out."

"Dominic, she hates me. I could see it in her eyes, she'll never forgive me for this."

He pulled her close to his chest and kissed the top of her head. "She will love. Just give her some time."

Charlotte sprinted down the main road. Tears streamed from her eyes. She just wanted to run and never stop. Her life was in tatters and from the second her mother had told her who her real father was, she couldn't help her stomach churning over. She wanted to be sick, spew her guts up. She was rotten, born from a dirty seedy sin that her real father had committed. Charlotte stopped in a side street and hid away from the world. She fell to the floor and curled up in a tiny ball. She wished she was dead, how could she ever get over this? She had no boyfriend and now, no real father. Her world was upside down and there was fuck all she could do about it.

Footsteps crept towards her. Her body was being turned over. "Are you alright love? Come on, let me help you up."

Charlotte opened her eyes and jumped to her feet. She was in real danger and she knew it. She was out of public view and no one could have saved her. The man kept his identity hidden, a thick black scarf covered his nose and mouth. All she could see were his eyes. It was too late, he whacked her over the head with the half brick in his hand and she fell to the ground like a lead weight. No screaming, no pleading for help. The man checked her pockets and pulled out her mobile phone to switch it off. He was sweating and struggling to lift her to her feet. He was on the move. Her arm draped around his shoulder until they got to the end of the side street. A car waited with the boot open.

Charlotte was slung into the boot of the car and her attacker jumped into the driver's side. This had all happened so quickly and there were no eye witnesses, nothing. Poor Charlotte, she was up shit street now.

CHAPTER THIRTEEN

TOM SAT IN THE LOCK-UP with his head hung low, drooling. He was off his napper and trying to roll a cigarette up. He'd planned this whole thing down to a tee. Every detail was precise. Two chairs faced each other, a small distance apart. His victims were both secured to them with black tape, pillowcases over their heads. This was his moment. His time to set the record straight. This was the same place his brother took his last breath. A cold, dark, deserted warehouse. It was time to show these cunts who he was and what he was capable of. Tom wanted to introduce these two properly as brother and sister. He'd watch their expression change in an instant. He'd tell them all about his brother Gordon and the man he was. Not a bad word would be said about him though. He was a legend in his eyes and nobody would say anything different. Not on his watch anyway. But what then? Had he not considered his next move? What an idiot, he was just like his brother.

After he'd told them they were brother and sister it would all be over. It was pointless really, nothing could be gained whatsoever, except heartache, a family ripped apart. Tom patted his coat pocket and slowly pulled out a silver pistol. What the hell did he have this for, this was never in his plan, something must have changed. He stroked the cold barrel along his lips and tickled the trigger with his finger, pressing at it, itching to pull it. His words were strange and not making sense. He was slavering, slurring his words. He'd had more than just smack today. He'd necked a load of tablets too and smoked some crack. Something wasn't right. He looked up towards the ceiling and held the gun up high, waving it about. "Our kid, look what I've done for you. We're equal now. You can set me free. I owe you fuck all now. This score is finally settled. Boom! Look, both of them in the same room. I wish you could have been here to see this bro." His hand dropped back down and he let out a menacing laugh. "Maybe they can come and meet you, maybe not. What's the point in them both living here on this earth anyway? She'll probably end up fucked in the head and he'll be like me or you, fucked. It's not good is it? I can end the misery for them both and send them to you bro. What do you think our kid? Shall I do them in or what, blow their brains out?"

Rico and Charlotte were stirring and Tom was alert, eyes rolling. He tickled the end of his chin with his index finger before he moved a muscle. He walked to Rico's side and yanked the pillow case from his head. "Sorry about this son. I had to do this. Your mam is a bad woman and she has to learn that you can't play about with people's heads like she does. She said she loved me once you know. Yeah, hard to believe now isn't it, but on my life, she was head over heels in love with me. We could have been good together me and her. I would have brought you up as my own. But she's a dirty cow and easy meat. I mean, how can you stop caring about someone just like that? A click of a finger and I was gone out of her life. No kiss my arse goodbye, no nothing. She's a twisted bitch. I'll show her who has the last laugh. You just watch me now, I'll show them all."

He was on one and his eyes were menacing, a vacant look in them. Rico looked shocking. The lad was so ill, his eyes bulging from their sockets, cheeks blood red, he had a high temperature, there wasn't an ounce of energy in his body. Rico tried to focus and he wasn't sure where he was. Taking a few seconds, he licked his dry lips. "I need to go to the hospital. Please take me Tom. I'm not feeling too good, honest my head feels like it's going to pop." His head dropped onto his chest and he was too weak to even lift it back up again without a struggle.

Tom jangled a bunch of keys in his hand and smirked over at his nephew. "I'll be back later. You two can get to know each other a little better while I'm gone." Tom yanked the pillow case from Charlotte's head. He was mumbling something under his breath but it was never heard. He shouted behind him as he started to leave. "See you two later. Look after each other." Tom staggered to the small iron door at the side of the room and switched his torch off. It was pitch black, no light whatsoever. Rico and Charlotte were his prisoners. Nobody knew where they were and the odds were against them. Their existence was now in the hands of a junkie who was unstable. Anything could happen.

Misty was crying her eyes out. She'd tried to get some booze down her neck but Dominic had made sure she was staying straight-headed. Max, Denise and Rob were all sat in the front room and none of them had a clue where Charlotte was. Anytime now, they were going to ring the police and report her missing. They'd have to tell them everything though. Share their secret once again. Rob was raging. "We should have put that cunt in an early grave from the moment he tried bribing us. I told her, I said 'Lisa, let me deal with him' but she wouldn't let me get involved. I would have shut him up good and proper. As God is my witness. I would have made sure nobody would have ever seen him again."

Max raised his eyes and shot a look over at Dominic. Was Rob chatting shit or was he really capable of ending another human being's life? He'd been in the army for a few years but none of them ever believed the gruelling stories he'd shared with them when he'd had one too many. The way he went on, it was like he'd been awarded the Victoria Cross for his courage during a war. Rob had been in the army and no one was taking that away from him. But the SAS, come on, really. Surely, he was lying through his teeth. Dominic sat twisting the newspaper in his hand, rolling at it, biting the end of it. "I'll kill the prick when I get my hands on him. All this could have remained a secret forever and no one would have been any the wiser. Once Charlotte is home, I'll go and find the junkie myself and put a bullet right through his head".

Max wasn't sure if he was hearing this right. These two men were as soft as shit and in all the time he'd known them both, he'd never heard them say a peep to anyone. Misty was the head the ball here, she was the one everyone should have been scared of. She was clever, cunning and played the game well. She never let anyone get the better of her. All was fair in love and war and she was willing to go all the way, especially now her cage had been rattled. "Ring the police Dominic. I can't stand it anymore. I just want my baby back home. I don't care what we have to tell them. Just make sure they bring her home. I need her home."

Denise was by her side trying to comfort her. There

was a knock at the front door. The room went completely quiet, not a peep, silence. Dominic stood to his feet and headed into the hallway. Was this the dreaded knock on the door that every parent thought they might get when their child was missing? Had they found her already, was she alive or battered within an inch of her life? Denise held her ear to the door, she held a single finger over her mouth at Max, who was still nattering.

"Ssshh, I think it's Mandy. If you shut up yapping for a single second then I'll be able to hear properly. Be quiet will you, gobshite." Max blushed and folded his hands tightly in front of his chest. Denise was always having a pop at him and one of these days, he was going to tell her straight. But not today, he could do without the drama. Max remained quiet. He knew what was good for him. Mandy was in the front room with them all now, distraught. She'd been sobbing her heart out all the way around here. Maybe she could have been a better friend, listened, given her advice instead of flying off the handle. She was riddled with guilt and wanted to clear her conscience before this got any deeper. "Misty, can I speak with Charlotte please? Is she upstairs in her bedroom, shall I just go up? We've had words so to speak and I want to set the record straight. It was both of us arguing so don't look at me with them eyes thinking it's me who kicked off. She played her part just as much as me?"

Dominic stood at the doorway and he knew now that Mandy wasn't aware that her best friend was on the missing list. He walked a few steps closer to her and patted his flat palm on top of her shoulder. "Love, Charlotte hasn't been home all night. We're going to ring the police in a minute. When I saw you stood at the front door I was hoping you knew something about her whereabouts. I'm gutted really that you don't know anything. At least then we would have had something to go on."

Mandy opened her eyes wide and looked bewildered. "What do you mean she's not been home all night? Have you tried ringing her phone? She won't be far, she probably just got sidetracked."

"Of course we have, we're not daft you know. We're on the blower all the time."

Denise shook her head and sighed. Mandy was as thick as pig shit sometimes. She must have been at the back of the queue when brains were being given out. Mandy smirked and sucked hard on her gums. "Well, she won't answer to you lot will she. Here, let me try." This could be a breakthrough, maybe she would answer to her best friend. They had a bond. The circle of trust. Mandy dialled the number and walked around the front room with her ear glued to the phone. Everyone's eyes were on her and Misty was sat on the edge of her seat, praying there was some response, anything to let her know her daughter was safe. This was their last chance saloon. "Come on girl, pick up, answer the call for crying out loud," Mandy mumbled under her breath. They all had hope in their hearts and they were never going to give up, no way. They would search high and low until Charlotte was found. No stone would be left unturned.

"Send her a text message, tell her to ring you as soon as possible," Misty panicked.

"And tell her auntie Denise is worried out of her bleeding mind. So if this is one of her little games to get us all worried then it's bleeding working. We're out of our minds here. Tell her to get her arse home and we can sort stuff out."

Mandy held a blank expression, what did they have to sort out? Her plan was to come here tonight and say she was sorry that's all. That was all it would have taken. She looked over at Denise and twisted her head slightly. "What do we need to sort out, it was a daft argument that's all? You know what us two are like. We'll always be best friends no matter what. So there's nothing to sort out really. It's just a minor disagreement."

Misty looked over at Mandy, she had to put her in the picture. Her daughter may have needed a friend to talk to about this in the future and she wanted to make sure she was fully aware of what was going on. There was no more thinking about it, it had to be done. "Mandy, something has happened and Charlotte…" she paused and looked at the other family members before she continued. "Well, she's had some bad news."

The cheek of this family. Were they trying to point the finger at her regarding her daughter not coming home? No way was she having this. It was a daft fallout, nothing more. If they wanted a beef she would tell them Charlotte hated her mother drinking. In fact, she'd called her a pisshead on one or more occasions. Yeah, let there be one word said here that she wasn't a good friend and she would take them all to the bleeding cleaners. The whole lot of them. Hypocrites they were. Trouble causers.

Misty popped a cigarette into the side of her mouth and they all sat waiting for her to tell Mandy the dirty secret the family had hidden from everyone for years. Here it was. Misty took a few deep breaths before she began. "Mandy, what I tell you stays inside these four walls. It's private and I want you to promise me you'll never breathe a word of what I'm about to tell you. I swear, if you tell a living soul you'll have me to deal with. I'm not kidding either."

Mandy looked around the room and realised this was hot news. She swore herself into the circle of trust with excitement. She loved gossip and this was right up her street. "I won't say a word, honest to God, cross my heart and hope to die."

Misty let out a laboured breath and rubbed her fingers over her head. Max was watching Mandy like a hawk, he wanted to see her face drop, her jaw swing low when she heard the news that Charlotte's real dad was dead. You could have heard a pin drop. "Dominic is not her proper dad. I told Charlotte this and that's why she's upset."

Mandy flicked her eyes one way, then another. Was this a prank, a practical joke? This was like the stuff she'd seen on Jeremy Kyle. Bleeding hell, who was the daddy then? Was there a DNA test involved here? Was Misty a slut who didn't know who the father of her child really was? No wonder Charlotte had got on her toes, this was shameful. She was a bastard child born out of wedlock. Her mother had told her about kids like this. Everyone's eyes were on Mandy, waiting on some kind of response. Charlotte's friend looked around the room, speechless for now. Should she tell them what she was really thinking, reveal that in her eyes Misty should have kept her legs crossed until she had a ring on her finger, or should she just keep her thoughts to herself?

Mandy twiddled her hair, she had to think about this before she dropped a clanger. It was too late, she just blurted it out. "This is bad. Charlotte must be heartbroken. Why have you never told her this before? You're proper shady if you ask me. If you were my mother I'd never talk to you again. I mean, her head must be all over the place. It's bad. You've let her down in my eyes. Yeah, the lot of you have fucked it big time. How could you keep something like this from your child?"

Mandy covered her mouth with her hand. For crying out loud, had she just said all that out loud? Denise snarled over at her. "Oi, it wasn't like that. Don't start judging people here when you don't know shit about the circumstances. There are reasons why Misty made the choices she did."

Mandy was in deep shit now, she'd dropped a bollock. But her words were out there and everyone in the room was aware that she didn't approve. She swallowed hard and swiped her hair back from the side of her cheek. "I mean, it's bad. I can't help being honest. Charlotte is my mate and all I have is her best interests at heart."

Dominic could see she was sinking, her cheeks going brighter by the second; he had to diffuse the situation before it all blew up. "Right, now you know. No one has died here so let's move forward. We've searched high and low for her so we have no other option than to ring the police."

Mandy's eyes were wide open. For crying out loud, the family were a load of grasses too. Charlotte would come home when she was good and ready, they just needed to chill the fuck out and let their daughter get her head around things. Misty reached over and passed the phone to her husband. "You do it, you're better than I am with stuff like this." She paced around the room and licked her lips frantically. She needed a drink to calm her nerves, to stop the tremors crippling her body every time she made a movement. But all the drink had been cleared out and she'd promised her husband that no alcohol would touch her lips again. Maybe she'd jumped in too quick with her promises. She was a pisshead and everyone knows you can't just quit like that. She was falling off the wagon, ready to run out of the house and down to the local off licence to feed her addiction.

Dominic held the phone close to his ear as Denise sat biting her fingernails. Hold on, there was a knocking at the front door. Praise the Lord, this could be Charlotte and their worries would be over. Mandy ran out of the living room, she wanted to see her first, to hug her and tell her that she still loved her even though she was a bastard child. Misty ran behind her and into the hallway. The front door opened and Mandy's face dropped when she saw who it was.

"Is Charlotte here?" Mandy placed her hands on her hips and shook her head at Francesca.

"Nah, she's missing and they're ringing the dibble to tell them she's not been home."

Misty was pushing Mandy out of the way, she wanted to see who it was. The colour drained from her, she knew this woman. Yes, she knew her alright. She was older than she could remember and she'd gained a bit of weight but she knew her on first sight. After the shock of seeing her, she snarled. "What the hell are you doing here?"

Francesca screwed her face up in confusion. She stepped back and checked the house number again. Maybe she had got the door number wrong. "I'm looking for my son. His girlfriend lives here and I wanted to see if she'd seen him."

Misty was suffocating, blowing rapid breaths. "What the hell are you going on about?"

Francesca shot a look at Mandy. Maybe she could shed some light on the matter. "Misty, Francesca's son is Reeks. You know, Charlotte's boyfriend?"

This couldn't be true. Misty gripped the doorframe before she lost her balance, her head was spinning, nothing was making sense anymore. Dominic was at the front door now and as soon as he saw Francesca his stomach turned, eyes wide open. This woman could only mean trouble. What the fuck did she want after all these years? He was having a panic attack, dragging his fingers through his hair. The penny dropped and Misty snapped.

"Get rid of that dirty slapper before I rip her fucking head off. Dominic, remove her from my door now before I do."

What the hell was up with Dominic? Why was he just stood there like a spare part gawping at Francesca? He needed to do something before it all kicked off. Dominic stood facing Francesca. There was no love lost with these two and he wasn't afraid to put her in her place. His emotions were all over the show and his eyes flooded as he remembered the hurt this woman had brought to his wife, to him. "I don't know what kind of sick twisted joke this is but we're going through enough shit here at the moment without you adding to it. My wife isn't in a good place and seeing you will just push her over the edge. Please, just fuck off and leave us alone."

Mandy started to defend Francesca. "Dominic, don't be snide on her. She's only looking for her son. He's been missing too, just like Charlotte. Maybe they have eloped, got married. Oh my God. She could be pregnant and had no one to turn to. Yeah, that makes sense now. The more I think about it yes, I bet she's preggers."

The penny dropped and Dominic put two and two together. "So, your son is Reeks?"

Francesca paused and eyeballed him. "His name is Rico, and yes he's my son."

Dominic continued and made sure he was clear of every word that was being said. "And he's the lad who has been dating Charlotte?"

Francesca was losing her rag, ready to kick off and put this little weasel right in his place. "For fuck's sake Dominic, yes. So go back inside and tell that barmpot of a wife of yours that if she's got any beef with me still, we can sort it out. Right here, right now."

This was sick, if this was true then Charlotte was dating her half-brother. This was getting worse by the minute; incest, a bastard child, what would be next? The facts were there for everyone to see. Charlotte and Rico were both Gordon's children, his bloodline. Dominic swallowed hard. He stared at Francesca for a little bit longer than he needed to. "You'd better come inside. This shit needs sorting out once and for all. I'll go and make sure Misty will talk to you."

Francesca scowled. "I don't need permission to talk to her. She was my best friend for years and surely if I'm here to find my son, she will understand that."

Mandy knew there was more to this than met the eye. What a fucked-up family this was.

Francesca marched in behind Dominic, she didn't need an invite. Mandy closed the front door and hurried in behind them all. She wasn't missing this for the world, not a fucking chance.

Denise ran at Francesca when she saw her. "Who the hell do you think you are, coming around here upsetting

Misty like this? Her daughter is on the missing list and she has better things to do than catfight with you over you sleeping with her boyfriend. But if you're here for a fight, then step outside and I'll bleeding murder you."

Mandy plonked down on the sofa and rubbed her two flat palms together. Go on Denise, smash her all over the show. Scratch her eyes out, drop her. Misty kept her eyes focused and shook her head slowly. She walked up next to Francesca and rammed her finger into the side of her head. "You daft bitch, have you not worked it out yet?"

Francesca shrugged her shoulders and looked over at Dominic. "What the fuck is she going on about?"

Misty could see she would have to spell it out for her. "Charlotte is my daughter and Reeks is your son, you thick cow. Come on, work it out. It's not rocket science."

Still the penny didn't drop. Denise couldn't stand it any longer and blurted it out. "Their dad is Gordon, which means they are brother and sister, well, half."

Francesca squirmed. "Gordon is not Charlotte's father so stop lying. Dominic fathered her. Everyone knows that. You two split up and then you got pregnant."

Misty stood up and looked her in the eye. She was going to have to tell her what really happened. "Gordon raped me, you remember that don't you? Or, was you that off your fucking napper that you remember nothing about what really went on?"

Francesca wobbled, she had to sit down, she was white. "But you married Dominic, you got pregnant straight after that?"

"No, Francesca, I married him after I found out I was pregnant. We wanted everyone to believe that Dominic was her father. No one would have been any the wiser if it wasn't for Tom. He's been bribing this family for years to hold this secret."

Francesca wafted her hand in front of her eyes. Her words were trapped on her tongue. Mandy could see she was struggling to speak and quickly rushed into the kitchen to get her a drink of water to help her continue. Francesca took a moment to digest everything that was being said. She shot a look at Misty. "So, Rico and Charlotte are... Ewww, that's hanging…and he's having sex with her." Francesca covered her mouth with her hands in disbelief. Mandy's jaw dropped. This was some seriously fucked-up shit. Just when she thought it couldn't get any worse...

Misty paced the living room. These two women had history and it now looked like they had to sit down and be civil to each other. They were both a mess, both destroyed by the man they'd loved at one point or another. Misty plonked down onto the sofa. "Dominic, just phone the police will you? For crying out loud. I need her home."

Francesca lifted her head. "Will you tell them my son is missing too? I think they could be together wherever they are."

Denise shook her head and sighed. "When it rains in this house it bleeding pours. For crying out loud, can we have any more bad luck?"

Max walked over to his sister and kissed her softly on her cheek. "I'm going to see if I can find her too. I can't just sit here on my arse doing nothing. Poor Rob has been out for ages looking for her. I'm going to join him."

Francesca piped up. "Tom is looking for Rico too so hopefully he'll come up trumps. He knows the crack around here doesn't he and if anyone can find him, he can?"

"Don't mention that smackhead's name again in this house. He's the one who's caused all this shit to start with. I mean, I begged him to back off. To leave us alone, but all he wanted was more money from us to buy his silence. He's rotten, pure evil," Misty snapped.

Francesca froze, her mouth moving but no words coming out. She held her flat palm over her heart and held her head to the side slightly. "You mean you've spoken to Tom about this and he carried on threatening you?"

"Are you deaf or what, I've just said that haven't I?"

Francesca blew a laboured breath and shook her head. "He's been at my house and never once has he mentioned it to me," she paused before she continued. "I bet he's got them both. He was acting strange when he was with me, saying stuff that didn't really make sense. Yes, the more I think about it. It must have something to do with him. Think about it Misty, if they are both Gordon's children he must have something up his sleeve for them?" She gasped her breath as she continued. "Am I fucking blind or what? Of course it's him. He's taken our kids, Misty. I'm sure of it."

There was a big panic on now, everything slotting into place. That no good slime ball had taken Charlotte and Rico. Dominic was on the phone to the police and he relayed his fears. He gave them Tom's full name and address and carried on speaking to them for a few minutes more, giving all the details he could about the missing people. Misty sat gnawing at her clenched fist. "I know where he lives. I'm going there. I'll rip his head off if my daughter is there with him. Dominic, you wait here with Denise and fill the police in when they come. This is my war and I'm going to end it once and for all."

Francesca jumped up from her chair. "I'm coming too. There's strength in numbers and I'll stab him to death if my boy is hurt in any shape or form. Come on then, what are you waiting for?"

Misty grabbed her car keys from the side of the table. Before Dominic could get a word out, the front door was slammed shut. These two women were on a mission. They could only pray they weren't too late.

CHAPTER FOURTEEN

IT TOOK EFFORT FOR CHARLOTTE to raise her head. Dark red claret was running down the side of her head and her forehead was swollen beyond belief. Rustling could be heard. Somebody was there with her. This place was pitch black, she couldn't see a thing.

"Hello?" she whispered.

Nothing, no response. She could hear squeaking as rats ran about near her feet. She could hear them but she couldn't see them. Their rancid smell, their germs, near her body. Somebody was coming into the room. Keys could be heard jangling and then someone coughing. Charlotte closed her eyes and prayed this ordeal would be over soon. "Please God, help me," she whispered. A small beam of light heading towards her, there was heavy breathing and the smell of stale tobacco.

Tom shined the beam of light over his hostages. He was ready now, to do what he'd set out to do. His mind was made up. It was D-day. Tom's cold hands grabbed Charlotte's face, pulling at her cheeks, slapping the side of her head to wake her up. She was alert now, eyes wide open as the light shone into her eyes. She couldn't see her attacker, she was blinded. He knew she was awake and smiled down at her. Staring at her, examining every inch of her identity, he bent down slightly and licked the side of her cheek.

"Are you not going to give your uncle Tom a kiss then?"

She quickly turned her head, wriggled about, trying

to break free. He chuckled and ran his fingers through her hair slowly. "I've got a little surprise for you, darling. You just hold on here while I get some light on the stage. This had to be perfect, just the way he planned it. Footsteps were heading away from her, water splashing on the floor as Tom waded through the large puddles. Charlotte jerked her body about in the chair, rocking in it, trying to move it any way she could. Noises came from behind her, warm breath tickled the back of her neck. Who was that, somebody else was here with her? Then there was silence, they were gone. Tom was singing as he wobbled back to his victims. There was light now and she could see someone else in the chair facing her. Tom walked to Rico's side, slapping his cheek firmly as he carried on singing a song by Oasis.

"Don't look back in anger, I heard you say. So, Sally can wait, she knows it's too late as she's walking on by."

Tom was belting this tune out now and you could see it was a song he loved. He was a big Oasis fan and whenever he could, he would sit down and listen to their tracks. Rico lifted his head and squirmed as the light from above hit his eyes. Charlotte was alert, shocked, the horror was evident as she saw Rico for the first time. Tom danced over to her and pulled the tape from her mouth with a quick movement. He jiggled back over to Rico and did the same. What was he doing now? For fuck's sake, this man was a nutter. He just sat down in between them both and broke out into a fit of laughter. "So, at last you two meet. Isn't it nice that all my family is under the same roof for the first time? Rico, meet your sister Charlotte. Charlotte, meet your brother Rico."

Tom placed the silver pistol on his lap and pointed it at each of them in turn. "My brother was a good man, he would have loved you both, looked after you. But I took his life because he took the only thing I have ever loved. Francesca. She was mine. He didn't love her, he loved no one but himself."

Charlotte sat frozen, not digesting a word he was saying. There was noise behind her again and she was listening carefully to it. Rico was alert and mumbling. "Tom, why are you doing this to me. I thought you loved me?"

"I do love you. I loved your mother too but she carted me. She never gave me a chance. Your dad saw to that, why do you think I popped a cap into him?" Tom's head was falling about from side to side, he had no control over it whatsoever. He was off his head. Every now and then he reached into his pocket and popped a handful of white pills into his mouth.

"Tom, it's all in the past. Just let us both go."

He snapped, waving the gun in his hands at his nephew, he was ready to blow his brains out. "It only takes me pulling this trigger and you can go and meet your old man." Then he pointed the gun in Charlotte's direction. "You can meet him too love. You can be my present to my brother." Tom was struggling to hold the gun up any longer, it dropped back into his lap and for a few seconds he just sat staring at it.

Rico began to cry, tears streaming down his cheeks. "Why have you brought Charlotte here too? Let her go, she has nothing to do with this."

Rico was unaware of what Tom had just said and this made him angry. He launched the torch over at him, just missing his head. "Have you not been listening to me you thick cunt? Charlotte is your sister. Misty is her mam. You know, the one your mother betrayed when she slept with

Gordon. Misty was her best mate." Tom held his head in his hands and tried to explain it further. "Your slut of a mother slept with our kid behind Misty's back. And to cut a long story short, he banged them both and they both ended up pregnant with you two bastards."

Charlotte was raging, her cheeks bright red. "Your brother raped my mother. He's a sex case, a fucking nonce. He's no dad of mine. Dominic is my father. I don't care whose blood is running through my veins, he's not my dad, fucking shoot me if that's what you want to do but that cunt will never be my dad."

Tom shot a look over at her and chuckled. "So, it's you who got your father's temper then? I thought it might have been this fairy over here, but no, it's you who's got the rage inside you isn't it. I don't know what happened to you Rico. I think you're a throwback, maybe a dud seed from our kid."

Charlotte screamed at the top of her voice in the hope that somebody would hear her, "Help me, somebody please help me!"

Tom laughed loudly and rubbed his hands together. "How does it feel to know you have been fucking your own brother, you dirty bitch. Eww, when I found out you two had hooked up it made my skin crawl; incest, fucking disgusting."

Rico was sobbing, anytime soon he would pass out and that would be the end of him. Tom rolled a cigarette and sat watching them both closely. His mind was made up. He cocked the gun and stood in the middle of them both with his fag still hanging out of the side of his mouth. "Who wants it first? Who's going to meet their daddy?"

He shot his eyes in Charlotte's direction, then towards

Rico. Why didn't he just get on with it, the sick twisted bastard. If he was going to do it, what the hell was he waiting for? Why wasn't he putting them out of their misery, for crying out loud.

Misty hammered her clenched fist on the front door. She was screaming at the top of her voice. "Tom, open the fucking door now. I know you're in there, so open up before I boot this door right off its fucking hinges."

Francesca started kicking the bottom of the door too, smashing her foot into it. "Open the door now!" she screamed at the top of her voice.

A light flickered from inside and the front door opened slowly. Melanie peered around the side and she looked petrified. "Tom's out. I'm here on my own. Has Paul Jones found out Rico has been here? Please tell him from me it had fuck all to do with me, it was Tom who was hiding him away, I had fuck all to do with it."

Misty pushed Francesca out of the way and barged into the house. She ran upstairs searching every room, every crack, every crevice in the place. She was screaming at the top of her voice. "Charlotte, are you here love, shout me if you are? Come on darling, I'm here to take you home!" There was nothing, not a peep.

Misty flew down the stairs to see Francesca pinning Melanie up against the wall by the scruff of her neck. "Tell me now where the fuck he has taken my boy, before I rag you about this fucking house by every hair on your bastard head."

Melanie feared for her life and she had no loyalty whatsoever towards Tom. He'd put her in danger, she owed him nothing. "He said he was taking him to the bang-up. Paul Jones was gunning for Rico and he said he had to take him somewhere safe. Rico is ill. I told him to take him to the hospital but he never took one bit of notice of me. Please, let me go. I'm fuck all to do with this."

Misty sprinted over and smashed her clenched fist into her face. Fuck being nice, this was serious, she wanted answers. "Listen you fat blob, where is my girl? Where has he taken her? I know you know, so you better start talking before both us smash your fucking head in. I swear, start chatting shit and I'll knock every one of them rotten brown scabby teeth out for you."

They both had her pinned up now, they were both in her face screaming. Francesca twisted her fingers into her hair and ragged her about the room as Misty flung punches at her. These two were crazy. They were like a tag team. Melanie was howling in pain as her body crashed to the floor. "I swear, on my life that's all I know. If I knew anything else I would grass him up. Honest, I'm telling you the truth." Misty and Francesca locked eyes. Bringing her foot back, Misty swung it straight into her victim's ribcage. "Let me find out you're lying and I'll be back. I swear I'll slice you up and feed you to the pigs."

Francesca lifted the junkie's body up from the floor and spat in her eye. "I hope for your sake we find them, otherwise I'll make it my business to come back here and finish you off myself," Francesca growled. Misty was already on her way out of the door. There wasn't a second to spare, the clock was ticking.

Francesca looked over at Misty as she was driving. She was speeding and taking chances on the road that were putting them at risk. She was going through red lights, driving on the wrong side of the road, Misty was dicing with death. "Fucking slow down will you. Where are you going anyway, do you even have a clue where he might be, slow fucking down I said?"

Misty hissed at her. "Since when have you been scared of anything in your life. I thought you were always out for a bit of a thrill. Have you gone soft in your old age or what? And while I'm at it," she sniggered and paused. "What's all this dress sense about? You look like Mrs Fucking Doubtfire."

Francesca smirked and looked out of the window. "I've changed. I know you might find that hard to believe but I have. I'm a teacher now."

Misty shrugged her shoulders. "You're a teacher, what, of bloody Karma Sutra or something?"

"No, I teach primary children for your information. I've not long been back in Manchester, I've been living in Leeds."

Misty hissed over at her. "Oh, what's wrong? Have you fucked all the men in Leeds now or stolen someone's husband and had to get on your toes?"

Francesca snapped, there was no way she was taking anymore of her insults. This mess was supposed to have been sorted out years ago, she thought her old best friend had forgiven her. How wrong could she be, but in fairness, do you ever forgive a friend who betrayed you in the worst way?. "Listen Misty, keep your snide remarks to yourself. I made a mistake that's all. And I think you know I have paid for that. So stop going on, move on and put it behind you. I have."

Misty growled as she gripped the steering wheel with both hands. Her emotions were high and even though she thought she was over her past, she still couldn't come to terms with it. "Fuck off. Who do you think you are telling me to move on? You're a Judas, you betrayed me. You were my best friend, somebody I thought I could trust. You're a dirty slapper, always will be in my eyes. So if you think I've changed my mind about you, give your head a shake. As long as I have a breath inside my body, you will always be a dirty slut. There you go, at least you know now so don't bother trying to patch things up with me. You deserved everything you got from Gordon. That was God paying you back."

"Misty, I've heard all this before. Look at yourself before you start judging me, Mrs Perfect. As I see it you're anything but perfect. Charlotte told me all about her mother being a pisshead and how she never listens to her, so put a sock in it. As I see it, you've turned out worse than me."

Misty gripped the steering wheel, her knuckles turning white. "No she didn't say that. You're making it up. My daughter loves me."

"Nope, it's the truth. Every single last word is true and you know it. So shut the fuck up and just let's find our kids. If you've got nothing nice to say, then say nothing at all."

Misty kept her eyes on the road and carried on driving. Francesca had changed, she wasn't the girl she used to be anymore, she'd grown up, changed her outlook on life.

★

Tom was talking to Charlotte and Rico. He was telling them stories about their father. He was making him out like a legend one minute and cursing him the next. This man was unstable and needed sectioning, potty he was. The victims were in floods of tears, aware that their lives could end at any second now. They loved each other so much and now their time on earth was nearly over. How could they carry on with their relationship now they knew they were related? It was all sick and twisted, there was no way out for them. Maybe they could run away together. Change their names so no one would ever find them again. It was such a crying shame for them both. Every time Charlotte looked over at Rico, her heart broke and tears just poured from her eyes. This was the worst pain she had ever felt in her life. Why her, why couldn't she just be happy for once in her life? Today had been the worst day of her life. Maybe her life ending wasn't such a bad thing after all. What did she have to live for now? Nothing. It was all ruined.

Tom paced about the floor. It was time to end this now, put it to bed once and for all. Set the record straight, get revenge. His nostrils flared as he pointed the gun at Rico's head. "You can go and meet your dad first I think. Then I'll send your sister straight after you," he chuckled as he continued to speak. "Don't worry Rico, you won't be on your own for long. Tell our Gordon I said hello. Tell him to sort me a gaff out up there too. I don't think I have much time left down here either. It's shit anyway, nothing to live for anymore. I'm done with life down here."

He smiled but suddenly he stopped. His expression froze, he was really going to do this. For crying out loud, surely he'd have some compassion for them. He only needed to look at them, they were the innocent ones in all this. They were kids with their lives in front of them. He needed to think about it, to not be so cruel, to just let them go. Tom rammed the cold pistol into the side of Rico's head and closed his eyes slowly. His finger was bending slowly against the trigger. For fuck's sake, he was going all the way with this.

Charlotte screamed at the top of her voice. "No! Please, think about this, please, don't hurt him."

There was rustling from behind her, her chair was being knocked to the ground with force. A gunshot was fired and she couldn't see what was happening as her body fell to the floor. There was heavy struggled breathing and footsteps pounding towards her. It was her turn now, he was going to finish her off. She sobbed her heart out. There was no fight left in her. The love of her life was gone, the bastard had shot him.

"Rico, please no!" A hand was dragging her up, no focus.

Rob lifted her up and quickly started to comfort her. "I'm here love, just you hold on and I'll get you out of here."

Charlotte looked around. Tom was lying in a pool of blood not far from where they stood. His eyes were still staring into space, wide open, like he'd seen a ghost. Rob hugged Charlotte with all his might as she broke down crying. It took a few minutes before her heart started to beat normally again, she was white, in total shock. Rob held her cheeks in his hands. "It's over, he can't hurt us anymore. You're safe. I'm here with you now, no one will ever hurt you again." Once all the tape was taken from her hands, Charlotte ran over to Rico and started to free him too. He was barely conscious. His head dropped low, he was on his last legs.

"Rob, please, get him some help. Quick, phone an ambulance, ring the police. Please, help him!"

Rob was a trembling wreck, his body shaking from head to toe. The man was telling the truth about being in the SAS. Well, fuck a duck fancy that, who'd have thought it? Rob was a hero, he'd saved the day. Without a second to spare, he left the room and went to find help. He'd tell the police the truth, tell them Tom kidnapped Charlotte and Rico. Yes, self defence, he would tell them Tom tried to kill them all. Surely if they all got their stories together, there would be no further investigation here. He would have to word the others up when he got back too, make sure they all kept to the same story, stuck together.

Charlotte held the love of her life in her arms and looked down at him. She was sobbing her heart out. "I don't care if you're my brother. I love you. I'll never give you up, ever. Please say you feel the same. Don't give up on us Rico. We can fix it, make it better. We're only half brother and sister anyway. We can make it work."

Rico looked deep into her eyes and a single fat, bulky tear fell down the side of his cheek. Taking deep breaths, he started to speak. His heart was racing inside his chest and he didn't know if was going to live or die. He was weak, sweating, ready to give up. "Charlotte, we can never be the same anymore. You're my sister. It's not right. It's all fucked up," he started to cough, blood spluttering from the corner of his mouth.

Charlotte wiped the blood with a single finger. Tears streamed down her eyes. "Tell me you don't love me and I'll walk away forever. Go on, tell me it's over and I'm gone."

Rico squeezed his hand in hers and slowly brought it up to his lips. He could never let her go. He knew that. Their heads touched together and he remained quiet for a few seconds. He kissed the end of her fingertips and tried his best to get his words out. "I love you Charlotte.

Somehow, someway we will get through this."

There was a loud bang and Charlotte and Rico fell to the ground together. Tom was stood behind them, rocking from side to side, blood pumping from his chest. The wanker had shot straight through Rico's head, straight into Charlotte's. Good God, surely this wasn't happening. They both remained still where they lay. Rob hobbled back into the room and pulled his gun from his pocket. He blasted Tom again and again and again until he dropped onto the floor. Tom's body shook for a few seconds and then remained still.

Rob screamed as he ran to Charlotte's side.

"NOOOOOOO!!"

★

Misty had been driving for over fifteen minutes now. It was no use, there was no sight of their children. Francesca was on the verge of a nervous breakdown and she screamed at the top of her voice as Misty pulled over at the side of the road. "He's all I've got. If anything has happened to him, I'll never be the same again. He's my world, my life."

Misty sucked hard on her bottom lip. Yes, she hated this woman with a passion but she couldn't just sit here and let her cry like this. She had a heart after all and she tried to console her. "The police will be out looking for them both. Just stop crying will you. Tears will do you no good, just be strong."

"I'm not strong anymore Misty. I've got no fight left in me anymore. I'm weak."

Misty examined her further. Surely this was bullshit, she was trying to have her over for sure. "Francesca, you're not weak so don't give me that. You're a fighter, always will be. You're a survivor."

Misty pulled two cigarettes from her packet and lit them both. She passed one over to Francesca. "Here, you still smoke don't you?"

Francesca looked at the fag and closed her eyes. She'd been trying to give up for months now but if she ever needed a cigarette, it was now. She gripped it tightly in between her fingers and sucked hard on it. It seemed to be working, she was calming down. Misty opened her driver's side window and Francesca did the same with her window. A gentle breeze filled the car. It was much-needed to calm these two down. Francesca shot a look over at Misty and examined every inch of her face before she started to speak.

"We've really never spoken about what happened have we?"

Misty rolled her eyes and gasped her breath, taking on a sarcastic tone. "There's nothing much to go over, you slept with my boyfriend, end of."

"It wasn't like that and you know it."

Misty leaned closer to her and was nearly nose to nose with her. "It was like I said, you shagged my fella end of."

"Can you at least let me try and explain? I probably should have done this years ago but let's say the time was never right. I was going to write a letter to you but I suppose I lost my bottle in the end, I didn't have the words to say I was sorry." Misty's jaw dropped, she wasn't expecting this, not now. Francesca was hardcore in her eyes and always would be. What the hell had happened to her? "He always loved you, Misty. I was just kidding myself that he ever loved me. I could see it in his eyes. It was you he was thinking about. It was you he wanted. I was jealous of you. You were what all the men wanted I suppose. You were pretty, loving and caring. Whereas me, well, nobody has to tell you what I was like. I thought men would love me if I slept with them but they never did. You're right. I was a slag. I was probably searching for someone to love me, to hold me, to tell me everything was going to be alright."

"You could have found someone of your own. Gordon was mine. I thought he was my true love but you made sure you spoiled that."

"I'm sorry. I could never say how sorry I am. I just got mixed up in his world. The drugs, the drink. I hated myself, hated who I'd become." Tears streamed down the side of her cheeks and this woman was speaking from the heart, no gimmicks, no lies, this was the truth. "You had a lucky escape if I'm telling the truth. The man was an arsehole. A selfish bastard he was, who treated me with no respect. I was his doormat and he crucified me in the time I was with him because he'd lost the woman he loved. He loved you."

"He never loved anyone but himself, Francesca. I can see that now. You were the only person in my life that I trusted. My home life was crap, you know that more than anyone, and Gordon was my escape. I know now that I never loved him. I just thought I needed him. You were welcome to him."

Francesca dropped her head. "He told me all the time that he still loved you, yet I stayed with him hoping he would learn to love me the way he loved you. I hoped when he found out I was pregnant that he would change his mind but if I'm being honest, he never did. He never wanted Rico, he just wanted you. I used to watch him when he was sat down in a world of his own. He was thinking about you, hoping that one day you would have him back, forgive him even. I was just a back-warmer, somebody to keep him warm at night when he was lying in bed. He never kissed me, never showed me any affection. His heart was yours and even until his dying breath, he only ever loved one woman. And that was you."

Misty was digesting everything she'd just heard. Maybe after all these years, they could be friends again. Gordon meant nothing to her anymore. Her heart was with her husband and always would be. Maybe today was the day that they both said goodbye to the past. It would help them both, stop Misty's nightmares, her anger, her demons. Should she reply to Francesca or just let sleeping dogs lie? She wasn't sure. Misty tapped her fingers on the steering wheel, thinking, debating. "I'm shocked. I never thought you had it in you to say you're sorry. Losing you as my best friend was harder than losing Gordon, you know?" It was Misty's turn now to open up. This was really happening, after years and years of hatred for this woman, Misty was finally setting the record straight. About time too. This had gone on for way too long. The pain in her heart needed to be dissolved, got rid of forever so she could move on with her life, get closure. "My life has been shit lately if I'm being honest. And yes, Charlotte was telling the truth to you. I have been drinking too much. In fact, I've been drinking a lot. It's nearly ruined my marriage."

"Why are you drinking? You have everything you want in life. Why would you wreck it? I would give my left arm to have a husband who loves me like Dominic loves you."

"My mam left me with a lot of baggage. Stuff I saw growing up I suppose. Do you know she was always trying to take her own life? When Rob came along I thought it was all over but no, she became aggressive, abusive. She liked a drink too, probably trying to forget all her problems. She told me she hated me, said Gordon should have finished me off, yeah, killed me."

Francesca rubbed at her arms as goosepimples started to appear on her arms. "She never meant that, surely. Your mam loved you. Alright, she was a bit nutty every now and then but aren't we all? She had a lot on her plate. And you probably don't know the half of it. At least you had a mother, mine disowned me. Honest, she never once tried to find me to see if I was alright. She just left me to rot, as my auntie did. When I left Manchester, all I had was my son. A son who had no dad, no family. I'd never felt so alone in my life and let me tell you, I had a few dark days myself. Times when I couldn't see the light at the end of the tunnel. But do you know what? I got sick of feeling sorry for myself and did something about it. I had to learn to love myself again. To be proud of what I'd achieved. And, do you know what? I am proud of what I've done. I dragged myself out of bed each day and went to college, then university. It was hard, so bleeding hard, but I got there in the end. I can honestly say now that when I look at myself in the mirror, I like myself. I never ever thought I would say that, but I do. I've paid for my mistakes, Misty, more than you will ever know."

Misty choked up, her eyes flooding with tears. Was this the end of the rift between these two or what? Was it finally water under the bridge? Misty stared over at Francesca. She was older now but Misty could still see her old friend there. The girl that made her laugh. The friend that always sat with her when her head was mashed with family problems. Misty edged closer and wrapped both her arms around Francesca's neck. She squeezed her with all her might and sobbed her heart out. Today was a day of forgiveness and after all these years, these two had finally had the talk they should have had years ago. Misty's mobile phone starting ringing. She pulled away from Francesca and quickly dried her eyes.

"Hello, Dominic, has she been found?"

Misty listened at the other end of the phone and held a serious look. She was screaming down the phone. "She's been found where? Is she alright! I'm on my way home now!" The phone call ended and Misty turned the engine over.

"Thank God, they've found them."

Francesca burst out crying and shook her head. She made the sign of the cross across her body. "Thank you Lord above. Thank you so much for keeping my boy safe."

Misty pulled onto the main road. "Dominic sounded strange. He wouldn't tell me much, just to hurry up home."

"At least they're safe and that's all that matters." Misty was thinking aloud. "Maybe she's pregnant. For crying out loud. I can't cope with much more stress. Francesca, you do realise that our kids can't be together. They are half-brother and sister for crying out loud. Charlotte's head must be mashed with everything that's gone on lately. And this now with Rico, for fuck's sake she must surely see it's wrong?"

Francesca was thinking and what she was about to say would put a spanner in the works for sure. "Is it that bad really? Love is hard to come by and in my eyes, if it makes them both happy who are we to say what is right and what's wrong?"

Misty nearly collapsed at the wheel. "Are you right in the head? It's sick. It's incest. You better sort your head out, girl. Don't you be saying you think it's alright when we get home and make me out to be the bad one. Charlotte is already angry with me. It's a wonder if she ever talks to me again. I swear, I've ruined her life telling her Gordon is her father. See, even from his grave he's still messing things up in my life. He won't rest until I'm totally ruined."

The rest of the journey was spent in silence.

★

Misty pulled into her street. Lots of police vans were parked up, neighbours were out talking over the fence. The two women shot a look over at each other. "What the hell are the police here for? Oh, for crying out loud, I hope they're not in trouble. Our Charlotte has already got a police record longer than my arm and the courts have told her that if she doesn't sort her head out, she'll be going to jail if she appears in front of them again."

Francesca was observing the activity in the street. "Our Rico would never break the law. No way, he's as good as gold."

Misty snarled over at her. "Don't you be blaming my daughter for any of this! If he's landed up in trouble then he's got a mind of his own, just as Charlotte has."

Misty opened the car door and headed towards the house, with Francesca following closely behind her. As she walked a few steps closer, she could see Dominic and Max stood in the front garden. Her pace quickened. "Where is she, why are the police here? Is she alright?"

Francesca was as eager as Misty to get a reply. Dominic walked closer to his wife and dropped his head onto her shoulder. Max placed his arm on her other shoulder and sobbed his heart out. Misty pushed them both away and stood facing them. "What the hell has happened?"

Francesca piped in. "Where is Rico? Is he here?"

Dominic struggled to break the news. He took Misty's hand gently and led her inside the house. Max urged Francesca to come with them too. The living room was full of coppers, everywhere, reading through all her private stuff, sentimental stuff. A female officer looked at Dominic and spoke. "Does she know?" This was serious, what the hell had her daughter been up to? No matter what she would declare her innocence, tell them it was a misunderstanding, try and make things right.

Francesca and Misty were asked to sit down. Two police officers were sat near them. The news was going to break their hearts, nothing would ever prepare them for what lay ahead. Francesca was agitated, fidgeting, eager to know if she needed to get her boy a solicitor. Dominic sucked in a large mouthful of air and sat next to his wife. "It was Tom who had them both." Francesca's eyes were wide open, sat on the edge of her seat as he continued. "Rob found out where he was holding them both. He had them tied to a chair. God knows how long he had them."

"I'll cut his balls off. I swear I knew from the second I seen him, he was up to something. Where is he? I hope he's been arrested. I'll make sure that prick stays behind bars for as long as I can."

Max was at Francesca's side trying to comfort her. "Come on love. Just try and be calm."

Dominic had to dig deep to get his next words out. His wife looked him straight in the eyes and she could tell there was something more. "Dominic, you're scaring me now, please tell me everything is alright?"

If only he could, if only he could have made everything

all right, he would have. "Tom shot Charlotte and Rico. Rob thought he'd shot him first but when he went to get help, the bastard was still breathing and he shot them both with one bullet through their heads."

The police woman was on standby, ready to restrain her, to help her calm down, try and explain what had happened.

Francesca wasn't sure she heard him right. "So, are they in hospital? Bleeding hell, I wish you would have said this on the phone, we could have gone straight there. Which hospital are they in, I'm going to make my way there?"

The policewoman came and sat next to Francesca. She was ready to drop the bombshell. "I'm sorry but neither of them survived. The medics did their best but they were both dead before they got to them."

The screams filled the room, howling pain straight from the heart. Francesca dropped to her knees and pounded her clenched fist into the carpet. "No, please tell me it's not true! He's not dead, please tell me he's not dead!"

Misty was in shock, her lips trembling, body shaking. "Dominic, please tell me this isn't true. I want my baby, please bring my baby to me."

This was heart-wrenching to watch. The pain these mothers were going through was like something you've never seen before. Francesca was hyperventilating, she was having a panic attack, unable to speak. "I want to see my son! Take me to my son now. He needs me, please, take me to where he is."

★

Misty and Francesca sat outside the mortuary. This was never going to be easy. No mother should have to go through the pain of burying their child, their flesh and blood. It should have been the other way around. These women were past child-bearing age now and neither of them would ever conceive again. This was the end of the road for them both. Maybe it might have been easier if they'd had other children. At least then it might have eased the pain in their hearts. How could a parent ever truly forget a child they'd nurtured in their womb? Held in their arms and loved since the minute they were born? There would be a void in their hearts now, a vacant space that nobody would ever fill again.

Dominic held his wife's hand and stroked his finger across it. "Love, you don't have to do this. I will identify her. It's too much for you to take. Please, let me do this."

She looked deep into his eyes and her words were choked. "I need to see my baby girl. Dominic, I need to hold her and tell her everything is going to be alright." Misty could see Francesca at the side of her. She had no support, no one to hold her. She reached over and held her hand tightly inside hers. "We'll do this together. I'm here for you. You're not alone. We'll get through this together. Honest, we will get through this."

These were such endearing words to hear at this moment. Dominic looked deep into his wife's eyes and knew how hard that must have been for her to say. The police officer appeared from a room nearby and nodded his head slightly to Dominic. "We're ready when you are." Misty's legs buckled and her husband had to support her.

Francesca sat rocking in her chair, trembling from head to toe, eyes streaming. "I can't do this. Please, I can't see him lying there." A female officer came to her side and sat down next to her. Her words were comforting but not what she needed to hear. Francesca snapped and she was hysterical. Misty walked slowly to her side and took her hand with a firm grip. "We can do it together I said. I'm here with you all the way." As if by magic, Francesca froze. She took a deep breath and her chest expanded. They walked hand in hand into the mortuary.

The air was cold, hairs on the back of her neck standing on end. It was time to see their children. Misty prepared herself, sucking in large mouthfuls of air. She needed a drink, something to calm her down; tranquillisers, drugs, anything to keep her calm. The plastic cover was over Charlotte, she knew she was lying underneath it. With a trembling hand, she slowly lifted the cover. Sobbing, gagging into her hands, her legs gave way from beneath her. There she was, her baby, her daughter. Dominic tried to be strong but this was all too much. He walked to the cold slab and took hold of his daughter's hand, lifting it up towards his mouth. She was cold. He could see the bullet wound now and his eyes cringed. Slowly his finger touched her forehead.

"Sleep tight baby. We'll never forget you."

Misty's body folded as she saw Charlotte's face for the first time. Her princess, her life, just lying there, her life stolen from her, with no second chance. "I need to talk to her Dominic. I need to tell her how sorry I am."

Dominic shot a look over at Francesca, who was on the other side of the room with her son. Her cries were like that of an injured animal. He dropped to his knees and dragged his fingers through his hair. He was taking this badly. Was this family cursed? How could they have so much bad luck? Misty's mother, his own mother and now Charlotte. This family would never recover from this.

It was too much to bear, even the strongest family would have struggled here today. Misty looked down at Charlotte. This would be the way she would always remember her now, her last image. There would be no memories of her stood in her wedding dress, memories of when she gave birth for the first time, nothing, all that had been taken from her. Misty's face creased with pain, a stabbing pain deep in her heart, savaging her breathing, strangling her lungs.

"Baby, it's me, your mam. Charlotte, I'm so, so sorry for everything. I should have told you sooner but it was so hard for me. There is so much of my life that I wanted to keep away from you. It was toxic, bad, evil. I never wanted you to know." Misty stroked her hand across her daughter's head. "You're beautiful, so pretty. I always told you that didn't I? You were the apple of my eye. I lived and breathed for you, from the moment I set eyes on you. Dominic loved you too, he was the one who got up each night with you when you were teething, when you fell, he was the one who picked you up. He was your dad. He always will be. How can I ever say goodbye to my baby? You're all I've got. Charlotte, you're all I've got, do you hear me? I'm not ready to say goodbye, not now, not ever."

Francesca was a mess. Once she'd identified her son she had to be escorted out of the room. She was having a full-blown panic attack. She was with the doctors now, having emergency treatment. Dominic could see she was in trouble and followed her outside. It was such a shame, this woman had no family who were willing to help her, no one to comfort her. The police had contacted her mother to see if she was willing to stay with her or help in her time of need, but they were told straight never to contact them again. Her mother's words were, "She's dead in my eyes, leave her to rot." How cruel was that? Surely, there should have been an ounce of forgiveness in her heart. How could she turn her back on Francesca when such tragedy had struck?

Dominic sat next to Francesca and held her hand as she sucked on the oxygen they had provided for her. This man didn't have a bad bone in his body and even though this woman had made his life a misery in the past, and said some hurtful words to him, he was still willing to support her. There were good people in this world and Dominic was living proof of this fact. Even though he just sat holding her hand, it was enough to show that someone cared about her. Today was a sad day. A time both Misty and Francesca would never forget until the day they died.

CHAPTER FIFTEEN

ROB SEEMED TO BE in a world of his own. Since Charlotte's death and after what he'd witnessed, he'd hardly said a word to anyone. He was shell-shocked, traumatised. Maybe if he'd done things differently and involved the police from the start, this might have turned out for the better instead of two innocent teenagers losing their lives. How did he ever think he could tackle Tom on his own without there being some kind of comeback? Was it his big ego that had caused Charlotte and Rico's deaths? He was riddled with guilt. He kept getting flashbacks every time he closed his eyes. He had regrets over the choices he'd made. He wasn't in a good place right now and the last few weeks had taken their toll on him.

He could feel Misty's staring over at him. Her eyes sinking deep into his soul. Oh yes, she was gunning for someone and he was the main target. Every day since her daughter's death, she'd been the same. Nobody could reach her anymore, she'd lost the will to live. Dominic had tried every day but nothing worked anymore, she just sat crying every single hour of every single day. Misty sparked a cigarette up and rolled her eyes over at Rob. Here it was, he knew it was coming, it was just a matter of time. This was long overdue. "Why didn't you tell anyone you'd found out where Tom had them locked up? At least then the police could have intervened and stopped him dead in his tracks and saved their lives! How on earth did you think you could tackle that prick on your own?"

Rob dipped his eyes down low. "Misty, please, don't you think I've thought that myself. It all happened so fast and before I knew it, I was involved in the situation and it was too late for me to stop, to back down. The police wouldn't have got there in time anyway. As soon as I followed Tom back to the warehouse, it all happened so fast. I'd been waiting for him for ages, sat near his house to see what he was up to. I didn't even know he had them there. I just had a hunch, a gut feeling."

"A hunch you should have told someone about. A phone call to me or Dominic, anything that might have helped."

"Misty, you know my legs are bad. It took me ages to find out where he was going. I lost him at first but once I'd found him again, all I could see was him holding the gun to that poor lad's head. I had to act fast, do something to stop him. What else could I have done? If I would have left him alone, he would have blasted Rico there and then. At least I bought them some time. I thought he was dead. A bullet to the chest usually drops any man."

Misty knew she was being unfair. Her own grief had taken over and even though this man had done everything in his power to protect her daughter, she just needed to get it all right in her own head. "It's just all so sad. My baby, gone forever. Never coming back. I'll never see her face." Misty sobbed, head in hands, desperate, heartbroken.

The funeral was in two days and the priest had been coming to the house non-stop. A pain in the arse he was. Nobody wanted to hear that their loved ones were in a better place, with the big man in the sky; a place with no pain and no crime. All they wanted to hear was how they could get them back. Maybe to have one last conversation with them, tell them how much they loved them. Why do people always wait until someone has left this earth to tell them all the things they should have told them when they were alive? Doesn't make sense really does it. This life is not a rehearsal, it's the real thing. There will be no second chances, no reruns. This is it, one life only. If you love someone, for God's sake tell them. Cherish every minute you have with them.

Father Ged was a lovely man, his heart was in the right place, but all his Catholic faith rubbish was doing Misty's head in. Dominic had been a rock and he'd made sure everything was running smoothly; the flowers, the hearse, the times of the burial. It was all taken care of. Rico and Charlotte were being buried on the same day at the same church. Dominic had suggested it. It was only right that they should share a funeral. They were in love, after all and Francesca had no family. No one who could support her.

Dominic was being so nice to her and maybe he was warming to her after all these years. They used to fight like cat and dog in the early years. And many a night he'd chased her down the street ready to floor her. She was a cocky cow, she made his blood boil. Misty had made it clear from the start that she would speak on the day about her daughter. Francesca had given her some notes about her son too. Dominic had added some words about his life and the person he was. He was good with emotions and putting pen to paper, and Francesca was more than happy for him to help get her feelings down too.

The news of Charlotte's and Rico's deaths had hit the neighbourhood badly. No one was safe anymore. Not even living in this close-knit community could save anyone's life. But when your number was up, it was up, nothing could save you. Father Ged sat talking about how he was trying to change the area to be a better place to live. But no one was listening to a word he was saying, he was just rambling on and on. Misty sat staring out of the window as Francesca appeared in the front room. Dominic smiled at her and shook his head. These two women were broken, joined together by grief, by the loss of their children. Misty watched a brown sparrow hopping about in the garden. The bird was so light on its feet. It was free to fly away wherever it wanted to. If she had wings, she would have flown away too. Up, up and away. To a private place that only she knew about. An island where nobody could find her. One that was far, far away.

Dominic sat near his wife and gripped her shoulder tightly. "Come on love, we have to help Father Ged with the hymns. We need to pick some. I think we should have Amazing Grace. It's a lovely song and our Charlotte loved it. What do you think Francesca? You like that song too don't you?"

There was sobbing, her shoulders were shaking. There was a stabbing pain deep in her heart. "I would like to play it on my guitar if I can. Rico loved that song."

Dominic raised a soft smile and spoke directly to her. "I didn't know you could play a musical instrument? You're a right dark horse aren't you," he winked over at her and smirked.

"Can you play anything else?" Misty was alert. Bleeding hell, Francesca had changed for sure. Since when had she had any interest in playing a musical instrument?

"I can play the violin too and the flute. Let's say I had a lot of time on my hands in the past and thought I would make the most of it. I loved playing the guitar and when Rico was a baby, he used to sit for hours listening to the melodies I played to him. It soothed him, especially when he was teething. Do you play anything?"

All eyes were on Misty. She played the fool a few times but no, she was never into the creative arts. She blushed and dropped her head low. She was feeling slightly embarrassed. "No, I've never really done anything with my life after having Charlotte. I had a few jobs but they never lasted long. Charlotte was a handful as a baby and anyone who was minding her always struggled tending to her needs. She needed my attention twenty-four hours a day. Honest, from the moment she opened her eyes she insisted on my total attention."

The women sat remembering their children as babies. As Dominic sat watching them both, he flicked his eyes from one to the other. It was heart-warming really, to hear about each of them and the things they used to get up to. Rico was a joy as a baby. He ticked every box. His mother had made sure of that. When Rico was old enough to read, Francesca used to take him to the local library and help him choose the right books for him to read. Rico was a bookworm. He loved a great story line and more often than not, he could be found with his head buried inside a book. He was nothing like Gordon in his mannerisms, and if she was being honest he was nothing like her. He was laid back and always there to help anyone. He had such a caring nature. As a small boy he would always find injured animals and bring them home to care for them. Usually birds or squirrels that had been injured. If the animals died, it would break his heart and he'd cry for days. Francesca hated the way he cared so much about God's creatures.

Each one that never made it always had a funeral. Yes, he would make them a coffin and say a few words before he laid them down to rest. He was a geek really, not very manly.

Misty was showing Father Ged to the front door. He'd been there for hours. He'd definitely overstayed his welcome. He couldn't take a hint either. Misty had told him several times how tired she was and that she was going to have a lie down but he still carried on talking, completely unaware that he was boring them all to death with his tales from the Bible. Dominic watched Misty leave the front room. He looked over at Francesca and could see she was really struggling. "You just need to be strong for these next few days love. Just take every day as it comes. God knows I'm dying inside but I have to carry on too. I need to support you both."

"You've always been a nice guy haven't you Dominic?"

They stared at each other and he smiled gently over at her. "I suppose so, but we all have crosses to bear don't we?"

Misty stormed back into the room. "Please Dominic, if he comes again tell him to piss off. I know he's a man of the cloth but he could talk a glass eye to sleep. He watched my eyes closing and still he carried on waffling on and on. I know he means well but bleeding hell, he can't half talk. I thought he was here for the night."

Francesca was still staring over at Dominic in a world of her own, deep in thought. Rob was asleep and Misty was ready for a bit of shut-eye herself. Even a few hours, anything to stop her head from pounding.

Francesca snapped out of her weird mood and gasped her breath. "I'm going to head home. I just need some space. Thank you so much for all your help. I would have been lost without you two, especially you Dominic. You have held us both up when all we have wanted to do is curl up in a tiny ball and die. Misty," she paused and her words came straight from her heart. "You've got yourself a good man there. Look after him, he's special."

Dominic was humble and bowed his head slightly. His cheeks were slightly red and his bottom lip started to tremble. His mouth was moving and he was trying to get his words out but nothing, not a word. Misty checked the time. "Dominic, can you drive her home? She can't get the bus when her head is like this."

"Yes love. I can grab us a pizza or something on the way back. I know you don't feel like eating but you have to try and get something down you. You've not eaten anything proper for days."

Misty was about to decline when Rob opened his eyes. He stretched his hands above his head and yawned. He was just like everyone else in the room, he'd not slept properly for days and every now and then, his eyes just closed and he drifted off to sleep. He was exhausted. "Rob, do you want some pizza?"

Rob was a fussy eater and all this modern food was something he was trying to get his head around. Garlic bread, pizza, whatever happened to a good old neck-end stew? "No thank you. Honestly, my stomach is playing up and that pizza shit could push me over the edge. It's all the herbs and spices. My palate isn't used to it."

Misty raised her eyes over at her husband. "Can you nip to the chippy and get him fish and chips? He needs to eat too."

"No worries. Misty, why don't you get a bath and put some lavender in it? It'll help you relax." Misty nodded. He was right and since being off the booze, her nerves were in tatters. She'd done so well not touching a drop of alcohol too. Of course, every morning when she opened her eyes she wanted to hit the bottle and get steaming drunk but her husband helped her remain strong and kept her sober.

Francesca stood up and walked over to Misty. She wrapped her arms around her neck and squeezed her with all her might. "I'm so sorry Misty. Honest, I'm sorry."

"Francesca, none of this is your fault. I don't blame you." The two of them hugged each other and just before Francesca walked away, she kissed Misty on the cheek. "I'll be back tomorrow, I just need to spend some time alone. I can't focus or even think straight at the moment. Maybe after a lie down, I might be able to face a few things, but my plan is to pop a few of them tablets the doctor gave me and just lie in bed. My head feels like it's going to explode."

Dominic and Francesca left the room and Misty collapsed back into her armchair. Rob dropped his head back and closed his eyes again. Exhaustion, pure exhaustion.

Dominic flicked the engine over and waited for Francesca to get into the passenger side. Once she was inside, he drove from the street. Francesca tapped her head against the window and her heart was heavy. "You'll get through this. You're stronger than you think," Dominic whispered. His hand reached over and patted the top of her leg. Francesca turned to face him and shook her head.

"It's all secrets, isn't it Dominic? Maybe that's why Rico was taken away from me."

"Don't be saying things like that. Tom was unstable, off his head. How was anyone to know what he was capable of? He was just after more money for drugs to feed his habit. I think it just all got out of control."

Francesca dropped her head low. "It would kill Misty if she ever found out Rico was your child. I hate that, yet again, I have betrayed her."

"Don't you ever breathe a word. You promised me, Francesca. You always said you would say he was Gordon's. That's what we agreed. Please, don't give me anymore grief to deal with. Please. It would break me. How do you think it feels keeping this a secret? Don't you think over the years I've wanted to blurt the truth out and come clean? But I'm a coward. I can't face destroying Misty like that."

"It should never have happened. We were fools. I know you were upset when you found out about Misty with Gordon but we should never have slept together. It was so wrong."

"We were drunk Francesca. We were both involved in this web of deceit. I kept Misty's secret regarding Gordon being Charlotte's father and you don't know how much it killed me to watch my own son growing up and not be able to do anything about it. I should have come clean. She would have understood how weak I was, how mixed up my head was at the time. It was wrong, I know that, but at the time we both needed a shoulder to cry on. It's our secret and always will be. I loved Rico, you know that don't you? When we lay them both to rest, you know the tears I'm crying are for my boy too. I loved him from afar, always have."

Francesca sucked hard on her bottom lip. "You're a good man, Dominic. I'll never breathe a word about our son. As far as anyone's concerned, Gordon was his father and I'll take that to the grave. I owe you for all you have done for me over the years. It was hard for you I know, but I'm grateful for everything, the money you sent, the presents, the voice at the end of a phone when I was low. Thank you."

What a bleeding bombshell this would have been. No one could have called it. Dominic had always been whiter than white, he had pulled the wool over everyone's eyes on this one for sure. They made out they hated each other. What a crafty fucker he was. They say the quiet ones are the worst, maybe this time they were right.

Today was the day when it was time to say goodbye to Charlotte and Rico. Mandy sat with Misty and she was heartbroken. "I wish I could see her one last time. My mam said I need to go for counselling. I'm just not functioning anymore. I can't seem to get out of bed. It was always me and Charlotte. I miss her phone calls, I miss doing stuff together. She's left a massive void in my life. Nobody will ever fill it, ever."

These were such lovely words from her best friend. Her heart was in the right place and even though sometimes she was a livewire, she was a true friend until the end. A lot of Charlotte's college friends were attending the funeral too, along with Rico's few friends. Misty made sure that Mandy kept her mouth shut about what she knew and reminded her every day that if her daughter's memory was tainted, she would be gunning for her. Mandy would never tell anyone what she knew, her lips were sealed. Dominic came into the room and spoke in a calm voice. "The cars are here. We need to let the men in to help put all the flowers in the hearse."

Misty swallowed hard, her breathing struggled. "I can't do this. How can I say goodbye to my baby?"

Denise and Max came to her side and both held her up before her legs buckled from underneath her. The family was devastated and there wasn't a dry eye in the place. Rob stood up and flicked the dust from his black suit. It was the same one he'd bought for Lisa's funeral. As soon as this was all over, he was burning it. It was cursed in his eyes, bad luck.

Misty was escorted outside. There was a sea of people all lined up on the streets; sobbing, crying, mourning for the two young teenagers who were taken too soon. The flowers were in the back of the funeral cars and they were ready to head for the church, which wasn't too far away – just ten minutes or so from where they lived. Just as Misty was about to step into the vehicle, a woman came behind her and touched the top of her shoulder softly. "Misty, I know you probably hate me for what happened but from the bottom of my heart, I'm truly sorry for what Tom has done."

Misty twisted her head back and met the eyes of Melanie. She was well groomed today and her usual grey-looking skin was full of colour. Denise was on standby and she could tell by her niece's expression that this woman was no friend of hers. Melanie quickly passed a small bouquet of pink carnations over to Misty and her eyes clouded over as she spoke. "I'm trying my best to sort myself out. I've been free from the drugs since Tom went gone. I know I'll never get my own children back in my life again but as a mother, I understand your loss."

Denise had heard enough. Bleeding hell, Misty was burying her daughter here today and she didn't have time for any sob stories, for Melanie's guilt trip. "Come on love, leave her alone. Don't you think she's been through enough without you adding to it. Thanks for the flowers but we don't have any time today to listen to your life story. Good luck with it by the way but do us a favour and piss off."

Melanie dropped her head. What did she expect though, a round of applause? She turned to walk away when Misty called after her. "Thanks for the flowers." Misty climbed into the car and never looked back. Melanie inhaled deeply and looked up to the high heavens.

"Thank you Lord, thank you," she mumbled under her breath. Maybe all she wanted was forgiveness, to cleanse her soul, who knows.

The two light oak coffins stood next to each other at the front of the church. Father Ged welcomed the congregation inside and spoke about how Jesus had died on the cross for his children. Dominic sat in the middle of Misty and Francesca, holding his wife's hand. He could see her pain, feel her heart breaking as the priest spoke about their daughter. Father Ged spoke well of both the teenagers and told the people there about the lives they both led. One thing was for sure, Rico and Charlotte were loved by all who knew them. Mandy had stood at the front of the church and told the mourners all about her best friend. It was endearing, a true friendship that no one would ever break. She broke down during the speech and her mother had to come up to the front of the church to support her, she was nearly collapsing. It was just too much for her in the end.

Misty swallowed hard, it was her turn to speak about the children who'd lost their lives. Her body quivered and her legs buckled as she tried to stand up. There was no way she could do this, she was weak, broken in two. Dominic helped his wife sit back down and looked around the church. He had to step up and do his daughter proud. Misty passed him a small piece of paper and nodded at him as she sobbed her heart out. "Thank you love. I thought I'd be able to do it but my body won't let me."

"Sssh, you sit there I'll do it." Dominic moved out from the wooden bench and headed to the front of the church. His heart was beating rapidly and his mouth was dry. Deep breaths, lungs filling with air. His eyes dropped to the note his wife had given him and he prepared himself to talk to everyone gathered there. Father Ged was at his side and patted the middle of his arm softly before he began.

"Thank you all for coming today. Charlotte and Rico would be proud to know they had so many people who loved them," he choked up and took a few seconds to compose himself. Everything that has happened in the last few months was now there in his head tormenting him. His mother's death, his marriage falling apart, and now the secret he had shared with Francesca for all these years. How could he tell anyone that Rico was his son? It would finish his wife off, break her in two. He stared over at her and then shot a look over at Francesca. What had he done, he was no better than Gordon, he was a liar, a cheat and a hypocrite. For years he'd played the victim and Mr Nice Guy but now he stood there in the house of God, preaching to everyone about being honest and how secrets ruin families.

Have some balls man, he thought, tell your wife the truth. Dominic did what he'd set out to do there that day and in fairness he made everyone proud of the way he held himself, the way he spoke about Rico and Charlotte. But he was far from proud. You could see it in his eyes as he returned to his seat next to his wife. His body was shaking as he sat back down, lip quivering. Misty dropped her head onto his shoulder and looked deep into his eyes.

"I love you Dominic. Charlotte would have been proud of you."

He looked into her eyes and licked his dry lips before he spoke, stuttering. "Misty, when we get home, I need to sit down and talk to you. There is something I need to tell you. Something I should have told you years ago."

THE END